Petals & Portals

Enchanted Realms: Crossroads
Book One

MICHELLE MILES

Book Cover by Covers in Color

First edition 2026

ISBN: 9781969164095 (eBook)
ISBN: 9781969164125 (paperback)

For everyone who has ever found their way home through grief, through love, and through a little bit of magic.

Chapter One

Ten years had passed since I set foot in Hickory Hollow, Texas.

Ten years, almost to the day.

I hadn't missed it. Not the humidity that felt like breathing through a wet towel. Not the gossip. Definitely not the way the whole town still dressed like it was trapped in a 1987 Sears catalog.

I drifted along the edge of the crowded living room skimming faces the way I skimmed headlines. The threadbare carpet still had the same floral pattern I used to trace when I was bored as a kid. The furniture sagged in familiar places. The drapes—yellowed, heavy, absolutely not in style—hung in the exact same way they always had, like they were too tired to care.

Hushed voices floated through the room like the low hum of an air conditioner on its last legs.

"It was such a shock."

"She seemed fine the day before."

"It's such an unexpected loss..."

My throat tightened. Aunt Alice. Dead.

It still didn't feel real. Like a headline about a stranger I'd read on my phone between subway stops, instead of the woman who'd taught me how to coax seedlings into bloom and spin fairy tales out of nothing.

I tucked myself into a corner behind a side table stacked with deviled eggs and sympathy casseroles. My best impression of a wallflower—only I was the kind that cost four digits and came with red soles.

My couture black dress was sleek and city-chic. My four-inch heels were worth more than the combined outfits of half the room. I'd gone with minimalist gold jewelry and a sharp bob that skimmed my shoulders. Every inch of me screamed Manhattan fashion girl.

Every inch of the room screamed small-town Texas.

I'd never planned on coming back here. Ever. The plan—*the plan*—had been to die in Manhattan at a very old, very glamorous age after a long and scandalously successful career at *Glint* Magazine, with a walk-in closet the size of this living room and a partner who understood the sacredness of a sample sale.

Instead, I'd lost everything in a single spectacular, flaming dumpster-fire of a day.

Literally.

First, the job. My editor had called me into the office with that tight, apologetic smile that meant no one was "restructuring," they were getting rid of you. One HR meeting and a signed NDA later, I walked out of the glass tower with a cardboard box and no idea what I'd done wrong.

Then Preston.

I'd gone home early, planning to drown my humiliation in Thai takeout and terrible reality TV, only to find my long-term boyfriend in our bed with a runway model who looked like she'd been assembled out of designer toothpicks and sorrow.

And because fate liked to overachieve, an electrical fire broke out in the building that night. Sprinklers. Smoke. Evacuation. My apartment—and everything that said *this is my life now, this is who I am*—went up in flames.

I'd been standing on the sidewalk in bare feet, clutching my Hermès crossbody and my laptop bag, when my phone rang.

My mother's voice on the other end. Tight, thin, brittle.

"Piper. Alice is gone."

Job. Boyfriend. Apartment. Aunt.

A superfecta of catastrophe.

So, when my mother called again a day later, insisting—no, demanding—I come home for the funeral, I didn't have the energy to argue. I booked a cheap flight, packed what I could salvage into my ten-thousand-dollar Louis Vuitton luggage—a gift from my former editor, now saved in my phone as *That Woman (Do Not Answer)*—and let my uncle pick me up from the airport in his dented pickup.

Regroup, I'd told myself. Go to the funeral. Figure out the next move. Maybe LA. Maybe a different magazine. Maybe... something.

Because it sure wasn't going to be Hickory Hollow.

"You look like a city girl," my mother had said in greeting, standing stiffly on the front porch with a pinched mouth and a face that had forgotten how to soften.

"Gee, thanks, Mom," I'd answered.

"It wasn't a compliment. Your clothes are too expensive, and your hair is too short."

Classic Gladys Wakefield. Weaponized honesty.

The first thing I'd done when I got to Manhattan was chop six inches off my hair. I remembered watching blonde strands slide down the salon cape and feeling lighter with every snip, as if I were shedding more than split ends. Now I reached up and brushed my fingers along the sleek line of my cut, stopping where it sat above my shoulders.

"I like it this way," I'd said.

My father had come to my rescue, as he always tried to. "She likes it, Gladys. And it looks great."

My mother had made a noncommittal sound, the verbal equivalent of a shrug that said agree to disagree.

Now, as the last of the neighbors shuffled through the living room with their Pyrex dishes and condolences, I watched my mother work the crowd. Black dress, pearls, hair in a tight bun, jeweled reading glasses hanging on a chain. She accepted every hug with a tremble of her bottom lip and a damp handkerchief pressed dramatically to her nose.

If grief were a performance, Gladys deserved an Oscar.

Every so often, she shot me a sharp look over someone's shoulder. The look said, *They're asking about you. You're a problem.*

I lifted my chin and pretended not to care.

People came. People cried. People left. Eventually the house emptied, the murmur of voices fading until only family remained. My parents, my older sister Iris, my brother Clay... and one stranger in an expensive suit.

The stranger set a leather briefcase on his knees and flipped the latches with quiet precision.

"Good afternoon," he said, his voice smooth and practiced. "My condolences to you all. I know this is a difficult time—"

"Can we get on with it?" Iris cut in.

She lounged on the far end of the sofa, long legs crossed, arms folded, posture coiled like a cat ready to pounce. She was our mother's twin in temperament and looks. Tall, sleek, blue-eyed, dark hair flowing down her back in a glossy sheet. Even her glare matched Gladys's—cold and sharp enough to nick skin.

She was also six years older than me, which meant she'd had a solid head start on perfecting the art of being terrifying.

Clay slouched on the opposite end of the sofa in jeans and boots, his black cowboy hat tipped back on his head. He looked like he'd been born leaning against a fencepost. Boredom rolled off him in lazy waves.

Across from them, Gladys and George Wakefield sat on the love seat. Gladys clutched her shredded handkerchief. George tamped fresh tobacco into the bowl of his pipe with the careful focus he reserved for small tasks that allowed him to avoid big emotions.

I perched in the ancient wingback chair across from the lawyer, hands clenched together in my lap. Waiting.

Waiting for this to be done so I could book the next flight out of here and never look back.

Alice had been larger-than-life for as long as I could remember. Summer days in the greenhouse, surrounded by flowers that felt like something out of a storybook. Dirt under my fingernails. The warm, loamy smell of soil and something else—something I'd once called magic before I learned magic wasn't a word adults liked.

Alice had always had a way of telling stories like they were memories instead of fairy tales—about other lands, mirror-thin borders between worlds, and magic that didn't disappear so much as retreat. At the time, I'd laughed, thinking it was Alice being whimsical.

Now, the memory stirred something uneasy in my chest.

When I wasn't in the garden, I'd spent hours curled into the window seat in Alice's house, devouring novels about faraway kingdoms, enchanted forests, and girls who saved the day instead of waiting to be rescued. Alice never told me those stories were childish. If anything, she'd encouraged them—adding tales of her own about hidden realms and old trees that listened.

Those memories hit me now like a punch to the sternum.

Alice was gone. Not a phone call or a text. Gone.

I swallowed hard and blinked away the sudden sting in my eyes.

The lawyer's gaze slid from Iris to Clay and finally landed on me, lingering there in a way that made the hairs on the back of my neck prickle.

"Patience, Iris," Gladys said, casting her eldest daughter a reprimanding glance before turning on her best hostess smile for the stranger. "But we are anxious to understand why you've called us all together today, Mr. Schneider."

Roger Schneider was my aunt's attorney and executor.

He was tall and silver-haired, with an easy posture and a plaid blazer that screamed old-money subtlety. I clocked the cut, the stitching, the drape, the little details that separated off-the-rack from runway.

Ferragamo, I guessed. I'd seen the same blazer in a preview for the fall line, back when I still had access to those.

"It was part of Alice's final wishes," Mr. Schneider continued. His gaze flicked to me again, then returned to the folder he'd opened. "She requested the reading of the will on the day of the funeral."

The prickling on my neck intensified, a fizz of unease and anticipation that felt a little too much like stepping backstage before a runway show.

He cleared his throat. "This is Alice Hawthorne's last will and testament. Her estate is as follows: the house on Snapdragon Drive, including all furnishings; Enchanted Blossoms, her flower shop on Town Hall Street; her car; bank accounts totaling five hundred sixty-one thousand, four hundred thirty-five dollars; and investments valued at approximately five hundred thousand."

Clay let out a low whistle. "A million bucks?" He barked a laugh. "Who'd'a thought the old broad was rich?"

"Clay," Gladys hissed.

Holy. Crap.

My brain tried to assemble the words into something that made sense and... failed. Alice? A millionaire? She'd run a flower shop, for crying out loud. The aunt who wiped potting soil on her jeans and drove a sensible sedan—rich?

Beside me, Iris's spine snapped straighter, interest sharpening every line of her face. She practically vibrated with hungry expectation. If she'd been a cartoon, dollar signs would have replaced her pupils. I half-expected her to start drooling on the carpet.

"Clay, shh," Iris snapped without taking her eyes off the lawyer. Then, sweetly, "Please go on, Mr. Schneider."

Annoyance flared in my chest. Iris hadn't spent a single Saturday weeding flower beds or hauling bags of soil. She hadn't fallen asleep in the greenhouse listening to Alice's soft, soothing stories about other worlds and what-ifs.

I did, I thought. *And I didn't even know she had this kind of money.*

Mr. Schneider adjusted his glasses and cleared his throat again. "It is Alice's express wish that all assets I've listed, including all monies, go to Piper Wakefield."

Time hiccupped.

Iris shot to her feet. "What?"

Gladys's mouth fell open. Clay let out a loud, delighted, "Well, I'll be."

Heat rushed up my neck and into my face. For a second, the words didn't register. They were just noise.

"Sorry," I heard myself say, my voice thinner than I liked. "Yes. What?"

"You mean she's giving everything to Piper?" Iris rounded on me, blue eyes blazing. "You little suck-up."

Anger crackled beneath my skin, sharp and electric. "I am no such thing," I snapped. "I had no idea she was doing this. And anyway, I don't want this."

That part came out a little too honest.

I hadn't planned on staying. I had no idea how to run a business—much less a small-town flower shop. I could style a couture spread twelve ways from Sunday, but I didn't know the first thing about balance sheets or inventory.

"If you want it so bad," I added, my voice going cold, "you can have it."

"I'm afraid that's not possible," Mr. Schneider said calmly.

"Why not?" Iris sounded like a petulant teenager instead of a forty-something divorcée. "She doesn't want it. She said so herself."

"Alice stipulates, specifically, that Piper is to be the sole successor to her estate." He glanced at me again, expression unreadable. "There is no provision for transferring those assets to another party."

"She's left nothing for anyone else?" Gladys asked. Her tone was flat and brittle. Her knuckles whitened around the handkerchief.

"I'm afraid not," Mr. Schneider said.

"Oh, no," I muttered under my breath.

Clay let out another appreciative whistle. "How about that, sis?" He tipped his hat back farther with a grin. "You were Aunt Alice's favorite all along and no one knew it."

"Well, clearly *she* did," Iris snarled. "Didn't you, Piper? You're trying to hide it. You knew about this. You talked her into it."

"No, I didn't." My voice shook with fury. "I had nothing to do with it."

"She didn't," Mr. Schneider said, backing me up. "Alice stated you were the only one she trusted with her business."

That landed like another punch. I stared at him. Trusted? With what, exactly? The shop? The money? Something else?

Because sure, I'd always felt close to my aunt. But trusted? Enough to leave me everything? When I'd been a long-distance niece for the last decade, texting on holidays and liking Facebook posts?

"What about me?" Iris demanded. "What do I get?"

Mr. Schneider didn't answer. That silence was loud.

"Why is she getting everything?" Iris snapped. "Just because she ran off to Manhattan with her fancy degree and her fancy job? You're not as good as you think you are," she spat at me. "You can hide behind those expensive clothes, but we all know who you are underneath it all. Just a redneck like the rest of us."

My temper finally snapped. I stood, fists clenched.

"And you're nothing but a divorced middle-aged high school dropout," I shot back.

The words hung in the air like a slap.

Gladys gasped. Clay winced. For a heartbeat, no one moved.

Iris's face went rigid, her expression hardening into something ugly and sharp. Fury, jealousy, old resentment—all of it flickered in her eyes.

When we were little, Iris had shaved the hair off my favorite Barbie and called it a makeover. Some things never changed.

Mr. Schneider cleared his throat again, slicing through the tension like a knife. "There's one more stipulation," he said, addressing me. "Alice's last recorded wish was to ensure you understood that inheriting the flower shop comes with a condition. You must take it on and run it yourself. She specifically states that she does not want you to sell it. Ever."

Ever.

The word echoed in my skull. My stomach twisted into a knot that felt suspiciously like panic.

Ever meant no quick sale, no cashing out and fleeing to Los Angeles. Ever meant roots, permanence, being locked into Hickory Hollow—into Snapdragon Drive and Enchanted Blossoms and the life I'd worked so hard to escape.

"Why?" I rasped when I finally found my voice.

"She didn't say," Mr. Schneider replied.

"You conniving little snake," Iris spat, directing it at me like a curse.

Then she spun on her heel and stormed out of the room, out the front door, and into her car, punctuating the exit with a dramatic slam.

Gladys stood, smoothing her hands down the front of her dress as if ironing out wrinkles in reality. “Thank you for coming, Mr. Schneider,” she said tightly. Then she turned and walked upstairs without looking at me once.

The silence left behind felt heavy and deafening.

Clay stretched, joints popping, and then leaned down to kiss me on the cheek. “That was fun,” he said lightly. “Congrats, sis. I’m happy for you.” And I believed him. Clay never did drama. He existed, steady as fencepost. “See y’all later.”

His boots thudded across the worn floorboards as he ambled out.

Just like that, the room emptied—leaving me, my father, and the lawyer in a bubble of awkward quiet.

“So what happens now?” I asked.

“We’ll need to probate the will, of course,” Mr. Schneider said. He opened his briefcase again and pulled out a ring of keys, the metal clinking softly as they shifted. “In the meantime, I’m authorized to give you these. Alice wanted you to take possession of everything immediately.”

I stared at the keys.

House keys. Car keys. Shop keys. An entire life, jangling in a neat little circle on the coffee table when I didn’t reach for them.

“I’ll leave them here,” he said when I still didn’t move. He set them down gently and snapped his briefcase closed. “Do you have any questions?”

“Not right now,” I managed. My head felt stuffed with cotton.

He nodded, reached into his breast pocket, and handed me a business card. “If you think of any, call me.”

I took it automatically. Black ink on white stock.

Roger Schneider, Attorney at Law.

Then he was gone, the front door closing behind him with a soft click.

That left me alone with my father.

George Wakefield still looked like the quiet, bookish man who'd taught me the difference between a nebula and a galaxy using a National Geographic spread at the kitchen table. Brown cardigan. White dress shirt. Black polyester slacks. Horn-rimmed glasses perched low on his nose. Pipe clenched between his teeth.

For a second, I braced myself for some profound fatherly wisdom. Something like, *We'll figure this out together, kiddo.*

"Well," he said, removing the pipe from his mouth. "I think I'll make some coffee."

And... nope.

He shuffled toward the kitchen, as if his entire world hadn't tilted thirty degrees to the left.

I stared after him, then snatched the keys off the coffee table and followed, my heels clicking on the tile like punctuation.

I caught him as he reached for the coffee canister in the cabinet.

"Dad," I blurted. "Why would Aunt Alice do this?"

"Don't know, Piper." He filled the pot at the sink. "But clearly, she loved you. Or she wouldn't have willed you everything."

"But it doesn't make sense." I leaned against the island, the keys biting into my palm. "Mom is her only sister. Iris lives here. They've been in each other's pockets for years. Iris is right—I haven't set foot in Hickory Hollow for ten years and suddenly I'm... what? An heiress?"

He set the empty coffee pot on the counter, then circled the island and placed his hands gently on my shoulders. His eyes were kind behind the smudged lenses.

"I wouldn't worry so much about them. They're mad and hurt right now. They'll get over it. In time, they'll accept it."

"Dad—"

"Alice must've seen something special in you," he went on. "To give you her home. Her shop. All that money. She believed in you, Piper."

"But what did she see?" I asked, voice cracking. "What did she think I could do that no one else could?"

"Only Alice knows that, I suppose." He moved back to the counter, rinsed out the pot, and started filling it with water. "You spent a lot of time with her when you were a girl."

"Yes, but that was because I wanted to." I sank onto one of the barstools, elbows on the island. "The greenhouse, the garden..." I smiled faintly at the memory. "There was something magical about it. I used to pretend I was a fairy princess with iridescent wings, remember? I'd run between the tables and 'fly' between the flowers."

He glanced over his shoulder at me, eyes soft. "You were always my fairy princess," he said. "Still are."

The sting behind my eyes returned full force. "Thanks, Dad."

He smiled and flipped the coffee maker on. "For what it's worth," he added, "I'm glad you're back. And I'm glad you'll be staying. It was too hard to keep up with you on that MyFace thing."

I huffed out a laugh. "Facebook, Dad."

He waved a hand. "Whatever you call it."

Silence settled between us, thick but not entirely uncomfortable. The coffee maker burbled to life.

I twirled the keys around one finger. I wanted out. Desperately. A way to honor Alice without chaining myself to a small-town life I'd never wanted. Maybe Clay could take the shop. Maybe there was a legal loophole. Maybe, maybe, maybe.

Something about the word *ever* gnawed at me. Something about Enchanted Blossoms as more than a quaint small-town florist. About the way Alice used to talk about flowers like they remembered things, like they were listening.

"I guess I'll be here for a while, at least," I said finally. "Until I figure everything out."

"Alice wanted you to have her business and her home because she believed in you," my father said again, turning to look at me fully. "She loved you like you were her own. She worried about you in ways that were different from the others."

I thought about that. Thought about the rows of pictures she kept on the mantel. Thought about how she always let me stay with her whenever I wanted. Until my mother shut that down when I was a teenager.

"And I loved her, too," I said. Because we'd had a special bond.

"Don't ever feel guilty for accepting what she chose to give you," he said. "No matter what anyone else thinks."

I exhaled slowly. The keys were warm in my hand now.

"You're right," I said. "In the morning, I'll go to her house and check it out."

And maybe I'd figure out what on earth Alice had expected of me... and why the word *enchanted* suddenly didn't feel like clever branding anymore.

Chapter Two

I barely slept.

Every time I closed my eyes, the scene replayed on a loop—the lawyer's even tone, the way Iris's face twisted with hate, my mother's stiff back as she marched upstairs like I'd personally murdered her sister.

I lasted until dawn before giving up on sleep. A quick shower, a swipe of makeup to fake *rested human*, and I was zipping my life back into my absurdly expensive luggage which I shoved into a corner. No point dragging everything along until I knew if I was staying at Alice's house—or if there was some loophole that would let me escape Hickory Hollow without unleashing Iris the Destroyer.

Keys to Alice's place in hand, I crept down the stairs. My Manolo kitten-heel strappy slides betrayed me, each flip-flip-flip echoing through the quiet house.

I stepped into the kitchen and pulled up short.

My mother sat at the table with a mug of coffee and the *Hickory Hollow Mirror* spread open in front of her. The paper looked as tired and beige as the kitchen itself.

Gladys glanced up once, eyes cool behind her glasses, then went back to reading. "Nice write-up in today's paper about Alice."

She folded the paper, crisp and neat, and shoved it across the table without looking at me. "You might want to read it."

"Okay." I shifted my weight, the keys digging crescents into my palm. "Mom, about the will—"

"There's nothing to talk about, Piper."

My name hit like a slap. Somehow, Gladys could make two harmless syllables sound like an indictment.

"Alice and I never saw eye to eye," my mother went on, rising with her mug. "She got the last laugh giving you her estate." She smoothed a hand down the front of her dress, every line in her posture carved out of ice. "Now that you have a place to live, I assume you'll be moving your things out."

My spine went rigid. God forbid we share a roof for more than seventy-two hours.

"I'm heading to the house now to check things out," I said, keeping my voice level. "I'll have my stuff out by the end of the day."

"Good."

Gladys swept past me in a cloud of cheap floral perfume, leaving the faintest wake of disapproval behind her.

The silence that followed felt heavy enough to smother.

I let out a long breath, the kind that deflated me all the way down to my bones. So, this was how it was going to be—frozen politeness and weaponized silence. Fine. Add it to the list. Fired. Dumped. Evicted. Disinherited emotionally, if not financially.

I bypassed the coffee pot. If I tried to drink anything right now, it would slosh in my already swirling stomach.

At the front door, I paused on the porch, blinking against the early-morning glare. The humidity hit me full on. It was like walking through soup.

Welcome back to Texas, sweetheart. Population: you and your bad decisions.

Alice's car was at Alice's house, and I hadn't owned a car in Manhattan because that would've been like keeping a horse in the living room. I was officially, absurdly car-less.

But I was not asking my mother for a ride.

It couldn't be that far. A couple miles, maybe. I'd walk, get some air, and avoid another round of Gladys Wakefield's frosty domestic terrorism.

I slung my cross-body bag over my shoulders, keys in hand, and headed down the gravel driveway toward the main road, each step a reminder that I'd dressed for cute, not practical. The strappy sandals were already cutting across the top of my foot and collecting rocks like souvenirs. Sneakers would've been smarter, but the slides did look great with my airy white peasant top and iridescent blue capris.

Fashion over comfort. Some habits refused to die.

At not-quite-eight in the morning, the air already shimmered with heat. Sweat gathered at the nape of my neck. This was why I'd gone north—why I'd traded small-town scorch for city skylines and industrial air-conditioning.

And now I was back. With a house. A flower shop.

And a million dollars I hadn't asked for.

At the end of the driveway, I turned left onto the two-lane road. A low rumble of an engine made me step closer to the shoulder. A blue extended cab pickup approached, slowed... then rolled to a stop beside me.

The passenger window hummed down.

"Good morning!"

The man leaned across the seat, smiling up at me like the heat didn't bother him in the slightest. He was handsome in that infuriating, easy way. Three-day stubble shadowed a strong jaw, and at the open top of his rumpled plaid shirt I caught a glimpse of a broad, lightly furred chest. His drawl slid over my skin like warm honey.

Sweet. Actual. Jesus.

"Need a lift?"

"Um. No. I'm good. I'm walking." I glanced down the road, where the heat turned the blacktop into a shimmering mirage. My feet throbbed in protest.

"Don't be silly," he said. "I'm headed into town. I can give you a ride. Besides, it's hot. And I have AC."

My resolve wobbled. Pride tried to rally. "I never accept rides from strangers," I said, giving him my best cocky smile.

"Oh, so that's it."

He laughed, a deep rumble that I felt straight through the soles of my fashionable shoes.

The truck eased fully onto the shoulder and stopped. He climbed out, sauntering toward me with a knee-melting grin that crinkled the corners of his dove-gray eyes. Up close he looked even more annoyingly attractive, his sandy hair an artful mess that belonged on some rugged cologne ad.

"You're Piper," he said.

"And you hold me at a disadvantage, sir."

"*Sir*?" He chuckled, amusement lighting his eyes. "Don't remember, do you?" One corner of his mouth kicked up. "Figured you wouldn't. You've been away a while. But you haven't changed a bit."

He stuck out his hand. "Mac."

"Mac," I repeated slowly, searching old yearbooks in my mental Rolodex and coming up empty. "Just Mac?"

"For now." The grin widened, pure mischief.

Cryptic. Great. Just what my day needed.

"Welcome home," he said. "Now that we've been properly introduced, how about that ride?"

This time when he offered, I took it. I did not want to arrive at Alice's house looking like I'd crawled out of a sauna.

"That would be great," I admitted.

Mac opened the passenger door for me like some old-fashioned gentleman. Once I was in and buckled up, he slid behind the wheel, rolled up the window, and cranked the AC. Blissful cold air washed over my face.

"Thanks," I said, trying not to sound as dazed as I felt. *Get a grip. He's just a guy with climate control.*

"Don't mention it." He pulled back onto the road. "Where you headed?"

"My aunt's house," I said. "But if you're going into town, you can drop me there. No need to go out of your way."

He shot me a sidelong grin. The cologne—some warm, spicy thing—coiled through the cab and took up residence in my nervous system.

"Hey, no problem," he said. "I can drive there. Snapdragon Drive, right?"

"You know it?"

"I sure do. Be glad to take you there."

Of course he did. Everyone knew where everyone lived in this town.

He cut me a curious glance. "You were going to walk all that way?"

"Well," I started, "I'm not exactly the favorite one at the moment, so yes."

"Hmm," was all he said.

I realized I was still worrying the keyring, spinning it around my finger like a nervous tell. "I know you from somewhere," I said. "Were you at the funeral?"

"I was."

"Where do I know you from?"

"We both grew up here."

Non-answer. Irritation pricked.

"Did we go to school together?"

I studied him while he watched the road—straight nose, strong jaw, a face teenage girls used to drool over. I tried to sneak a look at his left hand. No ring, but that didn't mean much. Guys could be commitment-phobic and still have girlfriends. Plural.

Not that I was in the market for one. Not after Preston the Human Dumpster Fire.

"Did anyone tell you staring is rude?" Mac asked, laughter threading through his voice.

I snapped my gaze forward. "Sorry."

"It's okay. Really."

"You didn't answer my question."

"Nope, I didn't."

"Are you going to?"

"Maybe." He shot me another sideways glance, gray eyes amused. "But not today."

I huffed. "You want me to guess."

"I like to build suspense."

"You are frustrating. Did you know that?"

"I've been told." He turned onto a narrower lane flanked by trees and scrub.

I let my head fall back against the seat. "I'll figure it out eventually, you know. Did you know my aunt?"

"I did," he said quietly. "And I'm sorry for your loss. It was a shock."

"It was?"

"No one told you?"

I shook my head, throat suddenly tight.

"She keeled over in her garden," he said. "It's what I heard, anyway."

"She did?"

That didn't line up with the Aunt Alice in my memory—sturdy, tireless, the woman who could haul bags of soil in August heat without breaking a sweat. When she wasn't elbow-deep in flower beds, she was in the greenhouse. When she wasn't there, she was running Enchanted Blossoms like a queen holding court.

"I'm sorry, Piper. They think it was a heart attack," Mac added.

"A heart attack?"

In all the years I'd known her, Alice had never been sick. Not a cold, not a cough, not even allergies.

"It's weird, right?" he murmured, dropping his voice like we were sharing a secret.

He glanced at me, and I saw genuine concern in those gray eyes.

"Yeah," I said slowly. "Weird."

"So, tell me," he went on. "Why are you headed to your aunt's house?"

I seized the change of subject like a life raft. "Well, it's my house now," I said. "She gave me everything in her will."

Mac slammed on the brakes.

The truck screeched to a halt so abruptly my seatbelt snapped tight, biting into my collarbone.

"What'd you do that for?" I demanded.

"Everything?" His hands tightened on the steering wheel. "Even Enchanted Blossoms?"

"Um. Yeah. Why?"

Color drained from his face. His knuckles went white.

"No reason."

Liar, my instincts supplied immediately. It wasn't surprise on his face. It was recognition. Like he knew something he wasn't willing to say.

"Nothing," he added, throwing the truck back into gear. "It's a surprise. That's all."

"Oookay."

I twirled the keyring again, unsettled. First my aunt's mysterious "heart attack," now Mr. Cryptic having a whole moment over a flower shop.

We turned down a red-dirt driveway and rumbled up toward the house on the hill. The place rose ahead of us—dormer windows, wrap-around porch, weathered boards that had seen decades of Texas summers. Alice's Cadillac still sat in the drive, sun glinting off the hood.

Mac killed the engine. For a moment we sat in silence, both staring at the house.

Memories rushed in on a tide of scent and sound—baking chocolate chip cookies, spice cake cooling on wire racks, the crackle of a winter fire even when outside was barely jacket weather. The wheeze of the old piano as Alice coaxed music from its yellowed keys. The bang of the screen door as neighbors came and went carrying casserole dishes and gossip.

The white rocker on the porch swayed faintly in the morning breeze. I could almost see my aunt there—telling stories about fairies and knights and hidden places between worlds where magic still lingered if you knew how to listen.

Potted flowers spilled color over the porch rail. Somehow, even without Alice, they were thriving. Of course they were.

A skinny orange tabby with an outrageously fluffy tail hopped off the porch steps, stretched luxuriously, and sat, fixing us with bright golden eyes.

"Who's been feeding the cat?" I asked.

"I have."

I turned to stare. "You?"

"Well, I couldn't let her starve." He shrugged, like it was nothing. "She's a good mouser, but she doesn't eat them." He hesitated. "Should I come in with you?"

My first instinct was to say no. This house was memories and ghosts and grief—none of which I wanted to unpack in front of a guy I half-recognized and half-suspected.

But the idea of walking into Alice's house alone after ten years made my chest feel tight.

"Sure," I said. "You can come."

We climbed out of the truck. The cat trotted over and bumped her head against my shin, purring like a tiny engine.

"You're a friendly one, aren't you?" I murmured, bending to scratch between her ears. The cat wound figure eights around my ankles. "What's her name?"

"Willow," Mac said. "She was abandoned. Showed up on Alice's doorstep one day, so Alice took her in."

Of course, she had. Aunt Alice collected strays—plants, people, apparently cats.

We ascended the porch steps. Mac pulled open the old wood screen door, and I unlocked the front door with fingers that didn't feel entirely steady.

The musty scent of a closed-up house hit me first—dust, old wood, and underneath it all the faint sweet ghost of Alice's lavender cleaning spray.

Willow padded in ahead of us, tail high, as if welcoming us to her kingdom.

The living room was frozen in time. Two sofas facing each other with a scarred coffee table between them. An oversized chair. Entertainment center and television on one end. Bookshelves sagging under the weight of long-loved paperbacks and hardcovers. The fireplace on the other with the mantel lined with framed photos.

One in particular drew me in like a magnet.

I crossed the room and picked it up. The little girl—me—in a pink tutu, grinning at the camera, Alice's arm around my shoulders. I remembered the sparkly tights, the plastic tiara, the way my aunt had clapped louder than anyone in the audience.

Other family photos dotted the mantel—my mother, Iris, Clay, even my dad—but there were far more of me than anyone else. And sometimes I wondered if it was more than "proud aunt" but that seemed ridiculous.

"I always thought you were her favorite," Mac said quietly from behind me.

"I don't know why," I murmured. "I never thought I was special."

"But she did."

I was about to set the frame down when a sliver of white caught my eye. An envelope edge peeked out from behind one of the photos.

Heart thudding, I eased the frame aside and pulled the envelope free. My name was written on the front in precise, familiar script.

"Oh my god."

Mac leaned in over my shoulder. "What is it?"

"It's from my aunt."

"A letter?"

My fingers shook as I slid a thumb under the flap and unfolded the neatly creased paper. My pulse roared in my ears as I read.

Piper, If you're reading this, then I'm dead and you have inherited my entire estate. I'm sorry to call you away from your fast-paced life in the big city. But this is far more important than a fashion magazine job.

The room tilted a little.

I backed up and dropped onto the edge of the sofa, the letter crinkling in my hands.

"Piper?" Mac's voice sounded like it was coming from down a long tunnel.

"I... I think I'd like to be alone now," I managed.

He didn't argue. The screen door creaked and banged shut behind him a moment later, leaving me alone with the letter and the quiet hum of the house.

I drew a breath and kept reading.

Something has gone horribly wrong. My death is not an accident, no matter what they say. I need you, my little sleuth, to find who killed me. I think I know the why of it but for reasons I can't write down—for fear someone will read this letter before you—I can't say. You'll figure it out in time. Because you're so smart. You always were my shining little ball of starlight. I'm sorry to have thrust Enchanted Blossoms on you in such a horrid manner, but I simply can't take any chances. You're the only one I trust. The only one who can take over where I left off. There will be more information waiting for you at the flower shop. Over time, you'll understand more and come to accept all that I've given you.

My breath hitched. Murder. My aunt was talking about murder like it was a puzzle I could solve between flower deliveries and family drama.

Ink had bled faintly through the page. I flipped the letter over.

P.S. Be nice to Owen. I think he's always liked you.

"Owen?"

The only Owen I knew was—

Realization slammed into me so hard I swayed.

That sorry—

I stared at the back of the letter. Owen. Not Mac. Owen McAllister.

I'd grown up with him. The antique store owner's son. The golden boy of Hickory Hollow—valedictorian, scholarship magnet, the guy who'd made AP coursework look like light reading while I'd mainlined caffeine and flash cards to keep up. Everyone had assumed he'd leave town in a blaze of academic glory.

But he hadn't. He'd stayed. I'd never understood why—and I hadn't exactly stuck around to ask.

And now here he was, strolling back into my life with a fake name and a flirty smile.

Why?

Heat flared under my skin. I crumpled the paper in my fist and surged to my feet. The screen door did its familiar bang-bang-bang as I stormed onto the porch.

Owen—Mac, whatever he was calling himself these days—was still leaning against his truck. When I barreled out of the house, he straightened and headed towards me, that same bright smile snapping into place like a reflex.

He hadn't left. He'd waited.

"You're Owen McAllister," I said.

My tone could have stripped paint.

His smile faltered. Color crept up his neck. "You figured it out."

"We went to school together," I said, descending the steps until we were a breath apart. "I've known you all my life. You jerk face. You lied to me. Mac is your father. Mr. McAllister."

"Hang on a second." He lifted his hands like he could physically push back my anger. "I didn't lie."

"When did you start calling yourself Mac?" I shot back. "When you saw me on the side of the road and decided to have a little fun? You sorry—"

"Piper—"

"Oh, my bad. Did I call you a name?" I waved the crumpled letter at him. "Poor baby. You'll live. It's bad enough you messed with me, but my aunt thinks someone murdered her. She told me so. In this letter."

His eyes widened. "She thought that?"

"She knew something was wrong." My voice shook, but I powered through it. I took the steps until we were nose-to-nose—well, as close as we could get with him a head taller. "She wants me to find the killer."

"How are you going to do that?" he asked softly.

I let out a short, humorless laugh. "I have no idea. Do I look like someone who reads the future in tea leaves? Or Sherlock Holmes?"

He snorted. "No. You're much prettier."

"Don't try that with me." I shoved at his shoulder with my free hand. "Compliments are not going to get you out of this. I hate lies, Owen. I hate them."

"I'm sorry," he said. And annoyingly, he sounded like he meant it. "I don't know why I didn't tell you who I was. I guess I wanted to see if you remembered me. I hoped you would."

Oh, I remembered him.

He'd been the boy all the girls had secretly plotted to marry. He'd been the impossible curve-setter in every class. He'd been the person I'd silently competed against for years and never managed to beat.

He'd also been the boy I'd harbored a mortifying crush on for the last two years of high school.

Not that I was telling him that. Let him sweat.

"I saw you yesterday at the funeral," he said.

"Why didn't you talk to me then?"

"Didn't seem right," he said, glancing away toward the yard. "With all your family around. I didn't go to the graveside." His gaze flicked back to me, warm and unnervingly earnest. "You sure looked pretty."

Heat climbed my throat, traitorous and obvious. Words deserted me. That was twice now he'd complimented me and I didn't know what to do with that.

"Can you forgive me?" he asked, looking like a kicked golden retriever.

I folded my arms, letter still clenched in my fist. "Don't do it again."

"I won't. I promise."

His gaze drifted to my mouth, then back up to my eyes, lingering like he was tasting the thought of something he wasn't brave enough to say.

"I could help you," he said.

I barked a short laugh. "I don't think so." I turned toward the door.

"Why not?"

"I don't want your help. I don't want anyone's help."

My hand closed on the doorknob.

"Piper, wait."

I paused, looking back at him over my shoulder.

"If you change your mind," he said, "let me know."

"I think I'd like to be alone for a little while," I replied. "Figure some stuff out."

He checked his watch. "I've got to get to the antique store anyway. My dad'll be looking for me." He hesitated. "You have a cell phone?"

Suspicion and amusement wrestled inside me. "Yeah. Why?"

He climbed the steps, closing the distance between us until I had to tilt my chin up. "Let me give you my number."

Smooth. I had to give him that.

I dug my phone out of my bag and handed it over. His fingers brushed mine as he took it, and the brief, accidental touch sent a spark racing up my arm straight toward my chest.

He typed, then glanced up at me. "Hold on."

A second later, my phone buzzed in his hand.

He passed the phone back. "There. Fair's fair."

Something warm and unexpected settled in my chest.

"If you need anything, call," he said. "Anytime. Day or night."

He held my gaze a heartbeat longer, then he headed for the truck.

I watched him climb in and drive away, dust kicking up behind his tires, the house and its secrets looming at my back.

Somewhere beneath the grief and the anger and the knot of fear over the word *murder*, something small and treacherous fluttered low in my stomach—an ember of attraction I absolutely did not have time for.

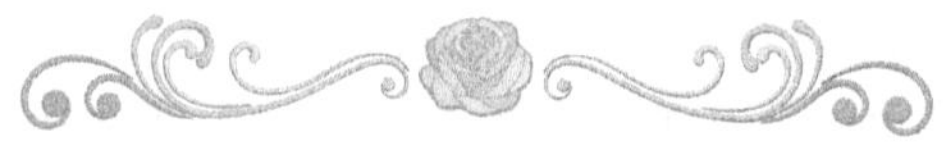

Chapter Three

I tore through the house like I was looking for a secret level in a video game.

The letter had blown everything open. *My death is not an accident. Find who killed me.* It looped in my head as I checked drawers, cabinets, under cushions. Nothing. No hidden folders. No conveniently labeled "Murder File."

When the walls started to feel too close, I gave up on the search and headed for the back door. The orange tabby—Willow, according to Owen—trotted at my heels like a tiny, judgmental shadow.

The greenhouse waited at the edge of the yard, just as I remembered it. A glass-walled, sun-soaked sanctuary. As a kid, it had been my castle, my spaceship, my secret portal to anywhere but Hickory Hollow.

I paused at the door, stroking Willow's head. "Here goes nothing," I murmured, and stepped inside.

Humidity wrapped around me like a warm, damp blanket. The air smelled of earth and chlorophyll, green and alive. Rows of plants lined the tables—daisies, daffodils, tulips, and dozens of things I couldn't name. Hanging baskets cascaded color from above. On the workbench, a pair of mud-stained gardening gloves lay exactly where Alice had left them, as if she'd stepped out for a minute.

I swallowed hard.

It looked like time had simply... stopped.

I ran my fingers over the edge of the workbench, a memory rising sharp and clear—Alice's hands in the soil, dark crescents under her nails, bright eyes dancing as she talked about bulbs that slept until the world was ready for them.

You've worked hard for this. Don't let anyone in this town make you feel bad for leaving, Piper.

Thanks, Aunt Alice. I'll miss you.

You'll be back someday, Alice had said. *I know it.*

At the time, I'd chalked it up to wistful aunt talk.

Now, goosebumps prickled down my arms.

Something buzzed past my ear. I swatted at it, expecting a fly. It buzzed back the other direction. I swatted again.

"Hey, do you mind?" a tiny voice snapped. "Trying to fly here."

I froze.

Willow sat primly at my feet, golden eyes wide. The cat meowed like she was commenting on the situation.

"Who's there?" I asked, scanning the greenhouse. "Owen? Is that you? Because if you're hiding in a fern, this friendship is over before it starts."

"Me. I'm here." The voice sounded equal parts annoyed and tiny.

A flutter brushed across my cheek—a faint puff of air—and then something zipped in front of my face and pinched my nose.

"Ow!" I stumbled back into the workbench, pots rattling. "What the—"

"Well, well, well." The little... being... hovered at eye level, hands on hips. "Who's the fancy-pants girlie?"

I stared.

Because there was no other word for her.

Fairy.

She was maybe six inches tall, wings a blur of glittering motion. Pointed ears peeked through short, choppy hair. Her clothes looked like someone had looted a Renaissance festival and shrunk it—tiny leather vest, leggings, and what was absolutely a miniature dagger at her hip.

I closed my eyes, took a steadying breath, and opened them again.

Still there.

“Okay,” I said faintly. “Either I’m having a full-on break with reality, or—”

“Or you’re rude,” the fairy said. “Staring is rude, FYI. Willow tried to warn me you’d be dramatic.”

The cat meowed, as if confirming it.

“You can... understand the cat,” I said.

“Obviously.” The fairy rolled her eyes. “And she doesn’t like being called ‘the cat.’ Makes her feel inferior.”

“Sorry, Willow,” I muttered, because apparently that was my life now.

I looked back at the fairy. “Who are you?”

“Wow, straight to the good questions.” The fairy zipped in a circle around me, inspecting my outfit like a critic judging a red carpet. “You must be Alice’s kid. You look like her. No wonder she hid you.”

“I’m her niece,” I said. “Piper.”

“Sure, sure. If that’s what you say.” The tiny eyebrows arched. “But yeah. Same eyes. It’s freaky.”

“No, it’s not,” I said automatically.

“Puh-lease.” The fairy thumbed her own chest. “I spent enough time with Alice to know. I’m Titania. You can call me Tani.”

“Tani.” My brain tried to recalibrate. “And you’re a...?”

“Fairy.” She flashed a grin. “Yep. Wings, tiny, devastatingly cute. What gave it away?”

“There’s no such thing as fairies,” I blurted. Part of me clung hard to that statement.

Tani snorted. "Right. And I'm a hallucination in good lighting." She buzzed closer and gave my cheek a light smack. "I'm literally in front of your face, doll. Where's Alice?"

Willow meowed again, tail flicking.

I dragged a hand through my hair. "Okay. Fine. Sure. Why not. Talking fairy. Talking cat. Next up, the roses sing show tunes."

"So," Tani said briskly, wings humming as she floated over to perch between two potted plants, "you never answered me. Where's Alice?"

My throat tightened. "She... died," I said quietly.

The fairy's wings stuttered and stilled. She dropped onto the workbench, shoulders sagging. Willow let out a low, mournful sound.

"No," Tani whispered. "No. No, no, no." She put her tiny face in her hands. "I knew something bad was coming. I told her she was in over her head, but would she listen? Of course not."

"You didn't know?" I asked. Somehow, the sight of a sobbing fairy made it all feel even more real.

Tani sniffled, wiping her nose with her sleeve. "I haven't seen her in days. I figured she was buried in orders or arguing with that ridiculous council again."

"The... what now?"

"Never mind." Tani waved that aside. "What happened?"

"Everyone says it was a heart attack," I said. "But Alice..." I took a breath. "Alice left me a letter. She thinks someone killed her."

Tani's head shot up, eyes huge and shining. "She wrote to you? Of course she did."

"She also left me everything," I added. "The house. The shop. Apparently, I'm in charge now."

Tani stared. "You?"

I bristled. "Wow. Try not to sound so horrified."

"Do you know anything about what she was doing?" Tani demanded. "About the shop? About—" She snapped her mouth shut.

"About what?" I stepped closer, folding my arms. "Because so far? No one seems to be giving me the whole picture. Owen gets weird when I mention Enchanted Blossoms. You act like I announced I'm taking over a dragon lair. So, if you know something, now would be a great time to share with the class."

"There's nothing to tell," Tani said too fast, pacing a tiny track between the pots. "And you're absolutely right. There's nothing to running a flower shop. Easy peasy. Petals and potions and done."

"Potions?" I repeated.

"Figure of speech." Tani flashed a strained grin. "Anyway, you'll be great. Alice said you would be."

Willow meowed, a questioning sound.

"Yes, I know, Willow," Tani said. "The cute guy coming by to feed you makes more sense now."

I blinked. "He's been coming here every day?"

"He has," Tani said dryly. "Seriously, try to keep up, girlie."

I filed that away for later. "Look, I need to get to the shop," I said, backing toward the door. "Apparently there's more waiting for me there."

Tani's expression softened. "You'll be back," she said. "You and I still have things to discuss, Piper Wakefield."

Not ominous at all.

I stepped out of the greenhouse, the heat hitting me in the face again. I jogged back inside the house long enough to grab my purse, then headed for Alice's enormous Cadillac. It was the opposite of my usual sleek city aesthetic—boat-sized, beige, and deeply uncool—but the AC worked and it was mine.

I slid behind the wheel. "Well," I muttered, turning the key, "at least I'll never have to worry about carpooling."

The engine rumbled to life, and I steered out onto the rural highway on muscle memory alone. Hickory Hollow might have shrunk in my rearview for ten years, but it was still mapped under my skin.

Town Hall Street came into view, with its neat line of brick storefronts and lampposts trying hard to look charming. The florist sat halfway down, big window boxes overflowing with blue roses in a shade not found in any garden or seed catalogue. The sign on the glass read Enchanted Blossoms in deep blue script.

As I parked, something prickled along my arms. Not nerves. Not exactly. More like static in the air, as if the world was holding its breath.

Great. Add "weird magical tingle" to my growing list of concerns.

I pushed open the shop door. The bell chimed, bright and oddly soothing.

Inside, a man at the counter turned toward me, a vase of flowers in his arms. Behind the register stood a girl with black lipstick, a streak of purple in her short black hair, and enough eyeliner to smudge into next week. Nose ring, choker, all-black clothes—goth chic in a town that still treated acid-washed jeans like a personality.

"That all, sir?" the girl asked, cracking her gum.

"Yes. Thank you." He paid, nodded, and brushed past me on his way out, the bell chiming again as the door shut behind him.

Before I could figure out what to say, a familiar voice called my name.

"Piper Wakefield."

I turned—and barely had time to register the voice before Halle Turner pulled me into a fierce, breath-stealing hug.

"Oh my God," Halle said, laughing a little as she squeezed tighter. "You're real. I was half afraid I imagined you."

Halle smelled like vanilla and something expensive I vaguely recognized. She looked exactly the same—golden hair, green eyes, cheerleader smile—small-town beauty that came with a built-in spotlight.

"I heard you were back," Halle said, pulling away enough to look me over. "You haven't aged a day."

"Liar," I said, smiling despite the strange knot in my chest. "You look exactly like you did at prom. It's suspicious."

"I'm here picking up flowers for a client," Halle said, then hesitated. "I saw you at the funeral, but... I don't know. I chickened out."

I blinked. That didn't fit with the fearless girl who used to drag me onto any dance floor within a fifty-mile radius.

"Intimidated," Halle admitted, cheeks pinking. "You looked so... New York. The magazine. The clothes. You got out. You did the thing."

Yeah. About that.

My smile tightened. "It's been... a ride."

"I'm sorry about Alice," Halle said, sincerity softening her voice. "She was wonderful."

"She was," I agreed, the ache flaring fresh and sharp.

"I should go—I've got a client waiting," Halle said quickly. "But lunch this week? Please. We'll do it right this time."

She kissed my cheek, then scooped up the enormous vase on the counter, and disappeared out the door before I could find my footing again.

The silence that followed felt oddly loud.

"Awkward," the goth girl behind the counter declared.

I huffed out a laugh. "You have no idea."

"So, hey." The girl gave me a chin-lift. "I'm Rylyn. Alice said you'd be the one."

"The one what?" I asked.

"To take over. Duh." Rylyn popped her gum again. "I'm the part-time help. Been keeping this place running since Alice kicked it."

I flinched. "That's... one way to put it."

Rylyn shrugged, like death was an unfortunate scheduling conflict. "I figured you'd show up eventually."

"Sorry it took me so long," I said. "I only found out yesterday about the will."

"Cool." Rylyn stared at me. Intensely. Unblinking.

I shifted. "What?"

"You look like her," Rylyn said. "It's kinda freaking me out."

"Everyone keeps saying that," I muttered.

"No, like." Rylyn leaned on the counter, eyes narrowing. "It's more than 'you have the same eyes.' It's like déjà vu. But, whatever."

A little chill slid down my spine. For the first time, the casual comments about my resemblance to Alice felt less like flattery and more like... something else.

"How long did you work for Alice?" I asked.

"Long enough," Rylyn said, which was apparently the default answer around here. "She was cool. Weird, but cool."

"Was her death... unexpected?" I pressed.

"You think so, too, huh?" Rylyn's gaze sharpened.

I dropped my voice. "Did you think she was murdered?"

Rylyn's fingers tapped a restless rhythm on the counter. "I don't know. She was acting strange the day before. Kept watching the front windows, muttering to herself. Like she was waiting for something bad to happen—and already knew it would. Then she's dead in her garden and everybody's, like, 'welp, heart attack.'" She shrugged. "Doesn't add up."

Before I could respond, Rylyn snapped her fingers like she'd remembered something. "Oh. Right. Hang on."

She disappeared through the door to the back, leaving me alone with the hum of the coolers and the faint chime of the wind bells in the window. Potted plants crowded the space, cheerful and oblivious. The blue roses in the boxes outside cast dappled shadows onto the floor.

Rylyn reappeared holding a large brown envelope and a small key.

She circled the counter and held out the envelope. "This is for you."

I stared at my name on the front in Alice's familiar handwriting, written in bold block letters. My fingers tingled as I took it.

"And this key," Rylyn said, dangling the key, "Alice said to keep it until you came."

I slid the key off Rylyn's finger, my heart thumping. "What does the key go to?"

She shrugged. "No idea. She wanted me to keep it for you, so I did."

Great. A mysterious key.

"How did she even know I'd show up?"

Rylyn snorted. "It's Alice. She knew stuff. Like when Mrs. Jenkins was gonna come in for sympathy lilies before her husband died. Creepy in a helpful way."

She turned toward the door.

"Where are you going?" I asked, clutching the envelope.

"Home. I'm done." Rylyn shrugged. "I've put in enough OT for a lifetime. So, like, I quit."

Panic clawed up my throat. "You can't quit. I need you."

"Alice said you'd know what to do," Rylyn said. "So, I'm out."

"I don't care what Alice said." I followed her to the door, heels clicking. "Rylyn, please. I don't have the first clue how to run a flower shop. My last job was at a fashion magazine. I know hemlines and color stories, not... watering schedules."

Rylyn hesitated, hand on the door. Her dark eyes narrowed, assessing.

"Stay through the end of summer," I rushed on. "Six weeks. Teach me how not to kill everything. Then you can leave, and I'll sign whatever glowing recommendation you want."

Rylyn sighed like the weight of the world rested on her narrow shoulders. "Fine. But come Labor Day, I'm gone. Vanished. Poof."

"Deal." Relief flooded me so hard I swayed. "Thank you."

"Don't thank me yet," Rylyn said. "We still have to get you through your first funeral order without making the lilies look like a threat."

I looked around the shop—at the flowers, the coolers, the secret envelope in my hand, the safe key burning a hole in my palm—and realized this was real.

I was no longer the girl who'd run away to the city.

I was the woman who'd come back to an enchanted flower shop, a dead aunt with secrets, a flirty almost-stranger who wasn't a stranger at all...

... and a mystery that might be bigger than Hickory Hollow—or my world—could contain.

Chapter Four

That afternoon, I moved my things from my parents' house to the one on Snapdragon Drive that now—apparently—belonged to me. The envelope was tucked safely into my bag, the key already on my keyring, cold and solid against my fingers whenever I reached for my car keys.

My mother had gone from icy to permafrost in record time. Every look said *how dare you be the one Alice chose* even though I hadn't asked for any of this. Gladys had all but stopped speaking to me, which made lugging my luggage past her a special kind of awkward.

Willow padded after me from room to room, tail high, as if personally overseeing the relocation. I hadn't set foot back in the greenhouse since meeting Tani. I wasn't sure if I was avoiding the fairy, the truth, or both.

The next two days blurred into a crash course in Florist 101 with Rylyn as my reluctant professor. Once you got past the eyeliner, the sarcasm, and the nose ring, Rylyn was sharp as a tack and stupidly talented. She did most of the arrangements herself, turning stems and greenery into miniature works of art.

It was... not what I'd expected from the girl who looked like she fronted a goth band.

Running the shop was easier than I thought it would be—phone orders, walk-ins, sympathy arrangements, birthday bouquets. I learned how to work the temperamental cooler, how to place rush orders, how not to murder delicate blooms with too much water. The work was steady, my hands were always busy, and for the first time since Manhattan imploded, my brain had something to focus on besides failure.

Not that I had a choice. This was my life now, at least for the foreseeable future. Florist. Small-town business owner.

Every customer seemed to remember me. Hickory Hollow never forgot anyone. There were the inevitable questions.

What are you doing back in town, Piper?

Why didn't your mama get the shop?

Why didn't Iris?

You gonna stay?

I smiled, deflected, lied by omission. *Just helping out... Still figuring things out... We'll see.* No way was I unpacking the "your aunt might have been murdered" part of my life over credit card receipts.

By the third day, Rylyn declared me "mostly competent" and took a hard-won day off. I opened alone, answered the phone without panicking, filled two orders for anniversary arrangements, and even managed not to maim any roses.

Late morning, when there was finally a lull, I grabbed a watering can, filled it, and stepped outside to tend the blue roses spilling from the long window box. I'd ditched the heels for flat leather sandals and rolled the sleeves of my linen blouse, the fabric already clinging in the Texas heat.

The sun beat down on my shoulders like it had a personal grudge. It wasn't even noon, and the pavement shimmered like a mirage.

I tipped the can, watching the water darken the soil. The simple, repetitive motion was weirdly soothing—until a shadow crossed the street.

My heart did a ridiculous little hop.

Owen McAllister crossed from the antique store, hands in his pockets, the morning sun haloing his messy hair. He smiled, slow and easy, and the hop in my chest turned into a full-on dance.

His shirt was open at the collar, sleeves rolled to his elbows like he was ready to pitch in if I asked. Faded jeans. Scuffed work boots. Nothing tailored, nothing precious. He looked like someone who knew how to fix things instead of billing by the hour.

He was the opposite of Wall Street polish—and I found, to my surprise, that I liked this far better. Especially on him.

"Morning," he called. "Aren't you giving those a bit too much water?"

I jerked my attention back to the window box. Water was spilling out the bottom and running over the lip like a tiny waterfall. I yanked the can upright.

"Great," I muttered.

He stopped a few feet away, all rumpled good looks and stubble and unfairly broad shoulders. Up close, he smelled faintly of soap and sun-warmed cotton, like he'd stepped out of the day instead of a boardroom.

"First day alone?"

"Yes." That came out way too bright. I tightened my grip on the can.

"How's the house?" he asked.

I shifted, suddenly aware of sweat trickling down my spine and the fact that my hair was probably doing something tragic in this humidity. Small talk. He wanted small talk. Why did small talk with him feel like an oral exam?

"How'd you know I moved in?" I asked.

He tipped his head, amused. "Everyone knows. Small town, remember?"

Right. Hickory Hollow. Where privacy went to die.

He nodded at the planter again. "You only need to dampen the soil. If the water's running off, you're drowning them."

"How do you know that?" I challenged.

He shrugged, unbothered. "I'm no florist, but I do a little gardening. Light gardening," he added, flashing that grin that made my stupid knees consider giving out.

He was drawing me in without even trying. I hated that. I hated that I liked it.

"I have to get back to work," I blurted, before my brain could betray me any further.

I flung open the door and strode inside. The bell chimed brightly, foiling my attempt at a dramatic exit. A moment later, footsteps followed. Of course he came in.

"Me too," Owen said easily, glancing at his watch. "I've got to get back to the store. But first—would you like to have lunch with me?"

I froze mid-step.

Lunch. With him. The town hottie. My stupid heart swooped, and heat flashed through my whole body before I could stomp on the feeling.

It was lunch. Not a proposal. Not a forever. But still—

"Stop looking at me like that," I said, setting the watering can in the sink a little too hard.

"Like what?" His smile softened into something shy.

Like he already knew my answer.

"All that smiling. It's unnerving."

He immediately sobered, though the corners of his mouth still wanted to curve. "Sorry. I can't help it when I look at you."

I snorted, because the alternative was melting into a puddle. "You're ridiculous."

"No, really. You have this... thing."

"Absolutely not," I said. "I do not have a thing."

"Well, I think you do, and my opinion is the only one that matters. So. Lunch?"

"No."

"Why not?"

"Because." I folded my arms.

"That's not a reason."

"It is for me."

"It's a lunch date, Piper. Not a life commitment."

"Date is a four-letter word, McAllister. I'm not ready for that."

He held my gaze, unoffended. Understanding flickered there instead.

Before he could reply, the temperature in the shop plummeted.

One heartbeat it was Texas-in-late-June hot, the next a cold draft slithered across my skin like someone had opened a walk-in freezer. My teeth chattered. My breath fogged in front of my face.

Black smoke seeped under the front door.

It crawled along the tile in a thick, unnatural wave, moving with intent—smoke that didn't drift so much as hunt.

I sucked in a sharp breath and instinctively backed up, bumping into the sink. Nowhere to go. No escape.

The smoke coiled up, twisting, stretching—and solidified into something straight out of my worst nightmare.

The thing that stood in front of me was massive, its horned head nearly brushing the ceiling. Coarse fur matted its body. Two curved tusks jutted from either side of a broad snout. Where hands should have been, it had cloven hooves.

It leaned in, bringing with it a wave of rancid breath that smelled like rot and brimstone.

"Piper—" Owen started.

The creature swatted him aside like he weighed nothing. Owen crashed to the floor, the impact rattling the card rack beside him.

The beast planted both hooves on the tile and leaned over the counter, bringing its glowing blue eyes level with mine. The pupils were slitted like a snake.

"Where is Alice?" it rumbled, its voice deep enough to vibrate in my bones.

My throat closed. I couldn't move. Couldn't think.

It inhaled deeply, nostrils flaring. "You smell like her. Where is she?"

"Alice is dead," Owen said hoarsely.

My gaze jerked toward him. He was on his feet again, hands fisted, jaw locked. Gone was the charming, easygoing guy. In his place was someone hard and dangerous.

"Get away from her," Owen ordered.

The demon snarled and drool flung from its tusks.

"I said, get away from her."

"Owen—" I whispered.

The creature charged him, head down like a bull.

Owen sidestepped at the last possible second. The beast plowed into the card rack, sending cards flying in a confetti explosion. The metal stand toppled with a screech as the creature crashed to the floor, dazed.

It shook its head, snorting, then fixed me with one last hateful look. In the space of a blink, it dissolved back into black smoke and vanished, sucked away as if through an invisible drain.

The room was suddenly, horribly quiet.

Only the faint sulfur stink lingered.

I stared at the place where it had been, heart pounding in my ears. The cards lay scattered like fallen leaves. My hands wouldn't stop shaking.

"What just happened?" I managed. "What *was* that?"

Owen straightened the card rack, then turned to me. The professor-serious expression on his face sent another chill down my spine.

"It was looking for Alice," he said. "That means someone sent it. I think we need to talk."

I flipped the sign to closed and locked the front door. Forget lunch rush. I needed answers and possibly a gallon of tequila.

We drove to a Mexican restaurant on the highway, far enough out of town that nosy Hickory Hollow eyes were less likely to peer over their chips and salsa.

As soon as I slid into the booth, I ordered a frozen margarita.

Owen lifted a brow. "Don't judge," I said.

"It's barely noon."

"It's noon somewhere," I shot back. "Spill your guts, McAllister. What was that thing?"

"That," he said, no hesitation, "was a demon."

I froze, chip halfway to my mouth. "I'm sorry, what?"

My drink arrived, all salted rim and artificial lime. I took a long pull, bracing for the brain freeze as much as the answer. It hit hard and sharp. I winced.

"I mean, I heard you," I said through the ice pick in my skull. "And normally I'd say there's no such thing as demons, but I met a fairy in the greenhouse, so apparently the universe is done pretending to be normal."

Owen blinked. "There's a fairy in the greenhouse?"

"Yeah. Little, mouthy, insults my wardrobe. Her name is Tani."

One eyebrow climbed. "And you didn't think to mention this?"

I threw up a hand. "Sorry, it didn't come up in conversation between 'hey, how are you' and 'maybe a demon tried to kill me.'" I leaned in, lowering my voice. "Was Alice in trouble?"

He toyed with his fork, jaw tense. "I'll tell you what I know. It isn't much. There's something... magical about Hickory Hollow. Something Alice was involved with in the woods."

"The woods?" I echoed. "What's in the woods?"

He glanced around the restaurant like he expected a demon to pop out from behind the salsa bar, then leaned closer until our faces were only inches apart.

"Have you ever heard of ley lines?" he asked.

"Sure. Vaguely. Lines of energy, sacred sites, England, Stonehenge, all that. But that's more New Age blog than science class."

His mouth twitched. "Someone was paying attention in something."

We were too close. His eyes were a soft gray storm and for a second, I forgot why we were whispering about magical geography. My pulse stuttered. A nervous giggle bubbled up and escaped before I could smother it.

Then I realized we were practically sharing air.

I sat back fast. So did he. I fidgeted with my napkin. He rearranged his silverware like it had personally offended him.

The waitress arrived then to take our order. When she was off with our selections, he continued.

"This is going to be hard to explain," he said finally. "Mostly because I don't have all the pieces. What I do know is... sketchy." He reached for a chip, dipped it in the salsa. "You know what I like about this hot sauce? The cilantro and the onion chunks. You can tell it's fresh."

I glared. "Do not change the subject, McAllister."

He sighed, set the chip down, and leaned in again, every trace of humor gone. "There's a hickory tree in the woods north of town. A big one. Old. That's where the ley lines converge."

He dropped his voice to a whisper. "Piper... they're magical."

I stared at him for a long beat, waiting for the punch line. "That's a good one. I believed you for a second."

His expression didn't budge. No smirk, no twitch, nothing.

Something cold slid through my stomach.

Because Owen never joked like this. Not about serious things. Not with that look in his eyes—steady, intent, worried.

And worse... some small, traitorous part of me didn't want him to laugh.

"Oh God," I whispered. "You're serious."

He nodded once.

The margarita turned to sludge in my stomach.

Before I could ask my next question, the waitress returned with our food. But I'd suddenly lost my appetite.

"How does a magical tree equal demon attack?" I asked.

"It's the hub," he said. "They call it the... supernatural superhighway."

"That is the worst name I've ever heard."

"I didn't name it," he said dryly. "But that's what it is. A portal. Or a junction. Or something. Your aunt—Alice—was the Guardian. Her job was to keep the gate closed and the bad things out."

Aunt Alice. With her gentle hands and dirt under her nails and stories about other lands told in the twilight.

A guardian.

"Portal," I repeated faintly. "Like... to where?"

"Whatever's on the other side," he said. "Other realms. Other dimensions. Places not here. I don't know. All I know is, every day she brewed a potion using flowers she grew herself. Then she'd go to the tree and use it to reinforce the barrier. Keep the evil out. Keep the gate sealed."

Other realms. The words slotted too easily into the memory of Alice's stories. Woods that whispered. Castles under starlight. Borders thin as glass.

"How do you know all this?" I asked.

Owen hesitated, then reached across the table and closed his hand around mine. His fingers were warm, solid, anchoring.

"Because my dad was helping her," he said. "They met at the shop. A lot. Behind closed doors. At first, I thought they were having an affair—"

I almost choked. Alice and Mr. McAllister having an affair was so absurd my brain refused to picture it.

"—but it wasn't that," Owen continued. "It was this. The tree. The ley lines. The gate. She needed help. He's... he knows things.

Old things. He said Crossroads work attracts the wrong attention. The kind that doesn't stay buried."

"Well that sounds ominous." I didn't like it at all.

He nodded agreement. "He was the one who told me about the demon, about how the wards worked, about what could happen if they failed."

Cold prickles raced over my skin. "Like demons showing up at the flower shop asking where Alice is."

"Exactly." He squeezed my hand gently. "You said you thought she was murdered."

I nodded.

"I think so, too, Piper. And I think my dad might know why."

I drew in a slow breath, the restaurant noise fading to a dull roar in my ears. Murder. Magic. Portals. Demons. Fairies. Hickory Hollow wasn't weird. It was... connected. To what, I still didn't know. But I could feel it now—a hum under my skin, like standing too close to a live wire.

"I think," I said carefully, "we need to go see your dad."

Owen nodded, eyes steady on mine. "He'll have more answers than I do. We can go after lunch."

I looked down at my untouched enchiladas. My appetite had fled somewhere between demon and portal. I slid the plate away.

"Good," I said. "Because I'm done pretending this is normal."

Chapter Five

I had the waitress box up my untouched enchiladas. My stomach still sloshed with margarita and nerves, the two combining into a lovely cocktail of acid and oh-no-what-have-I-gotten-myself-into.

Black smoke. A demon. A fairy in the greenhouse. At this rate, a talking llama would barely make the top five weirdest things that had happened this week.

I hadn't seen Dougal McAllister in years. I knew him—everyone in Hickory Hollow knew the man who ran the antique store across from Enchanted Blossoms. Owen's dad. Walking reminder that the past never stayed in the past around here.

As we drove back toward town, I stared through the bug-splattered windshield, my thoughts whirling faster than the passing trees.

"Mac is your dad," I blurted, breaking the silence.

Owen's fingers flexed on the steering wheel. "Yeah. He is."

"When you introduced yourself, you said your name was Mac."

"So, I took his name." He was quiet for a beat. "Honestly? When I saw you on the side of the road, I panicked. I didn't know if you'd remember me, or if you did, what you'd think. Dad's been 'Mac' my whole life—it just came out. And then I wanted to see if you'd figure it out."

It shouldn't matter. It did anyway.

"In my aunt's letter, she said you liked me. Do you?" The words tumbled out before I could stop them.

Owen's head snapped toward me, surprise written all over his annoyingly handsome face. Okay, maybe the tequila had been a mistake.

"Are you drunk?" he asked.

I flushed and stared hard at the road. "No. Answer the question, McAllister."

"So, I'm McAllister now, not Owen."

I blew a raspberry in his direction and crossed my arms, wishing I could crawl under the seat and stay there.

"Yes, Piper. I like you." His voice went soft, earnest. "I've always liked you. Since the day you pushed me down on the playground in kindergarten."

Heat rushed up my chest and into my cheeks. He remembered that?

And all this time I thought Hickory Hollow was in the past. Turns out, pieces of me were still living here.

I'd been six. Halle dared me to kiss Owen McAllister. He'd run; I'd chased him, grabbed his shirt sleeve, shoved him down, and landed on top of him to plant a quick kiss on his cheek. He'd shoved me off and stuck out his tongue like I'd given him cooties.

The teacher had caught us and hauled us both to the principal's office.

Maybe my crush had started way earlier than late high school.

"I don't remember that," I lied.

"Now who's the liar?" he said, but there was no heat in it.

I scowled out the window. "Can we go see your dad?"

He smirked, victorious, as he pulled into a space in front of Charmed & Vintage. The bell over the door jingled when we stepped inside. The familiar smell hit me first—dust, old wood, polish, and something sharper underneath. The place was crammed with furniture and objects that looked like they carried stories whether you wanted them or not.

Dougal McAllister looked exactly like a man who belonged in a shop full of secrets. Tall—easily six-three—with the same straight nose and square jaw as his son, he wore a white golf shirt, black pants, and polished shoes. Less rumpled professor, more retired navy captain.

"Owen," Dougal said, brows lifting. "What brings you here this time of day?"

"Hey, Dad. You remember Piper Wakefield?"

"Of course." He stepped forward and held out his hand. When I took it, he closed his other hand over mine, his grip warm and solid. "I was sorry to hear about Alice."

"Thanks," I managed.

"She was a special lady." His gaze softened, studying my face in a way that made something twist low in my chest. "You have large shoes to fill."

"So you've heard?" I asked. "About the will?"

He scratched his chin. "Hard not to, with Iris running around town spewing her nonsense."

I winced. Of course Iris was airing dirty laundry all over Hickory Hollow. The thought made my shoulders creep up toward my ears. Maybe Iris was owed something. Maybe I *was* the spoiled brat who got everything.

"Dad, we need to talk to you," Owen said. He glanced around the cluttered shop. "In private."

Dougal's expression sharpened. "What's this about, son?"

"Please, Mr. McAllister," I said. "It's important. And it's about my aunt. I was hoping you could answer a few questions."

Realization flickered through his eyes. He nodded once. "Of course. Follow me."

He led us through a maze of chairs, sideboards, and mysterious trunks to a door marked PRIVATE. Inside was a small, dusty office crammed with a desk, a computer, a filing cabinet, and enough floor space for two chairs.

He waved us into the seats and propped himself against the edge of the desk.

"You've come about the ritual, I suppose," he said. "I wondered when I might see you."

"I told her some of it," Owen said. "But I don't have all the details."

Dougal nodded. "I'll tell you what I can, but Alice kept most of it close." His gaze settled on me. "She didn't want it getting out."

"Why not?" I asked.

"She was afraid it would bring unwanted attention to the town."

I thought of the demon in the flower shop, the tusks and the drool and the smell of rot. Pretty sure the unwanted attention had already arrived.

"Do the townspeople know about this... supernatural superhighway thing?" I asked.

"Some of them," Dougal said. "At least in the old families. Alice took great pains to keep it under wraps. But over the last few months, something changed. She was afraid. Kept to herself more. She came to me a couple of times for help."

He cut a glance at Owen, then drew a long breath. "I tried, Piper. I don't think I was successful."

My fingers tightened around my knees. "What do you know about her death?"

Dougal looked to Owen again.

"I told her," Owen said quietly. "I think something killed Alice for what she was doing."

Dougal's shoulders sagged a fraction. He studied me closely. "How much do you know?"

"Not much," I admitted. "Just that there was some ritual she had to perform at the tree. That's what Owen told me."

Dougal nodded slowly. “That’s true. But what he didn’t tell you—because he didn’t know—is that the tree is dying. Alice was trying to keep it alive.”

Owen stiffened beside me. I felt my pulse jump.

“Owen told me she was a... guardian,” I said.

“Yes,” Dougal said. “Guardian of the Crossroads.” His voice went grave. “Her duty was to keep the gate clear of black magic and darkness. But over the last few months, dark things have been seeping into our world. Things out of our worst nightmares.”

His mouth flattened. “Someone—or something—has been stealing pieces of bark from the hickory tree. Alice believed that was what was killing it. And if the tree dies...” He let the thought hang for a beat. “There’ll be nothing left to stop them from coming through. Into Hickory Hollow. And then into the rest of the world.”

My aunt hadn’t been protecting a town. She’d been holding back the dark.

And Enchanted Blossoms, the house on Snapdragon Drive, the greenhouse, Town Hall Street—none of it was quaint small-town baggage anymore. It was the line.

If the tree died, Hickory Hollow wouldn’t be the place I’d come back to. It would be the first thing to fall.

He straightened and looked me dead in the eye.

“Piper, you’re her heir. It’s up to you to be the Guardian now.”

The words sat between us, heavy and unreal.

“No,” I said, shaking my head. “That’s not— I’m not—” I broke off, breath unsteady. “Alice never told me any of this.”

The shop. The house. The word *ever* in Alice’s will. I’d thought she was trapping me in Hickory Hollow.

But this was worse. She hadn’t trapped me here. She’d handed me the keys and expected me to hold the door against whatever lived on the other side.

Dougal didn't rush to fill the silence. Instead, he exhaled slowly, as if weighing how much truth I could bear.

"Hickory Hollow sits in a strange place," he said at last. "Some towns are just towns. Others..."

He hesitated, lips pressing thin, gaze drifting briefly toward the wall—as if he could see past it.

"Others exist where paths overlap. Where worlds brush too close. Your aunt used to say it was a Crossroads—whether people believed in that or not."

Silence slammed into the room.

I stared at him, the words ricocheting through my skull.

Guardian. Gate. Worst nightmares. Me.

My stomach cramped so sharply I folded in half, bracing my elbows on my thighs and dropping my head between my knees.

"You okay, Piper?" Owen's hand landed between my shoulder blades, warm and steady.

"I'm in a lot of trouble," I muttered. Then I jerked my head up and glared at him. "You knew and didn't tell me, didn't you? That's why you freaked out when I said Alice left me everything."

He had the decency to look guilty. "I knew... some. I didn't know what you knew, and I didn't want to be the one to tell you." He winced. "Sorry I was the one to tell you."

I pressed the heel of my hand to my forehead. "I think I'm going to be sick."

"Get her some water, son," Dougal said.

Owen slipped out, leaving me alone with his father.

"Piper," Dougal said gently, "I think there was a reason Alice left you her estate. I don't know what it is yet."

"You don't know," I said, "or you can't tell me?"

His gaze flickered, something unreadable moving there. "I don't know. Alice was a smart woman. She never did anything without a plan. She'd been keeping that gate at the hickory tree for a long time."

"How long?" I asked.

"Years." Dougal pushed away from the desk and moved to stand in front of me. He crouched until we were eye to eye. Up close, I could see the worry carved into the lines around his mouth. "Owen doesn't know this part, but I was helping her keep some artifacts."

My skin prickled. "What sort of artifacts?"

"Magical ones," he said simply. "I don't know where she got them. I didn't ask. She told me the antique shop would be the perfect place to keep them. So I agreed."

Because of course the place across from Enchanted Blossoms doubled as a magical storage facility. Why wouldn't it.

"Where are these things now?" I asked.

"In the storeroom. Locked up in crates like she wanted." Dougal straightened and paced the cramped office. "Also, Piper... your aunt was a witch."

My mouth went dry. For a second, I thought I'd misheard him.

Alice, with her gentle hands and dirt-smudged gloves. Alice, who told stories about other realms like they were half-remembered dreams. A witch.

Something strange flickered there again when he said *your aunt*, like the words didn't sit right in his mouth. It slid down my spine like a tiny shard of ice.

I might have laughed if Owen hadn't reappeared with a paper cup of water. Dougal fell silent while I gulped the cool liquid down in one go. I pressed the empty cup into Owen's hand.

"Another, please," I croaked.

Owen shot his father a look and slipped out again.

"You can't be serious," I said as soon as the door shut. "Witches are born, not made."

"Sometimes," Dougal said. His tone stayed calm, careful. "And sometimes people grow into what they already are. Or learn how to *use* things they didn't know they had." His gaze flicked to the door, then back to me. "Owen doesn't know."

Owen returned and handed me another cup. I drained it, grateful for the coolness against my raw throat and knotted stomach. Then I crushed the cup in my fist and stood.

"Well. Thank you for your time, Mr. McAllister."

He smiled faintly. "Let me know if I can be of further help."

"Oh, I will," I said. "Count on it."

I turned to Owen. "Can you take me home? I'm not sure I should be driving."

"Sure. No problem."

We said goodbye and stepped back out into the store, then into the bright afternoon. The drive to Snapdragon Drive was quiet, the air between us thick with everything unsaid.

"I heard what my dad told you," Owen said finally, eyes on the road.

"What?" I asked, though I already knew.

"He said your aunt was a witch."

A slow, shaky breath slipped out of me. "Yes." The word came out thin and cold.

"Do you believe him?" he asked.

"I don't know. Do you?" I studied his profile, the tight line of his jaw, the way his fingers tightened on the wheel.

"Maybe," he said. "Probably."

"I'm sorry he didn't tell you," I said. "No one told me, either."

He huffed out a humorless laugh. "I guess we're both in the dark. Just... different dark."

"Me more than you," I said softly. "I feel like I'm standing in a room with the lights off, and things keep moving that I can't see."

"I'm still willing to help you," he said.

"I know." And I did. "Thank you. I appreciate that. When I know what I'm doing, maybe you can."

Because whether I understood any of it or not, the tree was dying. Alice was dead. And Hickory Hollow was somehow mine now in a way I had never asked for and could no longer pretend didn't matter.

He pulled into my driveway and shifted into park. I rested my hand on the door handle, then paused to look at him.

"Thanks, Owen. For everything."

Our gazes caught and held. Now that I knew he liked me—had always liked me—I felt painfully aware of him. Of the warmth in his eyes. Of the air between us that felt charged, like right before a storm.

"You're welcome," he said quietly.

Before I could overthink it, I leaned across the console and pressed a quick kiss to his cheek. His skin was warm and faintly rough with stubble.

I didn't wait for his reaction. I bolted out of the car, heart racing, and climbed the porch steps. Only once I was inside did I dare peek through the window.

He was still sitting there, one hand on his cheek, as if he wasn't sure what had hit him. I didn't move away until I saw his truck finally back out of the drive and disappear down the road.

A pang of longing caught me off guard, sharp and startling.

Guardian. Witch. Ley lines. Demons.

And Owen McAllister, who had always liked me.

Welcome home, Piper. Whether I was ready for it or not.

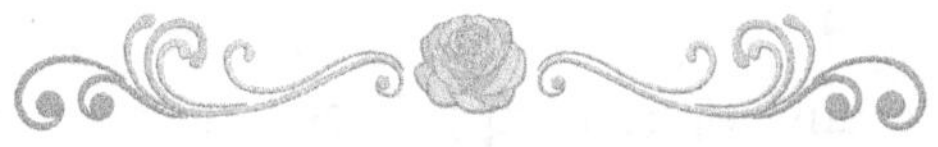

Chapter Six

I spent the rest of the afternoon—and well into the evening—unpacking the last of my clothes.

I couldn't bring myself to use the master bedroom. That room still belonged to Alice. Instead, I claimed the smaller guest room I'd used as a girl. The bed was narrower, the dresser scarred with age, the quilt faded—but it felt right. Familiar. Safe.

When I finished, hunger finally nudged its way past exhaustion. I reheated my boxed-up enchiladas and ate standing at the kitchen counter, not entirely sure why I couldn't bring myself to sit. A restlessness buzzed beneath my skin, sharp and insistent.

I opened a bottle of wine.

Willow stayed glued to my side—watching as I unpacked, settling in the center of the kitchen floor while I ate, weaving between my ankles when I poured a glass. I set out a can of cat food, but Willow sniffed it, flicked her tail dismissively, and followed me into the living room instead.

The envelope Rylyn had given me now resided on the coffee table.

That couldn't be ignored any longer.

I sank onto the sofa, legs tucked beneath me, wineglass in one hand and the envelope in the other. Willow leapt up beside me, golden eyes intent.

"You've been acting like you know something all day," I murmured, scratching behind her ears. "Want to share?"

Willow purred.

I opened the envelope and tipped its contents onto the table. Papers spilled out—scraps, sketches, lists in Alice's familiar handwriting. One page looked like a grocery list. Another held strange symbols and looping notes. And then I found the sheet of notebook paper, stained with a faded coffee ring in one corner.

A letter.

My chest tightened as I unfolded it.

Alice's handwriting marched across the page in neat, steady lines, so familiar it made my throat ache.

My dear Piper—I am sorrier than I can say for placing this burden on your shoulders. But the truth could no longer wait. Hickory Hollow is not merely a town. It is a crossing place, a place of old power. Long before it had roads or fences or a church bell, there were legends that named this land enchanted. Magical. A place where the borders between worlds wore thin.

By the third line, the wine turned sour in my stomach.

Everything Owen and Dougal had told me earlier wasn't just true—it was documented. Alice spelled it out plainly. The ley lines. The gate. The role she'd played as Guardian. The daily ritual that had kept Hickory Hollow from becoming a welcome mat for every nightmare with claws.

And now?

Now it was mine.

My hands shook as I kept reading.

You must take my place, Piper. I wish there had been another way, but there was not. You are the only one I trust to keep the gate, protect the town, and uncover what truly happened to me.

I pressed my lips together hard enough to sting.

"Of course," I muttered. "No pressure or anything."

Willow jumped lightly onto the sofa beside me, then settled with her tail wrapped primly around her paws, watching me with those unnervingly bright golden eyes.

I looked back down at the letter.

There is more you must know. Willow is not merely a cat. She is a witch under a hex, one whose name was once carried into legend and twisted into a children's tale. Long ago they called her a monster in the woods, the witch with the enchanted house and the sugared path. But stories told by the frightened seldom keep the truth intact. She was more guardian than villain, and I promised her I would break the spell laid upon her. If I could not, then perhaps in time you will.

I lowered the paper slowly and stared at the cat

"You're the witch from *Hansel and Gretel*?"

Willow blinked once, slow and unrepentant.

"Wow," I muttered. "Talk about a rebrand problem."

With the composure of someone who had clearly been waiting far too long for me to catch up, she tucked her paws more neatly beneath herself.

"Well," I said, rubbing my forehead, "that explains a few things."

Willow gave a soft, almost smug meow.

I looked back at the letter, pulse thudding in my ears.

Be kind to her. She has been my friend, my companion, and my guard in more ways than you yet understand.

That one got me right in the chest.

Alice hadn't asked me to stay in Hickory Hollow. She'd required it. Built it into the will. And somehow, impossibly, she'd trusted me—only me—to uncover the truth behind her death, guard the crossing, and one day un-hex a witch trapped in cat form.

I took a long drink of wine.

"Of course you did," I said softly.

I sifted through the remaining papers, growing more frustrated by the minute. Notes. Half-finished thoughts. Strange symbols.

No clear instructions. No handy beginner's guide to magical crisis management.

"How am I supposed to make a potion without a recipe?" I demanded the room. "Did you honestly think I'd just figure it out?"

Willow rose, hopped onto the coffee table, and nosed several papers aside before placing both paws squarely on one scrap.

I leaned forward.

It was a list—but not a mundane one.

Unpronounceable names sprawled down the page, each followed by a number.

Latin. Definitely Latin.

I looked at Willow. "You're a genius."

She flicked an ear.

Smiling despite everything, I reached out and scratched her beneath the chin. "I owe you tuna."

I started toward the kitchen—then stopped.

Something scraped upstairs.

Metal against wood.

Slow. Deliberate.

Willow's head snapped up, ears flat.

"Oh no," I whispered. "Nope. I am not doing attic horror-movie nonsense tonight."

Another thud echoed overhead. Then a dragging sound. I moved toward the stairs, one foot on the bottom tread staring up at the ceiling.

A faint orange glow leaked from the seams of the attic door at the top of the stairs.

My pulse spiked.

But I couldn't ignore it, could I? With my heart in my throat, I ascended.

I pulled the ladder down, heart pounding—and immediately realized it wasn't fire.

Light detonated from above, unnatural and pulsing.

"Fantastic," I muttered. "I love this for me."

I climbed.

At the top, a trunk glowed in the corner.

The lid blasted open.

Something massive surged upward.

I screamed and stumbled backward, barely catching myself before tumbling down the ladder. Below me, Willow hissed, body coiled tight.

Then—

Silence.

The light vanished.

The trunk was closed.

Nothing moved.

"I've officially lost my mind," I whispered.

I hustled down the ladder. As I shoved the attic door shut, a familiar voice chimed cheerfully behind me.

"That was a warning."

I nearly jumped out of my skin.

"Tani!"

The fairy hovered at eye level, wings a buzzing blur. "Relax. You're fine. Mostly."

"Oh, that's comforting."

"That thing wasn't fully here yet," Tani said. "It was testing the boundary."

I pinched the bridge of my nose. "Great. Love boundaries that test themselves."

I headed downstairs and snatched the wine bottle. Tani fluttered alongside me.

"You don't have much time," the fairy added. "Whatever Alice stopped is waking up."

"Of course it is."

When I showed her the list, Tani nodded. "Flower ingredients. You're missing the rest."

"Then how do I make the potion?"

"You find the rest the way Alice did."

I stared at her. "Cryptic is not helpful."

Willow brushed against my legs, then padded down the hall—stopping at the basement door.

I sighed. "Basements are never good news."

But I opened the door anyway.

The space below was transformed—clean, bright, orderly. Shelves lined with labeled jars. A worktable laid out like a laboratory.

"This," I breathed, "is definitely not normal aunt behavior."

Willow hopped onto the table and sat squarely over a locked drawer.

I dashed upstairs, returned with the keyring, and opened it.

Inside, a red folder.

A recipe.

Instructions.

Every ingredient listed plainly.

"Yes," I whispered, relief flooding me. "Thank you."

"Now you work," Tani said.

"Tomorrow."

The fairy yawned. "Every missed day widens the gate."

I squared my shoulders, staring at Alice's set up, at the tools I'd never asked for but now owned all the same.

"All right," I said quietly. "Let's get to work."

Tani disappeared in a puff of pink glitter, abandoning me to the basement, the potion notes, and what was rapidly becoming the weirdest night of my life—which was really saying something, considering I'd recently met a fairy, inherited a flower shop, and been informed I was apparently responsible for a supernatural superhighway.

I spent the next stretch of time elbow-deep in jars and labels, muttering terrible Latin to myself and trying to figure out which dried flower looked the least likely to accidentally summon a demon.

Somewhere overhead, the house settled into silence. Down in the basement, I lined up bowls, bottles, and the mortar like I had any idea what I was doing.

Chapter Seven

A pink cloud popped into existence over the worktable, dusting everything in a faint shimmer. Tani appeared in the middle of it, grinning like she'd photobombed reality.

"I'm back!" she announced.

I jumped, nearly dropping the mortar. "You are going to give me a heart attack one of these days."

"Please. Your arteries are fine." Tani planted her tiny fists on her hips. "All right, hit me. What do you need, oh mighty Guardian?"

I shoved the red folder toward her. "You. Reading. Me. Doing. That's the division of labor tonight."

Tani hovered over the pages, eyes skimming the neat type. "Okay, okay. This is the gate-warding blend. Starter-level apocalypse prevention. You got this, chica." She traced a line with one fingertip. "First, you need the daisy, the lily, and the gladiolus. Got that?"

I turned to the shelves, scanning the rows of jars until I found the Latin labels that now meant something thanks to Tani's crash course. *Thymophylla tenuiloba. Gladiolus callianthus. Lilium stargazer.*

"Got 'em," I murmured, pulling each jar down and lining them up along the counter, glass clinking softly.

"How many?" I asked without looking up.

"Let's see..." Paper rustled as Tani skimmed. "Four daisies, six lilies, and four gladiolus. And it says flowers, not petals. So full blooms, sunshine."

"Excellent." I unscrewed lids one by one, the faint ghosts of scent rising up—dry floral and something green and dusty. I counted the blooms out onto a clean ceramic plate. "Next?"

"Two bay leaves, a pinch of St. John's wort, and a teaspoon of vervain." Tani's voice took on a mock-authoritative tone. "Add all that to the mortar with the flowers and crush until it looks like you murdered a garden."

"Comforting," I muttered.

I dug out measuring spoons from a drawer, found the right jars, and measured carefully. Bay leaves. St. John's wort. Vervain. My hands moved on autopilot, but my brain hummed with every choice. This wasn't an aromatherapy experiment. This was the difference between "demon barges in" and "demon stays on its side of the fence."

I tipped the herbs and flowers into the mortar and lifted the pestle, rolling it through the ingredients. Stems snapped. Petals crumbled. The air filled with a heady, electric scent—sharp, clean, faintly citrusy under the floral.

I inhaled and, for a second, felt something loosen in my chest. "Okay. Pulverized garden achieved. Now what?"

"Now you need six drops of lime oil, two drops of patchouli, and twelve drops of yarrow." Tani's wings buzzed as she hovered lower, nose pressing close to the page. "Add to the dry ingredients and mix. Then pour into a vial."

I put three small bottles on the table, hands steady despite the late hour. I counted each drop into the mortar like it was holy water. One. Two. Three. Four. Five. Six. A bright, sharp citrus note cut through the earthier smells. Patchouli next—deep and grounding—then yarrow, grassy and strange.

I stirred slowly with the pestle, watching oil slick through the powdered herbs until everything darkened and clumped together. The mixture looked like something between mud and moss and smelled… weirdly comforting. Like a garden at midnight.

I grabbed a clean glass vial, wedged a tiny funnel into its mouth, and coaxed the mixture inside. When it was full, I pressed a cork into place and held the little bottle up to the bare bulb overhead.

My first real potion.

"Okay," I breathed. "Moment of truth. Now I pour this on the tree and chant, right?"

Tani kept reading. "When finished, pour the mixture at the base of the hickory tree. Take three deep breaths and say—ugh, Alice, you cheeseball—'Protect and save us from harm. Let these oils now work their charm.'"

I snorted. "That sounds like something out of a children's book."

"Yeah, well, children's books usually get the magic right," Tani said. "Don't knock the rhyme, doll. The gate listens."

I studied the vial again, trying to imagine that giant sacred tree, the invisible lines of power Dougal and Owen kept talking about, the way Hickory Hollow sat in the middle of some supernatural superhighway. A Crossroads. A place where worlds brushed too close.

"Still," I said. "That wasn't so hard."

Tani's brows knit. "Hold up. Not so fast, sister." She bent lower over the page, lips moving as she reread a section. "Uh. Whoops."

My stomach dropped. "Whoops? What do you mean whoops? There can be no whoops in demon-prevention magic."

"Relax. You're not about to blow up Texas." Tani winced. "We made the wrong potion."

I stared at her. "The wrong—what does that even mean? Wrong how? Like, now it summons raccoons instead of demons?"

"It's a house protection blend." Tani tapped the page. "Still useful. But not the one that keeps the gate from turning into a revolving door for nightmares."

I clamped my lips together, counted to five, and pinched the bridge of my nose. "Okay. Fine. We'll call this... Practice Potion."

"Love that for you," Tani said. "We'll label it later. Next one is the real gate-warding mix."

I exhaled slowly. "All right. One more round. Then I'm turning into a pumpkin."

Tani flicked to the next page. "Okay then. Round two..."

I woke to the shrill buzz of my phone screaming directly into my ear.

I fumbled for it, knocking something off the nightstand—maybe a hair tie, maybe my dignity—before finally managing to press it to my head. "Hello?" My voice came out rough, like I'd swallowed sandpaper and regret.

"Good morning," Owen said, sounding disgustingly chipper. "Or maybe I should say afternoon."

I squinted at the digital clock beside my bed. 1:07 p.m.

"Oh no," I groaned. Everything hurt. My head. My shoulders. My thighs from charging up and down stairs all night. "What time is it? Please tell me your watch is wrong."

"Sadly, my watch tells only the brutal truth. Thought you might need a ride to the shop, since you left your car there."

I groaned and put a hand to my head. "Oh, yeah. I forgot. I'm not dressed. When can you be here?"

He chuckled. "Already am. I'm standing on your front porch with a latte and a bag of donuts."

My stomach growled at the mention of coffee and food. "You're officially my hero. I'll be right down."

I rolled out of bed and realized with horror I'd gone to sleep in a tank top and tiny Juicy shorts. Perfect. Nothing like greeting the town heartthrob half-dressed and hungover on potion fumes. Excellent life choices, Piper.

I considered changing. Really did.

But he was already there. The coffee was already cooling. And the idea of making him wait while I spiraled over wardrobe choices felt… worse.

I padded downstairs instead, fingers combing through my hair in a useless attempt to make it look less like I'd lost a fight with a pillow.

When I opened the door, Owen stood on the porch in his usual rumpled button-down and jeans, looking like he'd stepped out of some small-town book boyfriend mood board. Latte in one hand, white paper bag in the other.

His gaze slid over me and stalled for the briefest second on my bare legs.

Heat prickled up my neck.

"I—uh." I snatched the coffee like it was a life raft. "Thanks."

"Long night?" he asked, stepping inside when I moved aside.

"You have no idea." I took a gulp of latte so enormous it was probably illegal in several states. Heavenly caffeine hit my bloodstream. "Owen, I found something."

His mouth curved as he stared at me a long moment. "You said my name. I like hearing it."

I swallowed. Then—

I gave him a look. "Do you want to see the thing that might keep our town from being overrun by demon cow-things, or flirt with me on my front porch?"

"Why not both?" he said easily, a lazy grin tugging at his mouth. "But yes—show me."

I grabbed his free hand before I could think better of it and tugged him through the kitchen toward the basement door. His palm was warm, callused, unnervingly nice to hold. I pretended not to notice. He pretended not to notice me pretending.

"Warning," I said as I flipped on the basement light. "It's a disaster zone."

He let out a low whistle when we reached the bottom. Glassware, bowls, and vials were scattered across the worktable. Herbs and petals dusted the surface like confetti from some unhinged botanical party. The only thing neat was the wall of labeled jars.

"Look, I put everything back in its place," I said defensively. "Mostly."

"It's... impressive," he said. And there was no sarcasm in it. Just honest surprise. "Like Harry Potter's Potions class got organized."

"I'm choosing to take that as a compliment." I set the bag of donuts on the edge of the table and snatched up the red folder, holding it aloft. "Behold. The Holy Grail."

He deadpanned, "It's a red folder."

"Check what's inside the red folder, McAllister."

He took it, balancing the latte in one hand as he flipped it open with the other. Pages crackled. His expression shifted from skeptical to intent to faintly stunned.

"This is..." He turned another page. "These are Alice's recipes. Full lists. Instructions. It's her entire potion book."

"Yup." I popped open the donut bag and pulled out a chocolate-glazed one. "I found it in a locked drawer in the basement lab. Willow and Tani helped."

He looked up at me. "You made the gate potion?"

I nodded, suddenly a little shy. "Took a couple tries. The first one was apparently a 'protect the house, not the world' blend. But we got it right."

He stepped closer without seeming to notice he was doing it. He was so near I could see the faint stubble along his jaw, the little flecks of darker gray in his irises.

"You've been busy," he said softly.

"Some of us were up all night saving Hickory Hollow," I said. Then ruined the moment by taking a giant bite of donut.

He smiled and reached up, thumb brushing the corner of my mouth to swipe away a smear of chocolate. The touch sent a bolt of electricity down my spine.

"There," he murmured. "You missed a little."

My heart thudded unevenly. My hand went slack around the donut. "It took a couple tries," I said again, voice a little breathless. "But the last one should work."

"Then we're one step closer to not getting eaten by whatever that thing in the shop was," he said. His gaze dipped to my lips as if pulled. "And we can test it at the tree today."

"Yeah," I said, half-dazed. "That's... what I was thinking, too."

On some ridiculous impulse, I lifted what remained of the donut. "Want a bite?"

I expected a joke. Maybe a polite refusal.

Instead, Owen curled his fingers gently around my wrist and guided my hand toward his mouth, eyes never leaving mine as he took a slow bite from the same piece of donut.

Time hiccupped.

Warmth shot through me, sharp and startling. It was such a tiny thing—shared sugar between breaths—but it felt intimate enough to tilt the room.

"Owen—" I started.

He paused, close enough that his breath brushed my cheek. Questioning. Waiting.

Whatever I was about to say dissolved when he leaned in and kissed me.

His lips were warm and soft and the right amount of firm, tasting of coffee and chocolate and something that was him. The world narrowed to the press of his mouth, the slide of his hand to my waist, the way my knees wanted to liquefy on the spot. Preston had never kissed me like this—like I was something he'd wanted for a long time and was finally allowed to touch.

My fingers curled in the front of his shirt, holding on. For a second, there was no demon, no dead aunt, no gate. Just this.

When we finally broke apart, both slightly breathless, he was smiling.

"There," he said.

My brain flailed. "What was that for?"

"You still had chocolate on your lips," he said. "Thought I'd help you out with that."

Heat flared in my face. "You're ridiculous."

"You taste like chocolate donut," he added.

"So do you," I blurted. "And you've... been waiting a long time to do that, haven't you?"

"Years," he said simply.

"So you weren't lying when you said you liked me."

"I never lie," he said. "I'm like Superman that way."

"Oh yeah?" I managed. "What other superpowers you got?"

His grin turned wicked. "Guess you'll have to find out in time, won't you?"

"Hey, Piper—whoa." A high, tinny voice sliced through the moment. "Heeeeeeey. Who's the hottie?"

We jumped apart like guilty teenagers. Tani zipped into view in a streak of pink and glitter, then hovered between us, giving Owen a slow, unapologetic once-over.

"Oh," she added thoughtfully. "You're a *very* hottie."

"Who's this?" Owen asked, eyebrows lifting.

"Titania," she said, landing on his shoulder and lounging there like a glamorous parrot. "But you can call me Titania." She batted her lashes. "Or just... call me."

I tamped down an irrational flare of jealousy. "Tani, this is Owen. He's a friend."

"Ohhh," she added brightly. "You're the one who's been feeding Willow."

"Nice to meet you, Tani," he said, completely unfazed by the fairy currently draping herself across his collarbone.

"Titania," she corrected primly. "And he looked like more than a friend, judging by the way you two were lip locked."

"I thought you liked being called Tani," I muttered.

"I do," she said sweetly, eyes never leaving Owen. "Just not by Mr. Hottie Hot Hottie." She flashed him another megawatt smile. "That name's already taken."

"You'll have to excuse my fairy," I said. "She's... a lot."

"I see that," Owen said, amusement tugging at his mouth.

"You're not freaking out that there's a fairy in my basement?" I asked.

"Why should he be?" Tani demanded. "Rude."

"Because normal humans don't believe in fairies," I said.

Tani planted her hands on her hips. "Is that an insult?"

"I think what she means is most people don't believe," Owen said smoothly. He met my gaze, steady and sincere. "But I do. In fairies. And magic."

Something in my chest gave a small, startled flip.

Tani drifted away at last, finally noticing the chaos on the table. "Ohhh. Nice." She nodded approvingly. "You figured out how to make the real potion."

"I did," I said. "Eventually."

"You better get going," Tani said, zipping close enough to tug on my tank top strap. "It's already late. You have to get dressed and get to the hickory tree. I'll stay here with Owen."

"You'll go back to wherever you came from," I said firmly. "Owen and I are going to the hickory tree."

Tani stuck out her bottom lip. "I can't go? Alice always let me go."

"I'm not Alice," I said gently but firmly.

"Killjoy." Tani blew a raspberry, then disappeared in a puff of pink dust.

Owen watched the empty air for a moment. "Maybe you should've let her come."

"Maybe next time," I said. "Right now, I need a shower, pants, and about six more donuts. Can you wait?"

"I'll wait as long as I need to," he said easily. "Go get heroic."

I grabbed the donut bag and headed upstairs.

The hot water helped chase away the lingering ache in my muscles and the fog in my head, but it couldn't wash off the weight of what I was about to do. Guardian. Gate. Crossroads town.

I dressed in baby-blue capris, a short-sleeved white cotton shirt, and—lesson learned—my worn-in Keds instead of anything with a heel. Practical over cute... this once.

When I came back down, Owen stood in the living room, studying the mantel. He turned when he heard me.

"You know," he said, nodding toward the photos, "your aunt must have loved you a lot."

I joined him, eyes tracing the frames. Baby me with frosting on my face. Kid me in a pink tutu. Me in my high school cap and gown. Then one from college, taken from a distance as if Alice had attended but stayed out of sight. Me with a suitcase, headed to Manhattan.

"There are pictures of everyone," I said automatically.

"Not like this," Owen said quietly. "She watched your life. Even when you weren't here."

It made my chest ache. "I sent her some of those from New York," I said. "The others… she must have stolen from my parents' stash."

Or maybe from somewhere else. Somewhere between worlds.

I pushed that thought aside. "I should grab the potion."

I ducked back to the basement, snatched the correct vial—labelled this time, thanks to Tani's nagging—and slipped it carefully into my pocket. Willow was nowhere in sight. Probably off hunting or doing whatever cursed witches in cat bodies did on their afternoons off.

When I came back to the living room, I squared my shoulders. "Okay. Ready."

Owen opened the front door for me, the afternoon light spilling across the worn threshold.

Together, we stepped out of the house and headed toward the hickory woods north of town—toward the ancient tree sitting at the place where paths overlapped and worlds touched, and toward whatever waited for me there.

Chapter Eight

"Can you stop by the library?" I asked.

Owen flicked me a look as he drove. "Why? I thought we were in a big rush to get to the woods."

"Tani is in a rush for me to get to the woods," I said. "I want to stop at the library because in my aunt's writings, she said there was an old legend about Hickory Hollow. I want to see if I can find anything about the town."

"Would it be in the library?" he asked. "If you're looking for old town history, the town offices might have more than a few dusty paperbacks."

"Okay, then, town offices. Wherever. I need to know."

"Why?"

"Because I do, okay?"

He flinched at my sharp tone. Guilt immediately pricked me. I dragged in a breath. "Sorry. I'm tired. I didn't sleep much last night."

He turned down Town Hall Street and parked in front of the town offices. After cutting the engine, he twisted in his seat to face me.

"Whatever this is, Piper, I'm here to help. We'll figure it out together." He reached for my hand.

His fingers closed around mine, warm and steady, and my heart did a ridiculous little jig. "Okay," I said softly. "I'm... scared. I don't know what to think about all this."

"I know. Me either." He lifted my hand and pressed a kiss to my fingertips.

The brush of his lips sent bright little zings straight to my chest. All I could think about was those same lips on mine, tasting chocolate and sugar and trouble.

Then he let go—far too soon—and climbed out. I followed him up the steps into Town Hall.

Louise Sandpepper was still stationed behind the front desk like a troll under a bridge. She'd been the town's unofficial gatekeeper since I was a kid. Back then I'd thought her name was Sandpaper, which honestly fit better. Now she was older, rounder, and still dressed in clothes that didn't believe in age-appropriateness. Today it was a black-and-white polka dot dress that showed more knee than anyone needed to see.

Her white hair was piled into a tight bun, her eyes as sharp as ever.

"Well, bless my soul, it's Owen McAllister," she cooed.

She bustled around the desk, skirts swishing, and enveloped him in a bone-crushing hug. He shot me a sheepish look over Louise's shoulder.

"Hey, Mrs. Sandpepper," he managed, patting her back before prying himself loose. "You remember Piper Wakefield?"

Louise gave me a once-over that managed to both judge and dismiss me in one sweep. Then she harrumphed.

"Hello, Mrs. Sandpepper," I said brightly, refusing to flinch. "You look well."

Louise pivoted right back to Owen and smiled as if I had ceased to exist. "What brings you here, dear?"

"I was wondering if you could show us the town archives," he said. He slipped his hand into mine, clearly making a point. "We're looking for some history."

I tried not to beam like a teenager at the small gesture of solidarity.

"For you, dear, anything," Louise said, then leaned in to Owen and stage-whispered, "I'm not sure about her, though."

"Hey—" I started.

"Piper is the new owner of Enchanted Blossoms," Owen announced like he was dropping a trump card.

Louise's eyebrows shot up. She spared me another quick look, then jerked her head. "Follow me."

"Why'd you tell her that?" I murmured as we trailed behind.

"I thought it would help," he whispered back with a helpless shrug.

Louise led us down a short hallway and into a small room. She flipped on the light. The "archives" turned out to be several tall, scarred filing cabinets lined up against the far wall. Late-afternoon sun streamed through wooden blinds, dust motes spiraling lazily in the light.

"Have at it," she said, and left without another word.

I stared at the cabinets. "That's it? How are we supposed to find anything in this?"

"I'll start down there, you start down here, we meet in the middle," Owen suggested. "Divide and conquer."

He looked so proud of himself I couldn't argue. "Fine."

I opened the top drawer of the far-right cabinet. It was stuffed with hanging files and old manila folders in absolutely no discernable order.

"Do you know what we're looking for?" Owen asked as he pulled open another drawer.

"Not really. All my aunt said was there was an old legend that mentioned Hickory Hollow. That long before it was a town, people said this land was... enchanted. A magical place. Somewhere the borders between worlds wore thin." The words felt strange on my tongue now that I knew magical wasn't exactly metaphorical around here.

Owen froze, eyes going wide. "Before it was a town?"

"Yeah." I glanced over at him. "Why? You know something?"

He snapped out of it fast. "No. Just... sounds familiar. Let's keep looking."

I frowned, but turned back to the cabinet. File after file yielded nothing helpful. Zoning disputes, land deeds, property taxes. Perfectly boring things for a perfectly boring town that apparently sat on a supernatural freeway.

Every so often I sneaked a look at Owen. He'd migrated to a shelf of bound newspapers, carefully turning the brittle pages of ancient editions of the Hickory Hollow Mirror. I could smell the mustiness from across the room.

I moved to the next cabinet and, to change it up, started with the bottom drawer. When I tugged it open, I expected more chaos.

Instead, there was only one thing inside.

A leather-bound book lay alone in the drawer, as if everything else had given it space out of respect—or fear. The cover was cracked and worn, held shut with narrow leather ties. Faded gold scrollwork had once been elaborate but now was ghosted by age.

"What have we here..." I murmured.

I eased the book out of the drawer, cradling it in both hands, and scooted back to sit on the floor. Carefully, I loosened the ties and lifted the front cover. The spine crackled in protest. And when it opened, it warmed against my palm.

An illusion, right? It had to be.

"What's that?" Owen dropped to the floor beside me, leaning in to see.

"A book," I said.

"I figured that much. What kind of book?"

"I think it's a grimoire. But I can't read this."

The inked lines were dark in places, faded in others. The handwriting was elegant and looping, more quill-and-ink than ballpoint. The letters themselves looked familiar and not at the same time—like English put through a blender.

"What language is this?" I asked.

"I don't know. I can't read it either. Turn the page."

I did, wincing as the paper rasped under my fingers. More of the same. Dense paragraphs, no illustrations, no helpful glossary saying Welcome to Your Magical Tree 101.

"What is this, Old English?" I asked.

He shook his head slowly. "I don't think so."

"Who could help us with this?" I asked. "Your dad?"

"Maybe. Maybe not."

I shot him a look. "That is not helpful, McAllister."

He smiled and, because he apparently didn't know the power he wielded, lifted my hand and kissed my palm.

My breath caught. Traitorous hand.

"My point," he said, "is I'm not sure my dad can read this. But Mrs. Rollins might."

I blinked. "AP English Mrs. Rollins?"

He nodded. "Remember how she made us memorize the first hundred lines of The Canterbury Tales?"

I laughed. "Yeah. For extra credit. '*Whan that Aprille with his shoures soote…*' That's all I remember."

"April with its sweet showers," he translated without looking up.

I groaned. "Now you're showing off."

He looked smug. "If she knows Old English, she might at least recognize what this is. Maybe she can translate the first page."

My mood lifted. "You're a genius, McAllister. Great idea."

I hugged the book against my chest and scrambled to my feet. "When can we go?"

"I doubt she's at school. It's summer."

I rolled my eyes. "I know it's summer. This is Hickory Hollow. We know where everyone lives by default."

He lifted a brow. "Aren't you forgetting something?"

I squinted. "What?"

"The potion?" he prompted.

"Oh. Right." I'd forgotten the whole reason we were going to the tree in the first place. "Do you think Mrs. Sandpepper will mind if we borrow the book?"

"I'll sweet-talk her," he said. "Give it to me."

I hesitated, hugging it tighter. I'd found it. Ancient mystery books shouldn't leave their discoverer, right?

"Really, Piper? You don't trust me?" he asked.

"Should I trust a man who kisses like that?" I blurted, then instantly wished I could rewind my mouth.

His grin turned slow and wicked. "You should always trust a man who kisses like that. By the way—like what?"

"Like... oh, never mind. Here." I thrust the book at him before I dug the hole any deeper.

Like he wanted to lay me out on the archive floor and kiss me until I forgot my own name, I did not say.

He chuckled as he took the book. "We'll circle back to that later. Don't think I'll forget."

"Let's go," I muttered, marching for the door.

He caught up easily and angled ahead of me, heading straight for Louise, who was now absorbed in some celebrity gossip site on her computer.

"Hey, Mrs. Sandpepper, we're going to borrow this, okay?" he said.

She peered over her black frames. "What is it?"

"A book." He flipped it around to show her.

I made a strangled noise, imagining centuries-old pages disintegrating under his fingers.

"See? Nothing special," he said.

Louise barely glanced at it. "Bring it back when you're done."

Outside, he handed it back to me with a flourish.

"That was easier than I thought," I said. "She must like you."

"It's because I'm so charming," he said.

I snorted, but I was still smiling when we climbed back into the truck.

Owen pulled away from Town Hall and drove through the sleepy streets, then turned down a narrow blacktop road that led north out of town.

"Do you know where you're going?" I asked.

"Trust me."

"Why does that always make me nervous?"

He didn't bother answering. Instead, he pulled off onto the shoulder and cut the engine.

"This is it?" I looked out the windshield. Trees. Just trees.

"Come on."

I slid the book under the front seat for safekeeping, then got out and followed him.

"How do you know where this place is? I thought only Aunt Alice knew where the tree was," I said.

"Most everyone knows where the hickory trees are, Piper."

"They do?"

"Yeah. In the woods. Duh."

I punched his arm. He laughed and kept going.

He walked a little way along the road, scanning the treeline, then veered off onto what might generously be called a path. He pushed branches aside and held them long enough for me to duck under, then let them snap back behind me.

The further we went, the quieter the woods became. Birdsong faded. The air grew heavier, tighter, like it was thinking about something it didn't like.

We stepped into a small clearing, and there—standing alone like a sentinel—was the hickory tree.

"That's it," Owen said.

It didn't look particularly magical. It looked... sad. Sick.

"This?" I asked.

As we approached, the smell hit me first. Sharp and rotten, like sulfur and burnt metal. The bark near the base was stripped in ragged patches. Leaves browned and curled on the ends of drooping branches. The wildflowers around it were mostly dead, stems blackened and bent.

"Oh, no," I whispered. "This must be what Alice meant when she said they were killing the tree."

"You have the potion?" Owen asked.

I pulled the small vial from my pocket. The liquid inside glinted sharply in the dim light.

"Right here," I said. "Where do I pour it?"

"On the tree?" he suggested.

"Helpful," I muttered, but there wasn't exactly a manual.

I ventured closer. At the base of the trunk, where roots met earth, a pool of thick, black sludge bubbled like tar in a slow boil. The sulfuric stench clawed at the back of my throat.

"Uh, Owen?"

He came up beside me and grimaced down at it. "What is that?"

"I have no idea. Do I pour the potion on that?" I looked up at him. His gray eyes mirrored my uncertainty.

"Try it," he said quietly.

"Here goes nothing."

I pulled the cork and forced three deep breaths into my lungs like the instructions had said. Then I tipped the vial and poured all four ounces straight into the bubbling black muck.

"Protect and save us from harm," I chanted. "Let these oils now work their charm."

For one long heartbeat, the bubbling stopped.

Then it exploded.

The sludge began to roil violently, burping and spitting like it was about to erupt. I staggered back, but Owen grabbed my arm and yanked me with him.

We'd cleared the worst of it when a geyser of black ooze shot upward, arcing through the air like corrupted lava. It sizzled when it hit the ground where we'd been standing seconds before.

Owen's arm tightened around me. "You okay?"

"Yeah. I think so." I turned—and saw the ooze boiling again. "Owen..."

"Let's get out of here."

We took a step back. The earth rumbled under our feet. A deep crack split the ground at the base of the tree. The black muck vanished into the fissure as a column of searing white light shot up, blindingly bright, swallowing the clearing in brilliance.

I threw up a hand to shield my eyes. Even through my fingers I saw a shape forming inside the light, sharp and tall and unmistakably human.

Then, like someone flipped a switch, the light snapped off.

In its place stood a woman in an enormous red ball gown trimmed in white iridescent jewels. Her brown hair was swept up in an elaborate style, crowned by a gold, jewel-encrusted circlet. Diamonds—or convincing fakes—sparkled at her throat. Her lips were blood red, her cheekbones sharp enough to cut glass. Her blue eyes were winter-cold.

She glanced down at the black sludge soaking the hem of her skirt and made a face of regal disgust. Lifting the heavy fabric, she stepped daintily out of the mess and straightened to her full, imperious height.

Then she fixed us both with that icy stare.

"Who are you," she demanded, "and why have you summoned me?"

"Summoned you?" I echoed. "I didn't summon you."

The woman scanned the clearing, frowning. "Where is Alice?"

Owen and I exchanged a look. The same question thudded between us.

"Alice is... gone," I said. "She died."

Shock flashed across the woman's face. Her hand flew to her chest. "Died? No. No, no, no. This is terrible. This is unacceptable." She paced in a small circle, the stained gown dragging in the muck. "Are you sure?"

"I'm afraid so," I said. "I'm her niece. Piper." I had no idea if I should curtsy or shake hands or run.

The woman swept closer and gripped my chin, turning my face left and right with clinical scrutiny.

"Her niece, you say?" she murmured.

"Yes."

"Are you her heir?"

My stomach did a small, traitorous flip. "I am. How do you know that? And who are you?"

The woman drew herself up to full offended height. "I'm the queen, that's who. And you will not use that insolent tone with me, young lady."

It was like being scolded by a fancy version of Gladys. My spine tried to shrink and straighten at the same time.

The queen's gaze finally slid to Owen. She circled him the way she had me, eyes narrowed.

"I don't know you," she said.

"Owen McAllister, Your Majesty," he said, bowing with alarming smoothness. "At your service."

I rolled my eyes. Of course he knew how to bow.

"You're the queen of what exactly?" I asked.

The woman turned that frostbitten stare back on me. "I'm the Red Queen," she said, in a tone that implied I should have embroidered that on a pillow years ago.

"The... Red Queen," I repeated. "As in Wonderland? Through the Looking Glass Wonderland?"

"I don't know what this 'through the looking glass' is," she sniffed, "but yes. I am from Wonderland."

The world tilted a little. I swayed and grabbed for Owen's arm.

"I think I need to sit down," I managed.

He guided me to a fallen log and eased me onto it. I clutched my churning stomach and stared up at him. "Seriously? The Red Queen?"

"Yes, my dear," the queen said crisply. "Did Alice not tell you?"

"Alice didn't tell me anything," I snapped. "About any of this."

"Well, she must have told you something," the queen said. "You conjured me with the potion, after all."

"I thought this was supposed to close the gate," I said, waving the empty vial. "Gate. Superhighway. Whatever we're calling it."

"Let me see that," the queen said.

I handed over the vial. The Red Queen sniffed the glass and made a small noise of dismay.

"Oh, dear. Oh, no. This is a conjuring potion," she said. "The superhighway is still very much open."

"Great." I sagged. "So I didn't make the potion right."

"Are you sure you read those directions right?" Owen asked gently.

I shot him a glare. "Yes, I'm sure."

Except now I wasn't. Not entirely. It had been late. I'd been tired and half-drunk and Tani had been chattering in my ear the entire time. There had been at least one "oopsie."

Tani.

"Tani was helping me," I said slowly. "She read the ingredients out loud. If I made a conjuring potion instead of a gate-closing one, she must've given me the wrong list."

"Titania, you mean?" the queen asked.

My head snapped toward her. "You know her?"

"Everyone knows her," the queen said. "She's the queen of the fairies."

"What?" I squeaked.

Owen let out a low whistle. "Well, that's... an interesting twist."

"I did suspect she was involved," the queen said. "Full of mischief, that one. I certainly wouldn't trust her. Why did you?"

"She told me she was Alice's friend," I said weakly. "She lives in the greenhouse. I thought she was a fairy, not *the* fairy queen."

"Well, Alice had many friends," the queen said with a sniff. "I am rather offended she chose to keep that particular annoyance around."

"Awesome," I muttered. "I've been taking magical advice from a chaos gremlin with wings."

"Oh, Oberon would be thrilled to hear that," the queen said. "If he weren't currently stuck in another dimension."

I blinked. "He's what?"

"Stuck," the queen repeated. "The Fae treasures were stolen. Her Majesty is here trying to recover them so she can rescue the king."

My brain tried to keep up. "Which Fae treasures are we talking about?"

The queen sighed dramatically. "Must I explain everything to you? The Sword of Light, the Club of Dagda, the Spear of Lugh. Useless in this land, powerful in Faery."

Owen's gaze slid to me, questioning.

But I was already thinking of the crates in Dougal's storeroom. Artifacts Alice didn't want in her house. Magical antiques in an antique shop that sat across from a flower store guarding a magical tree in a Crossroads town.

I swallowed. "You know something," Owen said quietly.

"No," I said automatically. Then amended, "Maybe."

"Piper," he said, squeezing my hand. "Tell me."

"Not here," I said. "I need to... put some pieces together first. Figure it out."

"Figure out what?" the queen demanded.

"How to get you back to Wonderland," I said, pushing to my feet. "Preferably without turning the whole town into a portal disaster."

"Oh, there's no rush," the queen said, slipping her arm through mine like we were old friends. "I haven't been here in ages. And I should pay my final respects to dear Alice."

Owen and I exchanged a silent conversation.

We cannot leave her here.

Nope. We absolutely cannot.

Owen gave a small nod. Decision made.

I plastered on my most diplomatic smile. "All right, Your Majesty. Let's get you out of the ooze and into something... less swamp-adjacent."

Together, the three of us headed back through the trees toward the truck—me clutching a mis-made potion vial, a stolen book under the seat, a fairy queen on the loose somewhere, and a real queen from Wonderland tracking black sludge across Hickory Hollow.

No pressure.

Chapter Nine

I'd managed to convince the Red Queen—whose actual name I still didn't know—to fold herself and her enormous gown into the extended cab of Owen's truck. It had taken some doing. Her Majesty had been adamant that she was not climbing into "that metal contraption death on wheels."

Owen had promised to drive slowly, hands at ten and two like some DMV poster boy. Even so, by the time we turned onto Snapdragon Drive, the queen was a bundle of frayed nerves, gasping at every passing pickup like it might veer across the line and obliterate us all.

I talked her into lying down in the spare bedroom to "recover from the journey between realms and interstate traffic." Thankfully, there was no sign of Tani. The last thing I needed was Fairy Royalty vs Wonderland Royalty in my hallway.

As soon as the bedroom door clicked shut, Owen said, "Tell me what you know."

I caught his hand and led him downstairs, putting as much floor and drywall as possible between us and the queen. Only when we reached the bottom did I turn to face him.

"Owen... when we were at the antique store before? Your father told me something in confidence. I don't think he wanted you to know."

His brows pulled together. "Know what?"

"He said he was keeping magical artifacts in his storeroom for Alice." My voice dropped on the last word.

For a heartbeat he stared at me, his expression going still. Then he pinched the bridge of his nose like he could press away a headache. "I knew he was keeping something from me. Why would he do that?"

"I don't know. Maybe Alice swore him to secrecy." Frustration bubbled up in my chest. "I need to see those artifacts, Owen."

"And you want me to take you there."

"Yes." I swallowed. "What if Aunt Alice was the one who stole them? The Fae treasures Titania's talking about?"

"Don't even think like that." His tone sharpened. "She wasn't a thief."

"Well, she was a witch, and I didn't know that," I shot back. "What else don't I know? What else did she hide? She had formulas for potions, ley lines under a hickory tree, a demon the size of a refrigerator, a fairy queen in my greenhouse—"

"Hey." He stepped in closer, hands settling on my shoulders, his thumbs brushing lightly against my collarbones. The touch helped. A little. "One step at a time, remember? Let's get to the antique store. Maybe my dad will have some answers."

I let out a long breath. "Okay. One step at a time."

We headed for the truck and this time Owen did not drive like a man promising to be gentle with someone's royal nerves. He gunned it back toward town, the engine growling as though it shared his mood. By the time he jerked to a stop outside Charmed & Vintage, my stomach was somewhere up near my throat.

He was out of the car before I could yell at him about his driving. I scrambled after him, jogging to keep up as he beelined through the shop toward the back.

We didn't make it.

Dougal McAllister intercepted us halfway to the storeroom, looming out from behind an armoire like a tall, stern haunted house prop.

"Owen, where have you been?" he demanded.

"Step aside, Dad." Owen didn't slow.

Dougal looked from his son to me and back again. I watched realization settle over his features in one slow, heavy sweep. When his gaze returned to me, his mouth flattened. "You told him."

"I had to," I said. "We found something in the woods."

"What?" he pressed, crossing his arms like a barricade.

"It's... complicated," I said weakly.

"We have reason to believe the artifacts you're holding were stolen," Owen said, voice hardening. "Now I want to see them."

"Stolen?" Shock cracked Dougal's composure. "Alice never said anything about them being stolen."

"She probably wouldn't have," I said. "She took secrets seriously."

"You think she did it?" Dougal asked.

Owen shook his head. "We don't know. Where are they, Dad?"

Dougal's shoulders sagged a fraction. His arms dropped to his sides. "Follow me."

He led us through the maze of furniture toward the back. I kept my gaze fixed on the line of his shoulders, ignoring the curious looks from customers as we slipped past carved headboards and dusty lamps. This town already thought I was the weird girl who'd inherited the flower shop. No need to add "artifact thief" to the list.

At the back of the shop, Dougal pulled a ring of keys from his pocket and selected a shiny gold one. He unlocked a metal door and swung it open, flicking on the light.

Fluorescent bulbs hummed to life, revealing a cramped storeroom packed with crates. Gun-metal gray shelving units lined the walls, sagging under the weight of box after unmarked box.

"I've stored them at the back here," Dougal said, nodding toward the far corner.

We followed him through the narrow aisles until we reached a cluster of crates stacked against the wall. All different sizes. None labeled.

"This is it?" I asked.

"This is what she brought me," Dougal replied. "I've never opened them. I didn't think it was my place."

I crouched by the nearest crate. The lid was nailed down. Of course it was.

"Got a crowbar?" I asked.

"Let me find one."

He disappeared back into the maze of shelves, leaving me and Owen alone with the crates and the scent of dust and old wood. Owen scanned the stack like he could see through them.

"Owen?" I asked.

"Yeah?" His eyes narrowed, fixing on one crate in particular.

"Are we in over our heads?"

My words snapped him out of whatever he'd been sensing. He looked down at me, the corner of his mouth twitching with something that was almost a smile but didn't get there.

"I don't know, Piper," he admitted. "Maybe."

I pushed to my feet and moved closer, needing the heat of him, needing something solid to hold on to. "I'm scared," I whispered.

Of what, I wasn't even sure anymore. Demons. Queens. Fairy lies. The possibility that my aunt—my anchor—had been tangled up in something darker than any of us realized. That the letter naming me Guardian had been less "inheritance" and more "last-ditch defense."

Owen caught my hands in his. "We'll get through it together," he said. "We're a team, remember?"

Before I could answer, Dougal returned with a crowbar.

"Found one," he said.

Owen took it before his father could even offer. "Which crate first?"

I pointed to the one nearest me. Owen attacked it with far too much enthusiasm, grunting as he pried at the nails, ignoring Dougal's attempts to "help." Finally, the lid gave with a groan. Owen and Dougal hauled it the rest of the way off.

Packing straw spilled out onto the concrete. I dug both hands into it, wading through the dry rustle until my fingers brushed something solid. I pulled out a shoebox-sized container and eased off the lid.

Inside was a pair of red slippers.

Not ordinary red—ruby red, impossibly vivid, with a faint shimmer and a low magical hum. Their surface caught the fluorescent light and fractured it, scattering tiny sparks of crimson fire as I tilted the box. The color seemed to run deep, as if the slippers weren't coated in color so much as cut from the heart of a gemstone.

They looked as though they were waiting for someone to slip them on and be carried away.

"What is it?" Dougal asked.

"A pair of red shoes," I said faintly, though the words felt inadequate. "And I have a feeling they're not meant for walking."

I dug deeper, straw scratching my wrists, but the crate held nothing else.

"That's all in this one," I said.

"Why would Alice have a pair of red shoes locked up like contraband?" Owen asked.

"I don't know." Although the word *relic* whispered at the back of my mind. Red shoes. Portals. Crossroads. I jammed the lid back onto the box. "Let's see what's in the next one."

We muscled open a second crate after several more minutes of swearing and lever work. Inside, nestled in straw, was a long, rectangular leather case. The leather cracked with age when I unfastened it, the hinges complaining as I lifted the lid.

Light caught metal.

I sucked in a sharp breath and stumbled back a step.

The sword lay in black velvet, its blade gleaming like liquid moonlight—clean, flawless, untouched by time. Not sharp in a way that promised violence, but bright in a way that felt… absolute. As if it decided where it belonged, not the other way around.

The pommel was pure gold, etched with symbols I didn't recognize yet somehow understood. They hummed faintly against my skin, a quiet answering call.

Silence fell. Even the hum of the fluorescents seemed suddenly intrusive.

"What is it?" I whispered.

"A sword," Dougal said softly.

"I can see that," I snapped, eyes locked on it. "But who does it belong to?"

Owen swallowed. "Do you think it's the Sword of Light? The one the Red Queen mentioned?"

"And if it is," I said slowly, "what's it doing here? In Hickory Hollow. In my aunt's crates?"

Dougal shook his head. "I have no answers for that. Alice only said it needed to be kept safe." His gaze lifted, distant, as if he were seeing something beyond the ceiling. "This town attracts things from the in-between. Relics don't simply wander into ordinary places, Piper. They arrive where the paths cross."

Right. Like Hickory Hollow.

My skin prickled.

"I don't get it," Owen said.

"Me either," I muttered. "I don't have answers. I have more questions."

Dougal exhaled. "I suppose we'll have to open the rest—"

"No." I snapped the case shut and stepped back. "Close them up. Both of them. They'll be safer here for now."

I turned to Dougal. "Who else knows about these crates?"

"No one besides you two," he said. "Alice didn't want anyone else involved."

"Good." I nodded. "Let's keep it that way until I can figure this out. In the meantime, I'm going to talk to Tani and see what she knows. If that is the Sword of Light, she'll want to take it back to Faery with her."

But I wasn't sure it was the Sword of Light.

"You believe all that?" Owen asked.

I met his eyes. "I think I have to believe it, Owen."

"I'm coming with you."

"I can handle Tani on my own."

"Too bad." He thumbed at his chest. "I'm your wheels, remember?"

He had a point. Hickory Hollow wasn't exactly overflowing with rideshares.

"All right," I conceded. "Mr. McAllister, thank you. For all of this."

"Anytime," he said. "You two be careful."

Owen nodded. We stepped out of the storeroom, then threaded our way through the main shop. We pushed out onto the sidewalk in front of Enchanted Blossoms—

—and stopped short.

A smear of black smoke hovered over Owen's truck like a storm cloud testing the wind. It twisted once, twice, then darted toward us as if it had caught our scent.

"Owen," I breathed.

"Piper, look out!"

He shoved me aside. My feet flew out from under me and I hit the pavement hands first. Pain tore across my palms, then up my arms as my elbows buckled and my cheek slammed into the sidewalk. The world flashed white for a heartbeat.

I rolled, heart pounding, and pushed myself up in time to see the smoke coalesce into the hulking demon from the flower shop. Horns. Tusks. Fur.

Owen stood between me and the beast, shoulders squared, fists clenched, staring it down like this happened every Tuesday.

"You're not wanted here," he said.

Before I could even form the word *run*, the door of Charmed & Vintage slammed open behind us.

Dougal strode out. And then everything went weirdly slow. Owen crouched, palms splayed against the asphalt. Dougal lifted his hands, fingers spread.

Fire spilled from them.

A ball of yellow-orange flame roared across the parking lot and slammed into the demon's chest. The creature shrieked, the sound high and edged with the crackle of something burning. Dougal didn't hesitate. He hurled another blast, and another, each one hitting with sickening precision until the demon buckled, melted, and collapsed into a wheezing heap.

Black smoke bled off its carcass in sluggish curls, then unraveled completely, disappearing on an unfelt breeze.

The demon was gone.

I blinked hard, my breathing ragged, half-expecting to see someone on the sidewalk pointing, screaming, calling 911. Instead, people strolled along the sidewalk, chatting, glancing into shop windows, completely unbothered.

As if nothing had happened.

As if there hadn't been a monster and a fireball in the middle of downtown.

"What..." My voice came out a croak. "What just—"

The last trace of smoke faded. Dougal wiped sweat from his brow with the back of his hand and turned to Owen.

"It shouldn't bother you anymore," he said.

"I could've handled it," Owen muttered. "I was handling it."

"Now it's done," Dougal replied.

"Wait a second." I pushed to my feet and planted myself beside Owen. My scraped palms stung; my cheek throbbed. "I don't understand any of this."

Neither of them answered me. Owen's hands were still fists. His jaw worked like he was grinding down words he didn't want to say.

"I was protecting Piper," he snapped at his father. "That's my job, not yours."

"Protecting Piper?" I echoed, my voice going thin.

They kept ignoring me.

"Next time, you get rid of the demon before it comes back a third time," Dougal said. "I saw it at the funeral home, son. You did nothing."

"I did what I thought I had to do," Owen shot back. "I was trying not to draw unnecessary attention."

I stepped between them, hands on my hips, forcing them both to look at me. My heart was still racing, fueled by fear and irritation in equal measure.

"What is going on here?" I demanded.

For a beat, both men blinked at me. Like they'd truly forgotten I existed.

"I think you'd better come inside, Piper," Dougal said at last. He jerked his head toward the door. "My son and I will explain everything."

Owen reached for my hand—then stilled when he saw my palms. His jaw tightened.

"You're bleeding," he said quietly. "Your hands—and your cheek."

"I'm fine," I said automatically.

His look said he didn't believe me for a second. "We'll deal with that," he murmured. Then, more firmly, "He's right. It's time."

I let him guide me back into the store and down the hall to Dougal's office again. This time, Dougal shut the door firmly behind us before leaning against the desk.

The fluorescent lights hummed overhead. I sank into the same chair as before, my scraped hands resting gingerly in my lap, palms still stinging every time I flexed my fingers. Owen sat close enough that our shoulders brushed—close enough that his presence felt steady.

"There is something you don't know about us, Piper," Dougal said. He looked tired. Older. "Your aunt asked us to protect you."

"Before she died?" I asked, glancing between them.

"Yes," Owen said. "She knew you'd come back to Hickory Hollow with no idea what was happening here. She didn't want you walking into it alone."

"That's right," Dougal agreed. "And we've been trying to honor that. But there are rules. Lines. Timing."

"Well, I don't know anything," I said, scowling. "And it seems like you two know a lot more than you're letting on. Why didn't you tell me from the beginning?"

"Because you weren't ready," Dougal said simply.

"That's not fair." The words snapped out before I could stop them. "If I'm supposed to do my 'job'—whatever that is—I need all the information. First Alice keeps me in the dark. Now you. And why did it seem like no one in town could see that demon? Or the light? Or the fire?"

"Because they couldn't," Owen said. "My father and I have the ability to conceal things like that from the general populace. Glamours. Veils. Call them what you want."

"How?" I demanded, looking between them.

Owen pressed his lips into a thin line. It was Dougal who answered.

"We are Druids, Piper. Most folks would call us witches," he added with a wry smile, "but our order is older—and a bit more particular—than that. We're Druids."

I stared at him. "Druids," I repeated flatly. "As in robes and stone circles and human sacrifice? That kind of druid?"

"Not that kind," Dougal said dryly. "We're Druids of the ancient Celts. Our clans survived. We moved. We adapted. But our purpose stayed the same. We're here to protect—this world, and the ones brushing against it—from evil and from those who would seize too much power. Though not all were interested in protecting the world."

"What does that mean?" I asked.

"Some decided guarding power wasn't enough. They wanted to wield it for themselves."

Demons. Ley lines. Druids. The potential Sword of Light sitting in a crate across the hall.

A shiver rippled over my skin.

"And my Aunt Alice was also a witch?" I asked.

"Yes," Dougal said. "She was born that way. Magic ran strong in her blood."

I thought of the pictures on the mantel. The way Alice always seemed to understand me without words. The way Gladys never did. "But my mother...?"

"Not a witch," Owen said quietly. "Not like Alice."

"If you tell me they're muggles, my head might explode," I muttered.

Owen snorted. Dougal's mouth tugged in something like a smile.

"No, Piper," Dougal said. "They're mortal. Human. Not everyone is born with magic."

"And you?" I turned to Owen. "You're... what? Also a druid? A witch? A wizard? A sorcerer with questionable fashion choices?"

"Druid," he said. "Magic manifests differently in our line, but the root is the same as my father's. Mine's... stronger. Wilder." He shrugged one shoulder. "More of a pain in his backside."

"That's why I'm angry he didn't deal with the demon sooner," Dougal said. "What were you waiting for?"

"I was waiting for the right moment," Owen shot back. "You jumping in the middle of the street wasn't subtle, in case you hadn't noticed."

"If I'd waited another second, that beast would have killed you and Piper," Dougal said sharply. "Then where would we be?"

I leaned back in my chair, pressing my fingertips to my temples. "I don't understand any of this," I said. "Guardians. Druids. A ceiling-high demon with tusks. Queen of Hearts cosplay in my woods."

"You will," Dougal said. "In time."

"Not the reassurance you think it is," I muttered.

But something else niggled at the back of my mind. Something the Red Queen had said at the tree.

"The Red Queen told us Oberon is stuck in another realm," I said slowly. "She said Titania is here trying to recover the Fae treasures to free him. Mr. McAllister, do you think Alice was keeping those treasures from Titania on purpose? Or does the queen not even know they're here?"

He spread his hands. "I have no idea what arrangements Alice had with Titania. Or what Titania knows."

I shot to my feet, ignoring the protest in my palms as energy buzzed through my veins like static. "Then I need to talk to her. Tani. Titania. Whatever she wants to call herself."

"Now?" Owen asked.

"Yes, now." I met his gaze. "You neutralized the demon. For the moment, at least. I need to get back to the house and find out what my fairy 'friend' has been lying about."

"I'm coming with you," Owen said immediately.

"Of course you are," I said, a little softer. "Apparently you're my official demon bodyguard."

"Be careful," Dougal warned. "That beast may be gone, but if the gate is still weakening, there may be more. And if someone was stealing bark from the hickory tree, someone else wanted that gate open."

He was right. The thought of Alice alone in those woods, knowing danger was creeping closer, made my chest ache. Someone had killed my aunt. My guardian. My witch. My... something more, if the town gossip and mantel photos were anything to go by.

Whoever had done it was still out there.

"We'll be careful," Owen promised.

He took my hand again, gently to avoid my scrapes. His fingers were warm and steady around mine as he led me out of the office, through the antique shop, and back into the small-town late afternoon sunlight that suddenly felt a lot less safe.

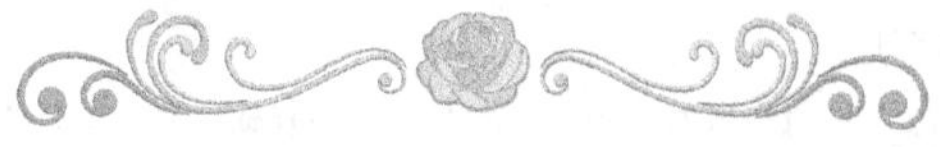

Chapter Ten

I chewed my thumbnail all the way back to the house on Snapdragon Drive. My knee bounced, foot tapping a frantic rhythm against the floorboard. I knew I was a nervous wreck.

"Hey, it's going to be all right," Owen said quietly.

"I know." I didn't.

"You should let me tend those scrapes."

"They're fine. I'm fine."

My thoughts spun in tight, panicked circles. Had Tani had anything to do with Alice's death? Why lie about the potion? Why give me a conjuring spell instead of something to seal the supernatural superhighway? And if the fairy queen had meant to summon someone else, who?

I would know soon enough.

Owen parked in the drive. I was out of the truck before he killed the engine. As soon as my feet hit the pathway, a loud crash sounded from somewhere inside the house.

We both bolted for the door.

I burst through first and skidded to a halt. Owen ran smack into my back, making me stumble a few steps into the wrecked living room.

The Red Queen was crouched behind one sofa. Tani—a life-sized Tani—hid behind the other. They were popping up to hurl things at each other. Breakable things. Lamps. Vases. A ceramic rooster I was pretty sure had belonged to Alice since the seventies. Shattered glass glittered across the hardwood like deadly confetti.

At least they'd spared the family photos on the mantel.

"What on earth is going on in here?"

"Uh oh. Mom's home," Tani muttered.

She straightened and smoothed her hands down her pants. Then she spotted Owen and lit up like Christmas.

"Oh. *Ohhhh.* He's even cuter full-size. I should be big more often."

She started to saunter toward him, but I threw out a hand.

"Stay where you are. I want an explanation."

Now that Tani was roughly my height, I finally got a good, full look at the fairy queen. She was unfairly gorgeous—more ethereal supermodel than woodland sprite—with pale gold hair, bright blue eyes, and delicate pointed ears. She still wore her tunic and vest, soft brown pants tucked into shiny black boots. More "Robin Hood's hot lieutenant" than sparkly pixie.

"She started it," Tani said, pointing accusingly at the Red Queen.

"I most certainly did not," the queen sniffed.

"I don't care who started it," I snapped. "Someone is going to clean up this mess."

Willow meowed from the staircase, then hopped down and twined around my legs as if in agreement.

"Well it won't be me," the Red Queen declared. She folded her arms across her bodice and turned away, chin tipped high. "I am a queen."

"You," I said, stabbing a finger in her direction. "I told you to stay in your room."

"Like a commoner? I think not. Queens do not languish in guest chambers."

"And she was hungry," Tani added. "I caught her rummaging through the fridge. And she can't cook."

"Maybe I should get the broom," Owen suggested, edging toward the kitchen—probably trying to stay out of the blast radius.

No way. I latched onto his hand, keeping him beside me. I was not being left alone between two supernatural monarchs.

"She doesn't belong here, Piper," Tani insisted.

"I belong here far more than you do, fairy," the Red Queen shot back.

"And you," I whirled on Tani, temper finally snapping. "She's here because of you. You gave me the conjuring potion, not the one to close the portal."

Tani at least had the decency to look guilty. "Oops?"

"No oops." My voice went sharp. "Why did you do it?"

"Yes," the Red Queen said. "Why did you?"

"Stay out of this, Red."

Tani glared at the queen, then turned back to me. "I didn't mean to. I thought it was something else."

"Like what?"

"Like... it was an accident, okay?" Tani waved a hand, irritation sparking in her eyes.

I didn't buy that for a second. "You are going to explain everything. Right now. Why is the Red Queen here and why is Oberon trapped in another realm?"

Tani's eyes widened, then narrowed into slits. She swung her gaze toward the queen. "You told her."

Red said nothing, gave Tani a frosty look.

"Okay, clearly I'm not getting anywhere with both of you in the room," I said. "Red—bedroom. Now. I want to talk to Tani alone."

When the queen didn't budge, I looked at Owen. "Would you mind?"

"Of course," he said, stepping aside and gesturing toward the stairs.

The Red Queen sniffed, scooped up her skirts, and swept toward the hallway with as much dignity as one could muster after a lamp-throwing brawl. Willow trotted after them like a furry little guard.

I waited until they were out of sight before turning back to Tani. "Explain."

Tani flopped onto the sofa, sprawled out like she owned the place. One leg hooked over the arm, boots dangling. Very un-queenly. Very Tani. She blew out a breath.

"It wasn't supposed to conjure her. It was supposed to conjure Oberon."

Finally. Something honest.

I folded my arms. "Go on."

"We thought we'd cracked it," Tani said, tapping a finger against her chin. "Alice and I spent weeks working the recipe. Alice was going to open the breach at the hickory tree, I'd go in, yank him out, close it again. Clean, simple, no demons invited."

"And?"

"And I think I messed up the formula." She winced. "Somewhere."

"Oh, you think?" I glared. "And the potion to close the portal? The actual gate-ward? We made several last night. Was that one of them?"

"That was the first one you made." Tani gave me a sheepish little smile. "I lied. I told you it was wrong so you'd make the conjuring spell. And it didn't work. I failed again."

My stomach pitched. "Where is he?" At Tani's blank look, I added, "Oberon."

"Stuck," Tani said quietly. "In another realm that's... not exactly friendly. We traced the ley line pattern, we thought we'd mapped the Crossroads right. This town brushes up against too many paths, and..." She sighed. "We miscalculated. I've been waiting for Alice to come back so we could try again. She was supposed to crack the gate for me." Her mouth tightened. "She never did."

At least that cleared Tani as the killer. Probably. But it still didn't answer the question of the treasures—or why Alice had kept so many secrets.

"What about the Fae treasures?" I asked.

Tani cut me a sharp glance. "What did Red tell you?"

"Not much," I lied, choosing my words carefully. "That they were stolen."

"Ha." Tani snorted. "Of course she did. They weren't stolen. I brought them here myself. Alice is keeping them safe in this realm until I can get Oberon out. Red always thinks everything is about her." She made a face. "Wonderland gossip is the worst."

"So you know exactly where the treasures are?" I pressed.

"Sure. Somewhere in this town." She waved a hand. "Alice didn't tell me the details. That way, if anyone tried to pry it out of my head, they'd hit a dead end. But I know they're close. I can feel them tugging on the ley lines."

My mind flashed to the sword in the crate. The ruby slippers. The way Dougal had said Hickory Hollow sat where paths overlapped. Crossroads. Ley lines. Other realms brushing too close.

"And you need them to rescue the king," I said.

"That much is true," Tani said. "The Sword of Light cuts through bonds that shouldn't exist. The Club of Dagda breaks doors that shouldn't stay closed. The Spear of Lugh finds what's lost. They're useless to mortals, but in Faery?" She whistled low. "Game-changers."

"So why does Red think they were stolen?"

"Because Red thinks everything that's not under her heel has been stolen from her," Tani said primly. "She lives in Wonderland. The name alone should tell you she's not exactly plugged into reality." She straightened and pinned me with her bright blue stare. "The real question is are you going to help me?"

"I have other more pressing matters," I said. "Like closing the portal before anything else crawls through. I need the gate potion. And I need to figure out who killed Alice."

"You're not going to figure that out overnight."

"I know. But I have to try."

Footsteps sounded on the stairs. Owen reappeared.

"Her majesty is sleeping," he said.

Tani snorted. "Must be nice. Some of us have to do all the real work."

"Did you find anything out?" he asked me.

"Yes," I said, already heading toward the basement door. "Tani brought the relics with her. Alice was safeguarding them. I'll explain everything on the way, but right now I want the right potion and I want to get back to the trees before the ley breach gets worse."

Owen fell into step beside me. Tani trailed after us.

"I'm coming with you this time," Tani announced.

"No. You're staying here." I halted and gave her the best intimidating stare I could muster.

"You're not the boss of me," Tani said breezily. "I'll meet you there."

Before I could object, the fairy queen vanished in a puff of pink dust.

I sighed. "Of course she will."

"Fairies," Owen said. "Zero respect for road trips."

I pushed open the basement door. "She told me she gave the treasures to Alice for safekeeping," I said as we descended the stairs. "She needs them to get Oberon out. Red's version is... not accurate."

"You think Tani's telling the truth?" he asked.

"Yes. Or as much of it as she ever tells." I stopped halfway down and turned to face him, closer than I'd intended. "Owen, what was my aunt into?"

"I'm not sure," he said. "My dad didn't know the whole story. He knew she was binding something nasty under that tree. It seems like she trusted you to finish what she started."

"Great. No pressure or anything." I exhaled. "Will you take me back to the woods?"

"Of course," he said. "I'm not letting you walk into a demon-infested Crossroads alone."

I grabbed the correct potion from Alice's neatly labeled shelves, tucked it securely into my pocket, and we headed for his car.

Chapter Eleven

By the time we neared the woods, a column of white smoke curled up from the tree line, smearing the sky.

My stomach clenched. "What is that?"

"Not sure." Owen parked on the shoulder and we both jumped out.

We ran through the trees. The smoke thickened the closer we got, carrying the bitter tang of sulfur and something burned. When we burst into the clearing, I skidded to a stop.

The ground at the base of the hickory tree roiled.

The black sludge that had bubbled there before writhed and heaved, pulling itself upright into a shape—a human shape. White smoke bled off its surface in curling strands, spiraling up through the high branches. That was the plume we'd seen from the road.

"What... what is that?" I whispered.

"Get down, you idiots!" Tani's tiny voice shrilled past my ear. The fairy, once again fun-sized, zoomed past our faces in a streak of pink.

Owen grabbed my arm and pulled me with him behind a screen of brush. We dropped to our knees and peered out.

The black sludge finished knitting itself into a man.

Tall. Dark-haired. Clothes as black as the muck he'd risen from. His eyes were closed as he took a long breath, chest expanding, then exhaled slowly and opened his eyes.

Thick black hair brushed his shoulders, threaded with faint silver, and his eyes were the color of a storm-tossed sea, blue-green shot through with gold.

Every fine hair on my body stood on end.

He took a step away from the tree. The last of the ooze sloughed off him and soaked into the ground. The smell of sulfur burned my nose. I shot Owen a look and mouthed, *Who is he?*

He shrugged and shook his head.

The man tilted his head up to the sky, closed his eyes, and inhaled the air like a man gulping in fresh air he hadn't had in years. Then he smiled and spoke.

"Come out, my friends. There is no need to hide."

His voice was a deep, resonant drumbeat that reverberated through my chest. The words sank into my skin and wrapped around something deep and lonely inside me, tugging hard.

I started to stand.

Owen caught my hand and yanked me down. "What are you doing?" he hissed against my ear.

His voice broke the spell for me to realize I was halfway up. I dropped back to my knees, heart hammering. "I—I don't know."

"Come, all of you," the man in black said. "You don't have to be alone anymore."

Again, the words pulled on me. On the hollow ache I didn't realize I'd been carrying since Alice died. Everything in me screamed that I needed to go to him. That he understood. That with him, I'd never feel this empty again. The ground tipped. Nausea slammed into me. I pressed my fingertips to my temple, trying to anchor myself in my own body.

"Piper?" Owen whispered.

I grabbed his hand and squeezed so hard my nails dug into his skin.

"What is it? What's he doing to you?"

"I... I don't—" The words shredded in my throat.

Tani zipped by again. "Get her out of here, Owen. Now."

"Why?" he demanded.

"He's riding the breach. Drawing on whatever's leaking through the ley lines. He's pulling her into his spell," Tani said. "Take her out of here."

"No." I shook my head, fighting the urge to stand. "I need to see. I need to know."

I forced myself to look back at the clearing.

Shapes rose from the ground—humanoid mounds shedding grass and wildflowers. As they shook free their camouflage, five other figures appeared—three men, two women—all dressed in black like him.

The man in black opened his arms. "My children."

They went to him in a rush. Touching, clinging, pressing their faces to his shoulders like lost souls finally coming home. Their sighs of relief blended with his low, satisfied laugh.

Another hard yank on that dark thread in my chest. Another swell of desperate longing—not for him, but for what he offered. An end to the emptiness. Someone who understood. A place to belong. I tightened my grip on Owen's hand until my knuckles ached.

"There is another," the man said. Slowly, he turned his head, gaze cutting toward the brush where we hid. "Come out, little one. You don't have to carry it all alone."

I flinched. I turned my face into Owen's neck and pressed my forehead there.

"Don't let him take me," I whispered.

"I told you to get her out of here," Tani snapped. "Now it may be too late."

"Who is he?" Owen demanded, never taking his eyes off the clearing.

"A demon," Tani said. "A powerful one. The breach gave him form. And he wants her."

"I need to go to him. He understands."

The words spilled out of me before I could stop them, muffled against Owen's skin but full of raw, aching truth—and it wasn't my truth at all. It was his. It was the spell.

I inhaled the sharp tang of Owen's cologne, clung to the memory of his thumb brushing chocolate from my lip. His mouth on mine in the basement. Anything that wasn't that demon's voice promising impossible things.

"It's the spell talking," Tani said. "He's using whatever power he's got to twist the grief that's already there. The loneliness. The gate's too open. He won't stop until he has her."

Owen wrapped his arm tight around me. "He can't have her."

"Then move," Tani snapped.

Owen surged to his feet, hauling me up with him. We barely took two steps before the demon moved—too fast, a blur of black.

He was suddenly there.

Smiling. Teeth sharp as knives.

"There you are," he crooned. "My lost little darling."

He reached for me.

Tani exploded into full size between us, a curved dagger flashing in her hand. She slashed, catching him across the upper arm.

He roared, a sound made of rusted metal and nightmares. Rage flared in his eyes, hot and molten.

Images slammed into my mind. Not my own—his. Tani broken on the ground, wings torn, blood on her lips. Then Owen sprawled in the dirt, ribs crushed, throat bruised where those clawed hands had squeezed—

"You shouldn't have done that," I gasped.

"Yes," the demon said silkily. "You shouldn't have done that, little fairy."

His voice wrapped around me like a shroud. My knees buckled. If Owen hadn't still been holding me, I would have crawled straight to the demon's feet and begged him to take away the ache.

The others were advancing, leaving the tree, moving in a slow, predatory circle.

"Owen, you going to stand there all day or do something?" Tani snapped.

Somewhere to the left, I heard the creak of a bow. I forced my head around in time to see Tani nock an arrow and let it fly. It hit one of the men square in the chest. He dropped. As if a puppet whose strings had been cut.

Another arrow. Another body.

The demon's snarl deepened. His outline began to glow faintly, as though lit from within by coals.

Owen shoved me behind him and stepped forward, hands curling into fists.

"You leave her alone," he said.

"Who's going to stop me?" the demon asked, amused. "You?"

His voice hit me like a physical blow. I dropped to the ground, palms scraping over dirt and leaves. The longing roared back, drowning me in promises of belonging and understanding and an end to carrying everything alone. My muscles trembled with the urge to crawl to him. To let him take it all away. His mind spilled into mine—images of myself curled up safe and understood, never lonely again, never grieving, never afraid.

"Yes," I breathed. The word hissed out of me before I could bite it back.

I found myself moving over sticks and stones, knees digging into the earth, hand slicing open on something sharp. I barely felt it.

He'll make it all stop, I thought wildly. He'll make it all stop.

"He won't," Tani said aloud, stepping in front of me again.

My vision blurred. Through the wash of tears I saw Tani loose another arrow. It drove into a woman's chest. She crumpled.

The demon's glow intensified.

"Be gone, fairy," he said.

He flicked his hand.

Tani flew backward like she'd been hit by a truck, crashing into the trees with a sickening thud.

My heart stuttered. I tried to scramble toward the fairy, but the demon's voice slid through my veins like poison honey and turned me around again.

I crawled toward him, hands bloody, breath coming in harsh gasps. Images flooded my mind—him holding me while I cried, him telling me it would all be okay, him promising I'd never be alone again. It was a lie, and I knew it was a lie but some part of me wanted to believe it, anyway.

"Stay where you are."

Owen's voice snapped like a thunderclap.

The spell wobbled. I collapsed where I was, cheek pressed into damp leaves and dirt. Shame mixed with relief, burning behind my eyes. I let out a strangled sob.

Wind whipped through the clearing, rattling the leaves overhead. The trees shuddered, branches bending low. The air changed—metallic and charged, like the moment before a tornado dropped out of a green sky. The temperature plummeted.

A raindrop splashed on my cheek.

"I said stay where you are."

I had never heard Owen sound like that. Dark. Commanding. Absolute. I turned my head enough to see his back—rigid, broad shoulders braced, fists clenched at his sides.

Lightning crackled across the sky, followed by a booming crack of thunder that shook the ground. The wind howled, ripping leaves from branches. The clouds above rolled in a churning, slate-gray mass, swallowing the sun.

Owen thrust his hands forward.

The gust that hit the demon was like a physical wall. The man in black went flying backward across the clearing, slammed into the hickory tree, and crumpled to the base of it, pinned there by wind that shrieked like a living thing. He was out cold.

The moment he hit the trunk, the roar stopped. The clouds broke apart as if ripped down the middle. Sunlight poured into the clearing. The wind died to a whisper. The suffocating pressure lifted.

Summer snapped back into place.

Owen spun and dropped to his knees beside me, hands closing around my shoulders.

"Piper. Are you all right?"

His voice—his normal, worried voice—flipped the switch inside me. The ugly, invasive longing evaporated like mist. I sucked in a lungful of hot, humid air and nodded.

"I am now," I managed. "What happened? Did you... use your magic?"

"Yes."

He helped me to my feet but didn't let go, arm steady around my shoulders. He brushed dirt and leaves off my cheek with gentle fingers.

"What did he do to you?" he asked, jaw tight.

"I—I don't know. Every time he spoke, it was like I had to go to him. Like he could make the loneliness stop. Like he understood everything, and I'd never have to feel this empty again." Heat flared under my skin—not desire, but shame at how badly I'd wanted to believe the lie. "He was pulling on the grief. On missing Alice."

The images still lurked at the back of my mind, false comfort wrapped around hooks.

Owen's jaw ticked. The anger in his eyes wasn't for me. It was for the demon.

A pained groan sounded from the edge of the clearing.

"Tani," I gasped.

We hurried toward the trees. The fairy queen lay crumpled on her side, still in her full-size form, one hand pressed to her head. Blood trickled down from a gash along her hairline.

"Why didn't you use your powers sooner?" she muttered, and gave Owen's arm a weak, annoyed punch. He didn't even flinch.

"You knew he has magic?" I asked, exasperated. "Why am I always the last to know everything?"

"You silly girl. He's an elemental," Tani said. "A Druid."

Druid.

The word landed differently this time.

"An elemental?" I said. "What does that mean?"

Owen met my gaze. "Elemental druid. We use the powers of the world around us. I can harness air. Hence the thunderstorm."

"That was... you?"

Realization slammed into me. The thunderstorm. The wind. The lightning. And then I thought of his father—the way Dougal had incinerated the other demon without hesitation.

Fire.

Air and flame. Father and son—guardians of a Crossroads town that sat where realms brushed too close.

"Help me get her back to the truck," Owen said. "She needs that cut looked at."

"I'm fine," Tani grumbled, trying to stand. Her knees buckled. Owen caught her before she face-planted. "Okay, maybe not fine."

"We need to move," Owen said. "I bound him to the tree, but I don't know how long it'll hold. He's drawing on the ley breach. He's stronger than me here."

"Who is he?" I asked, unable to stop myself from looking back.

Tani shuddered. "Something that should've stayed on the other side of the gate," she said. "And he's decided you're his new favorite prize. He'll use your grief like a fishing line until he reels you in."

I swallowed hard. I took one last look at the demon slumped against the hickory, shadows already coiling around him like smoke.

I had a gut feeling this wasn't the last time I'd see him.

And that terrified me.

Chapter Twelve

By the time we returned to the house, washed the grit from my scraped palms, bandaged them, and tended Tani's wounds, night had fully settled over Hickory Hollow. Darkness pressed against the windows, thick and listening, as if the world outside had leaned closer, curious what would happen next.

The house smelled faintly of herbs, old wood, and ozone.

Tani—pale, furious, and muttering under her breath—had shrunk back to her smaller form and vanished into the greenhouse with a promise of vengeance and healing salves. The Red Queen remained barricaded in the upstairs guest room under strict orders not to wander, sulking loudly enough to be heard through the ceiling. Willow perched regally on the arm of a chair, tail wrapped around her paws, golden eyes tracking Owen as he swept shattered glass into a dustpan.

I sat curled at one end of the sofa, one leg tucked beneath me, bandages snug around my palms. Every muscle felt hollowed out, wrung thin.

"Thanks for doing that," I said quietly.

Owen glanced up. "Of course."

He tipped the last of the broken glass into the trash and leaned on the broom, shoulders sagging now that the danger had passed.

"Piper... I'm sorry."

I frowned. "Sorry for what?"

"For not stopping it sooner. At the shop. In the woods." His jaw tightened. "I should've bound that demon the second I saw it. I hesitated."

"You didn't hesitate," I said firmly, pushing myself to my feet. Crossing the room felt like walking through water. "You protected me."

He shook his head. "Not fast enough. My father wouldn't have waited."

I took the broom from his hands and let it fall to the floor. Then I threaded my fingers through his, careful of the bandages. "You're not your father. And I'm alive because of you."

He searched my face, something raw slipping through the careful control he usually wore.

"I've wanted you safe for a long time," he said quietly. "Longer than I ever admitted to myself."

The words landed heavier than a declaration ever could. My chest tightened and my breath caught.

"Owen—"

"It's all right," he said quickly, already retreating half a step. "You don't have to answer that. I'll wait. However long you need."

No one had ever said that to me.

The realization hit harder than fear.

Emotion surged up fast and unmanageable. I stepped into him instead, pressing my forehead to his chest. His heart beat steady beneath my ear. He didn't kiss me. He didn't rush me. He wrapped his arms around me and held on, solid and unmovable, until the shaking eased.

Only then did he tip my chin up.

He kissed me like he'd been waiting—patient, careful, but unable to deny it any longer. His lips were warm and sure, fitting to mine as if they'd always known how. The world softened around us, the noise and fear falling away until there was only the quiet press of his mouth and the steady strength of his arms holding me in place.

It wasn't hurried. It wasn't asking for more. It was a promise made without words.

When I pulled back, breathless, it was only because I needed air. "There's something you need to know."

His expression sharpened instantly. "Okay."

"When the demon spoke..." My voice wavered. "It didn't scare me. It did something. Like it reached inside my head. Tried to convince me I'd never be alone if I went to him. Made me want to believe his lies."

His grip tightened, careful of my hands. "But you didn't choose it."

"No. And every time you spoke, it stopped." I swallowed. "If you hadn't been there..."

"Then I'm not going anywhere," he said without hesitation. "Not tonight."

Relief hit me so hard my knees nearly gave out.

We curled together on the sofa beneath my aunt's crocheted afghan, his arm firm around my shoulders, my cheek over his heart. The house creaked softly around us. Willow hopped down and curled near our feet.

Sleep came quietly this time.

A scraping sound tore me from sleep.

Scrape. Scrape. Scrape.

I bolted upright. Owen was already moving, eyes fixed on the ceiling.

"That's not the Red Queen," he said.

Cold fear slid through my veins. "I heard that before."

He was up the stairs before I could stop him reaching for the attic ladder. I hurried after him.

"Wait." I grabbed his arm. "It was... fire. Light. Power. It vanished."

"Then we'll find out why."

Willow appeared silently, staring upward, tail lashing once.

Owen pulled down the ladder and climbed first. I followed, heart pounding.

The attic was dark—until Owen lifted his hand, light crackling into existence in his palm like trapped lightning.

The sound came again.

From the trunk.

The lid launched toward us.

We ducked as yellow-orange light exploded upward, washing the attic in an unnatural glow. A shadow form surged out—thin, clawed, its eyes burning red.

It went straight for me.

I screamed.

Owen hurled the lightning, ripping through the specter—but it reformed, shrieking.

Wind roared suddenly as Owen raised both hands, forcing the thing back toward the trunk.

"Get the lid!"

I moved on instinct, hauling it across the attic floor—

And froze.

Something else came out.

This one was solid.

Scaled. Horned. Fanged. Holding a sword.

And it charged Owen.

Lightning struck again. Once. Twice. The blade flew from its grasp.

Owen snatched it mid-fall.

The sword hummed.

He swung.

The creature howled—and dissolved into black smoke.

More shadows surged upward behind it.

"NOW!"

I slammed the lid shut as something punched upward beneath it, nearly throwing me back. Owen leapt forward, white light flaring from his hands and sealing the trunk in a binding glow.

Silence crashed down.

I collapsed to the floor, shaking.

"That wasn't... a haunting," I whispered.

"No," Owen said grimly. "It was a containment anchor."

My breath hitched. "For what?"

"Unstable crossings. Alice didn't open doors—she locked them."

"They came for me," I said.

Owen knelt in front of me, firm grip on my shoulders. "Because you're the Guardian of the Crossroads now."

My blood ran cold.

"We need to move this," he said. "Before it tears wider."

"Where?"

He met my gaze. "My father."

The truth settled like a final, echoing bell. This wasn't Alice's legacy.

It was mine.

Chapter Thirteen

It took both of us to get the trunk out of the attic—and even then, it felt like it resisted every inch of movement.

The wood was heavier than it should have been, the weight uneven, as if whatever was inside shifted against us while we dragged it down the narrow stairs. My foot slipped, my heart lurching as the trunk tilted dangerously forward, and for one breathless second I was certain it would take me with it.

We wrestled it into the back of Owen's pickup, breathing hard, hands shaking.

I leaned against the tailgate, chest heaving—and then froze.

"The grimoire," I said suddenly. "I left the grimoire in the car."

I scrambled around to the passenger side and dug beneath the seat, pulling out the thick, weathered book. The leather cover felt warmer now, alert beneath my fingers.

Owen frowned. "That needs to be translated. Soon."

"Mrs. Rollins," I said. "Tomorrow."

He nodded, glancing toward the house. "Tonight, this thing doesn't stay here."

"Not without me."

His mouth curved into a quick, tight smile. "Grab what you need. I'll wait."

Gripping the book, I hurried back inside, heart pounding harder with every step. Halfway down the upstairs hall, something tugged at my attention.

The guest room.

I slowed, pressed my ear to the door.

Nothing.

Unease prickled up my spine. I opened it.

The Red Queen lay on her back, hands folded neatly on her chest, eyes closed. So still she looked like a queen laid out for a formal funeral.

At least she was quiet.

I closed the door softly, then hurried to my room and set the grimoire on my dresser. I stared at it for half a second—too long. Leaving it here felt wrong. Like leaving a live wire in my house.

With a muttered curse, I snatched it back up, tucked it under my arm, and grabbed my purse. I locked up. Owen waited beside the truck, his hand on the passenger door. When I approached, he opened it for me.

Ever the gentleman.

We drove to Charmed & Vintage. The road stretched too quiet, the darkness pressing close to the headlights. I found myself checking the mirrors over and over, convinced I caught movement beyond the edges of the light.

But there was nothing there. Just my hyperawareness and paranoia. The sooner we got rid of this trunk, the better.

We arrived without incident—but relief never came. Owen parked and cut the engine and we both hopped out. I scooped up the grimoire from the seat before I even unbuckled, as if leaving it behind would be an invitation. The leather felt warmer than it should've.

"I'll grab the dolly."

"You're leaving me out here alone?"

"For a minute," he said. "I won't be long. Promise."

The door shut behind him, plunging the street back into silence.

I clutched the grimoire to my chest, scanning the quiet storefronts, the single streetlamp casting a sickly halo of light. My imagination whispered.

Then one of the shadows moved.

Not flickered. Not shifted.

Moved.

My breath snagged.

The shadow slid along the storefront across the street, stretching unnaturally, peeling itself free from the darkness like ink lifting from a page.

"Owen, hurry up," I whispered.

The thing surged forward.

Owen burst back out of the shop, shoving the dolly aside as his hands flared with light. "Get behind me."

The creature took shape mid-charge—jaws splitting wide, stench of rot and sulfur hitting me like a physical blow. Owen released a blast of white-gold energy that sent it screeching backward—

—and then the air went cold behind me.

I spun.

Another one had formed.

Then another.

And another.

They were pulling themselves out of shadows, detaching from doorways, crawling out of the spaces between parked cars—too many, circling, hemming us in.

Fear crushed down on my lungs.

"There are too many," I whispered.

He saw them. I felt it in the way his shoulders squared, the way he backed us toward the shop. He shoved the keys into my hands.

"Get inside. Now. I'm right behind you."

"What about you—"

"I'll hold them off."

I fumbled with the lock, hands slick with sweat as the first key slipped uselessly against the metal. Light detonated behind me as Owen hurled magic into the street, demonic howls echoing in the night.

"Piper!"

"I'm trying!"

A set of claws slashed against invisible resistance inches from my face. I screamed, jamming another key into the lock—wrong again—

A demon lunged.

Owen's magic cracked like thunder.

The door finally gave way.

I stumbled inside as Owen leapt after me, slamming it shut. He slapped his palm against the doorframe, white light sealing the cracks—but the impact of bodies hit immediately, the magic shuddering under the weight.

"That won't hold them long," he said grimly. "Come on."

We ran.

The store felt endless in the dark, every shadow threatening movement. Owen navigated without hesitation, pulling me into the storeroom and flicking on the light.

I slapped the grimoire onto the worktable like it might bite, then wiped my damp palm on my jeans.

"The sword," I gasped. "The long box."

He wrenched the lid free and thrust the sword toward me.

The moment my fingers closed around the hilt, the world changed.

The blade warmed—not with heat, but with awareness. Power surged up my arms, not overwhelming, not violent. Recognizing. As if the sword had been waiting for this hand. For me.

Something deep in my chest answered.

Owen cracked open another crate and drew a second blade, its edge etched with ancient runes that flared briefly as he grasped it. “Stay close.”

The first demon tore through the sealed door like it was made of paper. He readied his stance. So did I. Together, we faced the door. Our doom.

The demon darkened the doorway. Then the fighting began.

At first, I moved on instinct alone—barely keeping my footing, swinging wide and wild. But the sword shifted in my grip. Adjusted my stance. Nudged my balance. Knowledge flowed not into my mind, but into my muscles.

I stopped thinking.

Stopped doubting.

I moved.

The blade sang as it cut through shadow and flesh alike, bright and sure. Shapes fell—shrieked—dissolved into black smoke at my feet. Each strike felt right, as if I were restoring something that had been broken rather than destroying it.

When the last creature collapsed, I staggered, breath ragged, every nerve alight and humming.

“You’re incredible,” Owen said hoarsely as he dispatched his final opponent.

“Your dad’s going to kill us,” I managed faintly.

Owen huffed a laugh—one quick, disbelieving breath.

And then the grimoire on the table thumped like it had a heartbeat.

The floor shuddered. Not from the fight. From the building itself—like the shop had taken a breath it didn’t want.

Cold swept the room without warning. Not a draft. Not air moving. Cold with intention.

The fluorescent lights snapped off one by one, plunging the shop into darkness until only the streetlamp outside cast a sickly glow through the storeroom windows.

He stood in the doorway. He didn't step inside. He didn't need to.

The same man from the woods. He'd found me again. Up close, I saw him more clearly.

And he was terrifyingly beautiful.

Tall and broad-shouldered, built like violence wrapped in silk. Thick black hair brushed his shoulders, threaded with faint silver, and his eyes—God—his eyes were the color of a storm-tossed sea, blue-green shot through with gold. Ancient. Appraising. Hungry.

His presence reached me first—pressure sliding along my skin, coiling tight in my chest. Not heat. Not magic the way Owen's was.

Something older. Darker. Power that didn't ask permission.

"There you are."

His voice—dark, deep, melodic—slid over my skin and straight into my bones.

My knees buckled. I sank to the floor, the sword dangling uselessly from my hand as something in me answered him in the worst way—like a part of my body recognized a command before my mind could refuse it.

The ache hit first.

A sudden, violent loneliness that didn't belong to me. Like someone had poured grief straight into my bloodstream and smiled while I drowned in it.

That same thought pounded through me. *Go to him.* Let him take away the ache of loneliness. Let him take that pain away.

"Piper!"

Owen tried to reach me. He took a step—

—and stopped.

I looked up in time to see him strain, muscles locked, boots rooted to the floor as if the boards had become a vise. His jaw clenched. Veins stood out in his neck.

He couldn't move. The sword in his hand was frozen.

The man's smile deepened, satisfied.

"Good," he murmured. "I was hoping you'd bring the caretaker."

"Stay away from her," Owen snapped, voice tight with effort.

The words cut through the haze—firm, commanding, grounding.

The pressure recoiled at the sound of him, lessened enough for me to inhale. Enough to remember myself.

But not enough to move.

The man's gaze dropped to the grimoire—where it lay on the worktable, half-shadowed, like it wanted to hide and couldn't.

"That book has been quiet for a long time," he said softly. "And then you picked it up."

My throat tightened. "Who are you?"

His eyes glinted in the windowlight—predator assessing prey.

"A problem you inherited," he said. "A door your aunt left cracked. My scout said you smelled like her. I had to find out for myself."

He paused, smile sharpening.

"You can call me Garrat."

He took one slow step forward. Every instinct in me screamed to back away.

The sword in my hand warmed—alert, offended—like it hated him on sight.

"Don't," Owen growled, and the lights above flickered as Owen's magic pushed against whatever held him.

Garrat didn't even look at Owen. He looked at me.

"Do you know what it's like," he murmured, voice lowering, "to listen to a boundary tear and not be able to reach through it?"

My stomach turned.

He lifted his hand—not toward my face, not to touch me—

Toward the grimoire. The leather cover shuddered. The shop groaned. And the air thinned, like something behind the walls had leaned closer.

"No." The word scraped out of me. "Don't touch it."

His smile sharpened. "Ah. There it is."

He shifted his fingers, delicate as a pianist.

The grimoire's clasp clicked.

Not open—

Just enough.

Like a lock testing itself.

The streetlamp outside flared, then dimmed.

Something moved beyond the glass, where there shouldn't have been movement—shadows gathering like they'd been called.

Owen swore under his breath. "Piper—look at me."

I tried. I tried so hard.

My vision tunneled, the compulsion dragging my attention back to Garrat's voice like a leash.

"You can't fight a pull you don't understand," he said kindly. "Not yet."

He stepped closer. Close enough that the cold in the room felt like it had teeth. And then—

"Stop."

The word cracked through the darkness like a whip.

The pressure holding me in place snapped. I jolted, gasping, as my muscles remembered how to work.

For a heartbeat I couldn't see anything but him—his halted hand, his smile frozen—

Then I became aware of the woman standing beside him.

She had not arrived loudly. There was no flash of light, no crack of thunder.

She simply was.

Full-size Tani stood there, her dagger in hand ready to attack. Her eyes were fixed on Garrat.

"Honestly," she drawled, inspecting the scene like she'd wandered into a mess at a party. "Could you be any more dramatic?"

Garrat's expression barely shifted. But I felt it—his attention flicked to her like a blade turning.

"You again," he said.

"And you," Titania replied sweetly. "Still skulking. Still sniffing around other people's thresholds."

She glanced at Owen—pinned in place, breathing hard—and made a face. "Rude."

Owen's jaw clenched. "If you're here to critique—"

"I'm here because something in this quaint little shop screamed across realms," Tani said, and her gaze snapped to the grimoire. "And I hate when humans ring bells they don't know how to un-ring."

My pulse hammered. "He—he was—"

"Trying to test you," she said flatly. "Trying to see if the book answers you."

Garrat's smile returned, slow and pleased.

"She's awakening," he murmured. "I simply came to confirm."

Tani's eyes flashed.

"Oh, darling," she purred. "You don't get to confirm anything in my orbit."

She lifted her hand—two fingers, lazy, like she was flicking dust from a sleeve—

—and the air tightened around him.

"You should go."

A pressure like invisible silk, pulling taut. The shadows at the windows hissed and recoiled as if burned. Garrat's gaze snapped to me one last time, eyes gleaming with dark promise.

"This isn't over," he said softly. "He's been patient a long time. You can't close what's already torn."

The darkness folded.

He vanished—not with a bang, not with a flash—with the sickening sensation of something being pulled backward through a hole too small for it.

The room exhaled.

What did he mean by *he's been patient a long time*? Add that to the list of mysteries I was investigating.

Owen staggered as the force holding him released. He caught himself on a shelf, breathing hard, fury carved into every line of his face. He gripped the sword tight in his other hand.

"Piper." His voice went low. "Are you hurt?"

I looked down at my hands—still shaking, still gripping the sword like it was the only solid thing in the world.

"I don't think so," I whispered. "But I—"

My gaze snapped to the grimoire.

The clasp had been disturbed.

Tani drifted closer to the book, her expression suddenly sharp in a way that wasn't playful at all.

"That book," she said quietly, "is not a cute antique problem."

Owen's jaw flexed. "We know."

"No," Tani said, and for once, her voice held something like warning instead of comedy. "You don't."

She looked at me—straight through me, like she could see every thread under my skin.

"Guardian grimoires are anchored to bloodlines," she said. "When Alice's heir touched it, the book woke. Recognized you. And when a grimoire that old wakes up..." She paused. "It sings across the veil. Like a beacon calling home."

My stomach dropped. "So anyone listening—"

"Knows exactly where you are," Tani finished. "And what you are. Alice kept it dormant for decades. You picked it up and rang every bell between here and Faery."

"That must be why it was hidden in the town archives," I said. "Alice was protecting me before I ever came back."

Owen swore under his breath. "And that's why he came."

"And why more will follow," Tani said grimly, "if that door at the tree stays open. The grimoire called. The crossing answered. And now everything on the other side knows there's a new Guardian in Hickory Hollow."

My mouth went dry. "How do I close it?"

Owen's fingers tightened around my elbow. "How do we make it stop?"

Tani's smile was thin. "You start at the tree. You seal the crossing properly—before it widens."

Her gaze flicked to the sword in my hand.

She went very still.

"Hey—" She stepped closer, eyes fixed on the blade. "That's not the Sword of Light."

She held out her hand.

I gave it to her, pommel first. The moment her fingers closed around it, she drew in a low, stunned breath. When she looked up at me again, her expression had gone almost reverent.

"Do you know what this is?" she asked.

"A sword?"

Her mouth flattened. "Not just any sword. Excalibur."

A startled laugh escaped me before I could stop it. "Funny, Tani."

But she wasn't smiling.

"Oh, God," I breathed. "It is."

Owen stared at the weapon in her hands. "Then what have I got?"

"The Sword of Light," Tani said, glancing toward him. "And she"—her gaze returned to me—"has Excalibur."

"Okay, great," I said faintly. "So between us, we're apparently running a two-sword special."

Neither of them laughed.

"Where did Alice get Excalibur?" Owen asked.

"The mystery deepens, McAllister," I muttered with a shrug, because Alice was clearly into a lot of weirdly magical, legendary things and I no longer had the energy to be surprised.

Tani looked between the two blades, then at the crates stacked against the wall.

"You have the Sword of Light," she said to Owen. "And Excalibur was hidden here, too." Her voice lowered. "Alice wasn't just safeguarding the three Fae treasures. She was hiding more than anyone knew."

She stepped toward the crates, eyes narrowed.

"How much do you want to bet the other two are in those?" I asked Owen.

He nodded slowly. "It's a good possibility."

"Well," I said, exhaling shakily, "this has all been deeply educational. But we still have the problem of the tree."

"Yes," Tani said. "And this time, Piper... you don't do it alone."

I swallowed hard, staring at the doorway where Garrat had stood, the air still wrong where his attention had touched me.

"Okay," I whispered. "Then we close it."

Owen's voice came out like a promise. "Together."

Chapter Fourteen

We were back at my house after hiding the trunk in the antique store's cellar, putting away the mythical weapons, wiping the black ash off the concrete floor, and locking up the shop. Dawn was still hours away, but exhaustion pressed down on my bones like lead.

Owen sat on the sofa, shoulders hunched, both hands wrapped around a mug of steaming coffee. His fingers weren't steady. Neither were mine. The heat didn't seem to help much—not with the aftershock still riding his nerves, his body unwinding from the night in small, involuntary tremors.

I hovered near the fireplace, arms wrapped around myself, pacing a groove into the rug.

I was still processing the fight in the shop—the shadow-things, the way the grimoire had *responded*, the man in the doorway who felt like hunger with a voice. I kept circling the same details, like if I replayed them enough times I'd find the moment where everything had gone wrong.

I didn't tell Owen what it had felt like when his attention touched me.

I wasn't ready to say that part out loud.

Finally, he let out a slow breath. "You're going to wear a hole in that rug."

I halted, looked at him. "Sorry," I muttered.

"That demon—Garrat—he tried to bind you to him again," he said after a long moment.

"Yes." My mouth went dry at the thought. "He wanted me to believe his lies. That I'm all alone. And that punch of loneliness was so deep, so raw... I wanted to believe him."

Owen placed his mug on the table and then gave me his full attention, leaning forward with his elbows on his knees.

"Piper," he said, my name quiet in his voice. "You aren't alone in this. You have me."

My heart squeezed.

"I know," I whispered. "And I'm glad."

"I won't let you face this by yourself."

He always knew the right things to say, to make me feel safe.

We looked at each other in the silence, but I didn't want to sit with those feelings too long. Otherwise, I would start to want something more with the man standing with me. And I wasn't quite ready.

"He looked at the grimoire like it belonged to him. Like he could pull on it," I said, changing the subject.

Owen's eyes sharpened as he picked up his mug again. "But the book answered you."

Guilt punched through my ribs. "I didn't mean to—"

"I know," he said, softer. "But intent doesn't matter if the veil heard it."

"Why?" I asked.

"I'll tell you why."

Tani appeared out of thin air beside the hearth in all her full-size glory.

"Ow—!" Owen jerked, sloshing coffee over his hand.

My hand flew to my chest. "Tani! Give a girl some warning."

The fairy queen winced. "Sorry. You want the explanation or not?"

"Yes," I said flatly.

"Please," Owen added, setting the mug aside.

Tani hesitated, glancing between us. Whatever humor she usually carried was gone. When she finally spoke, her voice was quieter. Heavier.

"This is complicated."

"Try," I said tightly. I'd never heard Tani sound like this—no slang, no sass. Just a queen speaking truth that weighed on her.

"There's a veil between realms," Tani began. "Between yours and mine. Between all of them. Human world. Faery. Wonderland." She drew in a breath. "That veil has been thinning."

"How?" Owen asked, instantly alert.

"I don't know," Tani admitted. "A few months ago, I felt it shift. Tear. Every spell I cast to stabilize it only made things worse."

"Worse how?" I asked.

"Like something pushing from the other side," Tani said. "Something that feeds on magic. Every attempt to stop it gave it more strength."

I leaned forward. "What took Oberon?"

Tani's jaw clenched. "Whatever this thing is—it tore a chunk out of Faery and dragged him into another realm."

"Why him?" Owen asked.

"Because he guards the Fae relics," she said bluntly. "Or because whoever's behind this thinks he does."

My thoughts immediately flew to the crates in Charmed & Vintage. To Alice hiding treasures away like landmines no one else knew how to defuse.

"If you knew any of this before," I said slowly, "why didn't you tell me?"

"I didn't know it was spreading," Tani said. "I thought it was contained to Faery. Until Wonderland started bleeding."

"That part is true," the Red Queen said from the staircase.

We turned as she descended, skirts gathered carefully in her hands. "Paths have been opening where none existed before. Places touching that never should."

"I tried sealing the boundaries," Tani said. "It worked—for a time. But it's temporary. The barrier's thinning again."

"What about Oberon?" I asked. "You said you found him."

Tani nodded. "He's alive. Trapped. I know exactly where he is. I can't reach him."

"I thought the hickory tree was the only crossing," I said.

"It's the strongest," Tani replied. "But it's not the only one. Standing stones. Old circles. Places where ley lines intersect."

My chest tightened. How many doors were there? How many chances for that demon to slip through?

"Did Alice know?" I asked quietly.

Tani hesitated.

Willow padded over and rolled onto her back at my feet, meowing softly.

Tani glanced down. "She did. She was trying to fix it."

I swallowed.

"So this... thing hit Faery," I said slowly. "And Wonderland. Which means it's only a matter of time before it pushes here."

"Holy jabberwocky," the Red Queen muttered.

"Closing the gate won't be enough," Tani said. "Not anymore."

"And we don't even know what it is," Owen added.

Silence followed.

"Then here's the plan," I said, straightening. "We stop broadcasting. We lock the grimoire down. We translate it. And we seal the tree properly—before the tear widens."

Owen's gaze held mine. "We?"

I didn't flinch. "We."

Tani's eyes narrowed—approval, sharp as a blade. "Good."

"And while we do that," I added, looking at Tani and the Red Queen, "you two keep an eye on the town. If paths open—if anything feels wrong—I want to know before it's in my driveway."

Tani yawned. "That's my cue."

The Red Queen nodded once and retreated upstairs.

Willow curled into the chair and was asleep instantly.

That left Owen and me alone.

I stepped closer to him, the weight of the night pressing in. Say something normal, I told myself. Something that belongs to the world before monsters and magic and doors that shouldn't exist.

"You'll stay?"

"I'll stay," he said softly. "As long as you need me."

The knot in my chest loosened a fraction. Enough to breathe.

"Owen… there's something I should confess."

His eyes drifted to my mouth. "Yes?"

The words that came out weren't the ones clawing at my insides. But they were safer. Familiar.

"I tried to beat you for valedictorian."

A grin broke across his face. "And failed."

"You were obscenely smart," I said. "It was deeply unfair."

"And you were relentless," he said. "I still have nightmares about you correcting the teacher."

The sound of his laughter—soft, real—felt like a lifeline. For a moment, I could pretend nothing had changed. That we were two people standing in a quiet house, trading old jokes, and not whatever the world had decided to turn us into.

I smiled—then sobered. "Why didn't you leave Hickory Hollow?"

"I stayed for my father," he said. Then, after a beat, "And because someone had to watch the Crossroads. Alice couldn't do it alone forever. I knew that even before I understood everything it meant. And…" He paused, his gaze meeting me. "Because I hoped you'd come back."

"Why?" The word came out quieter than I meant it to.

He didn't dodge it this time. "Because you were the one thing about this town that never felt small."

My chest tightened. "You never said anything."

"I didn't think I was allowed to want you," he admitted. "You were always going somewhere. I was staying."

I studied him, something clicking into place. "You could've left," I said softly. "Like your brother did."

His jaw tightened—not angry. "He wanted a different life."

"And you?" I asked.

Owen met my gaze. "I wanted this one."

"That's backwards," I said faintly.

He huffed a breath. "I know."

I studied him, seeing him differently now—not as the boy who stayed, but the man who chose to. "Did Alice know?"

His expression softened. "She knew everything. She always did."

That familiar ache stirred in my chest. "She watched over me, didn't she?"

"Yes," he said without hesitation. "In her own way."

Silence settled between us.

"I don't know what I'm doing," I said quietly.

Owen set aside his mug and rose. When he reached me, he took my hands, careful of the bandages. "Then we'll figure it out together."

Not forever. Not promises. Just together.

Since I'd come back to Hickory Hollow, that felt like enough.

Chapter Fifteen

"You're tired. Let's get you to bed."

I let him tug me gently toward the stairs.

Hours ago, we'd been curled together on the sofa, half-asleep beneath my aunt's afghan. Now everything felt different—shifted, rearranged—like the house itself had inhaled and hadn't exhaled yet.

It already felt distant. Like something that had happened to someone else.

He walked me upstairs in silence, our footsteps soft against the old wood. The house creaked and settled around us, familiar and strange all at once. At my bedroom door, he released my hand and started to turn away.

"Wait."

My voice came out thinner than I meant it to, scraped raw by everything I hadn't said.

He paused, half-turned back, one brow lifting. "Yeah?"

"Don't go."

One heartbeat. Two.

"You want me to stay?" he asked quietly. His gaze flicked to the bedroom behind me.

I nodded, stepping closer. My fingers curled in the hem of his shirt. "I want you to stay. With me. Tonight."

His breath caught slightly.

For a moment I thought he might argue. Be careful. Be noble. Make the sensible choice for both of us.

Instead, he stayed exactly where he was.

I slid my hands up his chest—and had a fleeting, startling thought that I must have missed something over the years. When had Owen McAllister gone from lanky, quiet boy to solid, warm, undeniably real man? Muscle shifted beneath my palms, heat radiating through cotton and skin.

Longing flickered in his dove-gray eyes.

His fingers closed gently around my wrists—not stopping me, exactly. Holding me there as if he were bracing himself against something fragile and precious all at once.

The memory of our kiss in the basement rushed back—the way it had made the rest of the world fall away for a minute. Right now, I wanted that again. Wanted something that wasn't fear or grief or unanswered questions.

"Owen," I whispered.

"Yeah?" His voice was rougher than usual, low and frayed at the edges.

"I'd like it if you kissed me again."

A soft, breathless laugh escaped him. "I was thinking the same thing."

His thumbs brushed along the insides of my wrists, sending a shiver skating up my arms. "But if I do," he said quietly, voice dropping into something warmer, "I don't know that I'll stop with kisses."

My pulse stumbled. "You want more than kisses?"

"I want you, Piper." His voice was earnest, unguarded. "More time. More closeness. More of whatever this is becoming."

My thoughts scattered. Heat bloomed fast and bright, making me sway a little.

"Oh," I managed.

"Is that clear enough?" His mouth curved faintly.

I nodded. "Crystal."

He leaned in—then stopped short, resting his forehead against mine, breath warm along my cheek.

"But not tonight," he said gently. "Not like this. You've had too much taken from you already."

My throat tightened. "Owen—"

"I want you," he said softly. "But I'll wait—until this isn't about holding on because everything feels like it's falling apart." His thumb brushed my cheek. "Until it's a choice."

Something sharp and aching bloomed behind my ribs.

He pressed a brief, tender kiss to my forehead instead—intimate in a way that somehow hurt more than stopping would have.

"I'll be downstairs," he added. "If you need me. And if you don't—I'll still be here in the morning."

I swallowed and nodded once. "Okay."

He stepped back, giving me space without making me feel abandoned by it. And for the first time in days, tomorrow didn't feel like something to dread.

Birdsong pulled me from sleep, followed by the faint clink of dishes and the unmistakable scent of coffee drifting up the stairs.

Someone had made coffee.

I rolled over, the echo of the night before still pressed into my skin—Owen's hands warm and steady, the way he'd held me like he wanted everything and yet had stopped. Not because he didn't want me. Because he did. Because he'd said he would wait until I was ready, until I wasn't reeling from truths that had cracked my world open.

My chest tightened.

I blinked up at the slats of sunlight cutting through the vertical blinds, then shoved back the blankets and swung my feet to the floor.

That was when reality settled in.

Alice was gone. The town sat on a thinning place between worlds. The veil was fraying—and last night something had reached through and looked straight at me.

And somehow, impossibly, I was now responsible for holding it all together.

I scrubbed a hand over my face, breath coming out shaky despite my best efforts. The room felt too bright. Too ordinary for a life that no longer fit inside neat edges.

At some point—soon—I was absolutely going to have a full breakdown about all of this.

Probably not before coffee.

I was about to slide off the bed when Owen filled the doorway, a steaming mug in his hand. His hair was damp and mussed like he'd taken a quick shower, his shirt slightly wrinkled—evidence it hadn't been on for long.

He paused when he saw me, gaze sweeping over my oversized sleep shirt and bare legs before a slow smile curved his mouth.

"Hey, there." He crossed the room and offered me the mug. "Thought you might need this."

I took it gratefully, fingers wrapping around the warm ceramic. "You are a saint," I said solemnly. "A magical, wildly overqualified barista saint."

One sip and I sighed. Exactly right. Of course it was. He retreated back to the door a safe distance.

"Sleep okay?" he asked, leaning a shoulder against the doorframe like he hadn't turned my world upside down and then made deliberate choices about not turning it further.

I peeked up at him over the rim of the cup. "Shockingly, yes. You?"

His mouth quirked. "Same."

We hovered there in the aftermath—carefully skirting last night's restraint, the truth bombs, the portals, and the minor detail that an unknown thing had tried to put its hands on the grimoire like it owned the right.

I cleared my throat. "I think I'd like to visit my parents today."

His expression softened instantly. "We can do that. After we go to the tree, though."

Right. The crossing. The dying hickory. The thing we were supposed to seal properly before it widened.

So far, my Guardian performance was... subpar.

"Of course," I said quickly. "After the tree."

"You forgot," he said, not even attempting to sound stern.

"No," I lied.

"Mm-hmm."

Instead of arguing, I rose from the bed, stepped closer, balancing my coffee one-handed and rising onto my toes to kiss his cheek. "Thanks," I said quietly. "For the coffee."

"You're welcome." His fingers brushed my hip, warm and deliberate, lingering long enough to remind me how aware of him I still was. "You know," he added lightly, "if you're planning to shower..."

I arched a brow. "Yes?"

"I'm committed to water conservation."

A laugh escaped me. "Tempting."

I was still considering poor but appealing decisions when the doorbell rang.

I glanced at the clock. Mid-morning. "Who on earth...?"

"I've got it." Owen's gaze flicked over me—bare legs, sleep-tangled hair, and precisely zero intention of modesty at the moment. "You might want pants before greeting the general public."

"Rude," I muttered, but he wasn't wrong.

He headed downstairs. I set my mug on the nightstand, tugged on the first pair of jeans I found, and swapped the sleep shirt for a clean T-shirt. No time for underwear.

Commando it was.

I added it to the rapidly growing list of things I was absolutely not explaining to whoever had decided today was a good day to show up.

Raised voices floated up the stairs—male, irritated. Owen answering, his tone tight and controlled.

Great.

Barefoot, I jogged down, heart thudding. At the front door stood a wall of a man, broad-shouldered and imposing, filling the threshold like he owned it. He wore a dark, structured coat that wasn't modern—heavy wool or leather, cut clean and severe, with subtle sigils stitched into the seams that caught the light only when he moved. It looked less like a uniform and more like something issued by an older, colder authority. His forearms were thick as tree trunks, tension carved into every line of him. Blond hair tipped faintly blue—because apparently even supernatural law enforcement had aesthetic choices—and eyes the color of Arctic ice swept the entryway with clipped professional judgment before landing on me.

He looked like he could punch through a brick wall.

Or a shadow-thing.

Or both.

Fantastic.

"I'm Piper Wakefield," I said, lifting my chin.

His gaze dragged from my bare toes up to my bedhead hair. Judgment flickered—quick, subtle, unmistakable. Of all days not to be wearing runway armor.

He reached into his pocket, flipped open a slim black wallet. Silver badge. ID.

"Agent Voss," he said. "Portal Enforcement."

I leaned in to read it. He snapped it shut before I got a good look.

"I understand there's trouble with the crossing at the hickory tree," he went on. "The Council sent me to investigate why it's still open."

"Wow," I said. "Word travels fast. How did you—"

"Where's Alice?" he cut in.

Owen shifted instantly, fractionally stepping in front of me. Protective. Infuriating. Comforting.

"Alice is dead," I said flatly.

The word still hurt—but at least it didn't steal my breath anymore.

Some of the fury bled out of Voss's face. "Dead."

"That's what I said."

"When?"

"A few weeks ago."

"How? And who's the new Guardian?"

I folded my arms. "Okay, bucko. I'd love to play interrogations with the Man of Mystery, but I don't know who you are beyond the shiny badge, and I've never heard of Portal Enforcement. Maybe enlighten me?"

His jaw tightened. Owen's hands flexed at his sides, the air around him humming faintly.

"Answer the questions," Voss said, clipped.

"Careful with your tone," Owen snapped, eyes flashing. Power rippled—controlled, but real.

I laid a hand on his arm, grounding him, then stepped around him.

"I'm the Guardian," I said. "What of it?"

The swear slipped out sharp and satisfying.

"Your crossing is failing."

"Thanks for that, Captain Apparent. I know," I shot back. "Because no one bothered to tell me anything until Alice was gone. I've been figuring this out blind—and shockingly, 'interdimensional maintenance' wasn't on my Manhattan résumé."

"She died suddenly?" he pressed.

"Yes. That's how dying tends to work."

Something flickered in his eyes. Calculation. Worry.

"That's... unfortunate," he said. "The Council will not be pleased."

I laughed, short and humorless. "The Council can get in line."

"Who's running the flower shop?" he asked. "That was Alice's cover."

"I am."

"And you're not?"

"I've been busy not dying."

"If you don't return to it, your cover will be compromised."

That was it.

I grabbed his bicep—solid as carved stone—and turned him toward the door, giving him a firm shove. To my surprise, he moved.

"That's enough. Bu-bye."

"You can't remove me," he snapped, bracing a hand on the frame, leaning in close. "You're making a serious mistake."

Owen was right behind me now—a presence, not a threat, but ready to become one.

I met Voss's gaze, voice low, dangerous. "I'm done with secrets. I'm done with everyone knowing my life better than I do. You explain what is happening—right now—or you leave."

Something in my voice—or the magic I hadn't learned yet—made him ease back.

"All you had to do was ask," he said carefully.

"Okay, then. I'm asking." I stepped aside. "Sit. We'll get you coffee."

I motioned to the worn sofa then gave Owen a pleading look. He muttered something under his breath but complied. Voss sat.

Willow immediately claimed his lap, purring smugly. He scratched her head between the ears.

"Your cat likes me," he said.

"Willow," I corrected. "She hates being called cat."

He blinked. I took the sofa opposite him, clasping my hands in my lap. Owen returned with coffee, handing one to the agent and one to me. I beamed as he settled next to me—close enough our knees brushed. Quiet solidarity.

"Tell me everything," Voss said.

He took a sip of coffee, then set aside the cup and pulled out a notepad and pen from the inside of his coat pocket—while still maintaining Willow, who seemed determined to fuse herself permanently to his lap.

I told him what mattered.

Alice. The will. The tree. The ritual. The attic tear. The shadow-things. The grimoire responding like it recognized me—and the moment in the shop when something on the other side had listened hard enough to find my name.

Voss's pen stilled.

"A listener," he repeated, quiet.

My stomach dipped. "That's what he is?"

His gaze lifted to mine. "Yes, and I know what it means."

"What does it mean?" Owen asked, voice flat.

Voss looked between us. "It means the crossing it's just open. It's loud. The portal at the tree is still open," he said. "That makes it accessible. Everything coming through is using your gate."

"I know."

"You need to close it."

"I plan to."

He stood abruptly. "Then my work here is done."

"Oh no," I said, springing to my feet. "Sit back down."

Owen stood too. "That wasn't a request."

Voss studied us for a long second. Then he sat. Willow immediately hopped back into his lap, turned once, and settled with a satisfied purr.

I blinked.

That... wasn't normal. Willow barely tolerated Owen.

Voss glanced down at the cat like he didn't know what to do with her, then sighed and rubbed a hand over his face. "The Council oversees all active crossings. All realms."

"How many realms?" I asked.

"Infinite."

I stared. "That's not helpful."

"It's accurate."

Pink glitter exploded at the doorway. The fairy queen was normal size, standing in the center of the room.

"Tani," I groaned. "We talked about poofing."

"Old habits," Tani said with a dismissive wave.

"Titania," Voss acknowledged with a dip of his head. His expression was grim.

"Insufferable man."

"You two know each other," Owen said.

"We have history," Tani snapped.

"A long one," Voss agreed, eyes narrowing. "Why aren't you in Faery?"

Tani's eyes flashed. "Because I can't get back without Oberon."

That gave him pause. "Where is he?"

"Trapped in another realm. I brought the Fae treasures to get him out. Alice was supposed to help me—but she died before she could."

Voss's mouth thinned. "Alice was a hedge witch. She wasn't powerful enough to pull that off."

I stiffened. "She said she found a way."

Voss looked at me then, really looked at me. Worry carved deep lines into his brow.

"How did she die, Piper?"

"I don't know," I said. "But she was afraid. She left me a letter because she thought someone might kill her."

"Do you believe someone did?" he asked.

"Yes."

"That could explain why the shadow-things are after you," Voss said.

He stood abruptly, dislodging Willow. The cat landed on the cushion with a disgruntled chirp.

Before I could comment, Voss reached into the air and pulled out a small, glowing device, pressing it to his ear.

"I need the Council. Immediately."

He turned away, lowering his voice.

I watched him pace, heart hammering. Where was this Council? Another realm? Somewhere watching us right now? I realized I hadn't asked—and that he hadn't offered.

Voss stopped.

The color drained from his face. His eyes went wide, unfocused, like he was seeing something no one else could.

"Right," he said finally. "Thanks."

The device vanished.

He turned back to us, expression grim.

"I know why the listener came," he said. "And why they're circling you."

Chapter Sixteen

Cold fear skittered up my spine like spider legs. Voss's expression—all grim lines and tight eyes—told me everything before he even opened his mouth.

"Well?" The word came out smaller than I intended.

"The things coming through your crossing weren't accidental," he said. "They were sent."

My muscles locked. Every single one. As if my body had decided that if I held perfectly still, the words would somehow unsay themselves. They didn't. They hung in the air between us, solid and real, and my worst fear had walked right out of my nightmares and into my living room.

"Sent by who?" Owen demanded, already tense beside me.

Voss shook his head. "It's not clear yet."

"Same people who killed Alice?" Owen pressed, glancing at me.

The name still did that thing to me—sharp, sudden pain, like hitting a bruise I kept forgetting was there.

"Possibly," Voss said. "Whoever it is, we need to identify them. Quickly."

"And the... listener," I said, trying for flippant and only half succeeding. "He wasn't exactly here to compliment my décor."

A grim look crossed Voss's face. "That's the part I don't like."

"Oh, good," Tani muttered. "I was worried this might not be apocalyptic enough."

Tani sprawled in Aunt Alice's antique armchair like she owned it. When Voss shot her a look that could freeze vodka, she waved a hand.

Voss didn't rise to it. "There are fractures," he said. "Not just at your tree. Across multiple boundaries. Places that were stable are... slipping."

"Like Faery," Tani said, all humor gone. "Same damage. Same signature. Like someone carved a hole straight through reality."

"Yes. Exactly." Voss turned back to me, and I wished he wouldn't. "Last night wasn't a random breach. It was an assessment. A confirmation that the grimoire answered you."

My stomach tightened. "So he came because of the book."

"He came because you lit a signal," Voss said. "And because whoever is pushing on the veil is looking for leverage."

"Not a what," Tani said softly. "A who."

Voss's voice dropped lower, grimmer. "Someone is doing it. Someone is prying open the seams between realms. Feeding on the strain. Using it."

The dread in my stomach rolled, then pitched. I swallowed hard. Voss didn't elaborate, which meant no one—not even Tani with her fairy intelligence network—knew who that someone was. Which meant we were all fumbling in the dark.

Could this someone be the one who sent the shadow-things?

And if so... why me?

"I can't worry about that right now."

I pressed cold fingertips against my temple and rubbed hard enough to hurt. Because I couldn't. I physically, mentally, emotionally could not worry about interdimensional invasions or shadowy puppet masters pulling strings. Not when there was a crossing hemorrhaging rot in my backyard. Not when the solution was right downstairs, purple and waiting.

"You should worry about it," Voss said, voice sharp as a blade's edge.

"I can't." The word came out harder than I meant it to. "I won't. Right now I have to seal that crossing. I have to get the potion."

I moved before anyone could stop me, heading for the basement door. My mind narrowed to a single point. Get the potion, get to the tree, seal the crossing. Everything else could wait.

"It won't help, you know."

I froze. Turned. "Why not?"

"Because the contamination is already here," he said, and the word contamination made my stomach twist. He walked toward me with a purposeful stride that said *I know things you don't.* "The rot doesn't politely stay inside a hole once it's been open long enough."

"What does that mean?" My voice came out thin.

"It means," Voss said evenly, "that after my call to the Council, I was formally assigned to this case—and I won't be leaving until the threat has been neutralized."

"You're not staying here." Owen moved instantly, stepping in front of me like it was instinct, not thought. "I won't allow it."

I bit back a laugh. Completely wrong moment—but, goodness it was endearing.

"There is a real threat here, sir," Voss said, unblinking. "I have to stay and guard her."

"I'll protect her," Owen shot back, crossing his arms.

"You're not trained to guard her," Voss countered, puffing up his chest like that was going to impress anyone.

"Oh my god," I groaned. "Is someone about to draw a line on the floor?"

"And what about me? I'm a queen. Shouldn't I be guarded?" Tani stuck out her bottom lip, arms crossed in mock-petulance.

"The entities aren't hunting you," Voss said, deadpan.

"Uncalled for," she sniffed.

"No one is staying here," I said, waving my hands, surrendering to the absurdity of it all. I hadn't even wanted houseguests, and now I had a fairy queen and a testosterone parade.

"Hey!" Tani's hands went to her hips.

I sighed. "Except you. You can stay, of course, though I'm still not entirely sure where you've been sleeping." The greenhouse, probably. Or maybe she hung upside down from the rafters like a sparkly bat.

The fairy beamed. "Greenhouse. Very cozy. Excellent moonlight."

"I've been ordered by the Council. I'm not leaving," Voss said.

"Then you can stay at the town bed and breakfast." My voice went flat. "I know Dolores. I'll speak to her on your behalf. Now if you'll excuse me, I'm going to get the potion and go to the tree."

This time no one stopped me.

I bounded down the basement stairs, heart hammering against my ribs, and searched for the vial. The basement smelled of herbs and old stone. I grabbed the purple potion from the worktable, fingers tightening around the glass like it might anchor me.

Owen appeared in the doorway and stopped short. "You're doing this."

"Yes."

"And you're fine with him hovering around?"

I smiled faintly. "No. But life's full of disappointments."

"I don't trust him," he said.

"I don't either, but I don't have a choice. He's not leaving, clearly. So he can stay in town—but not in my house." I tucked the potion carefully into my pocket. "I have to get to the woods."

His jaw tightened. "Whoever killed Alice wants you dead now. Because you're the Guardian."

"I know."

"That doesn't scare you?"

I straightened, meeting his eyes. “It scares me later. Right now? I have work.”

He studied me for a long moment, then nodded. “I’ll drive.”

Then his gaze landed on my bare feet. “Maybe shoes first, though.”

The motley crew descended on the hickory tree like a strange parade.

Voss folded himself into the extended cab of Owen’s pickup with all the dignity of an irritated linebacker. Tani rode shotgun, humming cheerfully.

I didn’t relax for a second.

Owen parked, and we all filed out.

I smelled it before I saw it—wet rot, smoke, rage. The ground at the base of the tree churned, black sludge bubbling like a wound that refused to close.

“The crossing’s compromised,” Voss muttered, already reaching for his communicator.

“No!”

I practically tackled him, knocking the device from his hands. It tumbled into the undergrowth. He stared at me like I’d lost my mind.

“Not yet,” I said. “Let me try the potion first.”

“Piper—”

“Let me try.”

He glanced toward the tree, then back at me. “Fine. But what’s wrong with the tree?” He peered at the spot where the bark had been carved away, leaving bare, vulnerable wood. “It looks sick.”

“That’s because the tree *is* sick. Someone’s been taking the bark.”

"And you're telling me this now?" He groaned. "I have to tell the Council."

This guy was seriously grinding my last nerve. "You don't have to tell them anything yet." The words came out in a low growl, my hand fisting. This mysterious Council could mind their own business for five minutes. I was going to fix the crossing. End of story.

Voss held up his hands in surrender.

"I'll cover you," Tani announced.

I glanced over and realized the fairy queen already had an arrow nocked in her bow, ready to fire—eyes suddenly all business.

Good enough for me.

I took a breath, stepped forward—and Owen's hand caught my shoulder.

"Be careful."

"I'm always careful." I flashed him a crooked smile and took another step.

His hand slid from my shoulder to my elbow. He pulled me to him in one swift motion, and before I could say a word, his lips were on mine.

The kiss was fierce, possessive, claiming—staking something in front of Voss and Tani and whatever watched from the other side of the bubbling dark.

Heat flooded through me despite the fear, despite the sludge and rot and certain doom. I kissed him back with a ferocity that surprised even me, a low sound vibrating in my throat.

When he pulled back, his eyes held mine, steady and sure.

"What was that for?" My voice came out breathless.

"Luck," he grinned.

I smiled back—couldn't help it—then turned toward the tree.

I pulled the cork from the vial and stepped up to the black sludge, its reek making my eyes water and my stomach pitch.

Without wasting another second, I poured the purple concoction over it.

A hissing sound erupted where liquid met mire. The bubbles stopped. All of them. At once.

I stepped back toward my friends, hope surging in my chest. Steam rose from the muck, curling upward toward the canopy of leaves overhead. The bubbling ceased entirely. The air lightened a fraction.

I'd done it. The crossing was sealed.

"Take that!" The words burst out of me, bright and triumphant.

But the peace lasted only a heartbeat.

The bubbles started again.

Steam rose again, thicker now, darker. The ground shuddered beneath my shoes.

And then a massive shadow-thing dragged itself up from the base of the tree—writhing and furious, its body made of darkness with too many angles, its eyes glowing like coals in the wrong place.

I swallowed.

"Okay," I muttered, fingers tightening around the empty vial. "So... plan B?"

Chapter Seventeen

The black shadow didn't dissipate.

It condensed.

One second it was smoke and consuming darkness. The next, it stepped free of itself—solid, whole, unmistakably male.

My breath caught.

Garrat.

He looked exactly as he had at the antique shop—tall and broad-shouldered, built like violence wrapped in silk.

Ancient. Appraising. Hungry.

And then he smiled.

That same slow, precise, calculated smile.

Like he knew exactly what that smile would do to me.

"Oh."

The word slipped out before I could stop it.

Heat bloomed low in my belly—sharp, dangerous. My body went rigid with want, my pulse kicking hard as something tugged at me from the inside. The pull toward him was immediate. Unnatural.

Magic.

Voss swore and lunged into my line of sight, shoving me backward hard enough that I stumbled. His gun came up in the same motion, aimed dead-center at Garrat's chest.

Owen grabbed my hand at the same time, yanking me back—

"Stay away from her," Owen snarled.

Garrat laughed, low and rich. "The druid's son. Still so protective."

"Piper, look at me," Owen said urgently, his hand gripping my arm. "Don't let him in your head."

But I couldn't move.

My feet were rooted to the earth. My gaze locked on Garrat as if invisible threads had wrapped around my spine.

Like at the antique shop.

"We meet again," Garrat said softly, his gaze burning into mine. "Though last time, the fairy queen interrupted our conversation."

"You can't have her," Voss warned, gun still raised.

"Oh, I merely wish to speak with her," Garrat said pleasantly. "I want to finish what we started."

"You can't."

"Oh, yes, he can."

The words tore free of me before common sense—or self-preservation—could intervene.

Owen hissed my name. I barely heard it.

"You are a pretty thing," Garrat said, taking one step. Then another. Each one deliberate. Measured. Until we were a breath apart and I could see the fine lines at the corners of his eyes, the glint of something feral beneath the beauty.

I was dimly aware of his hand lifting toward me.

"You touch her, you die," Owen said, his voice tight with fury. Thunder rumbled overhead.

Garrat glanced aside, amused. "So fiercely protective. These druids always are."

"What do you want?" I demanded, forcing the words past the pressure in my chest.

"Step away from the girl," Voss snapped. His gun never wavered.

"Now why would I do that?" Garrat's smile sharpened. "I've been looking for you, Piper. And I finally have what I came for."

My stomach dropped. "What?"

"The truth you've been searching for." His gaze burned into mine, dark and satisfied. "About who you are."

"Don't," Owen warned. "Don't listen to him."

But I couldn't look away.

Garrat's smile widened.

"You are Alice's daughter."

The words didn't stun me. They landed, hard and cold.

Silence crashed down around us. I couldn't move. Couldn't breathe.

Owen's grip tightened on my arm. Even Voss faltered, his gun lowering a fraction. I felt Tani's presence behind me, sharp and suddenly still.

"No," I whispered.

"Oh, yes. Quite true." Garrat laughed, deep and delighted. "She never told you? How delicious."

"I don't believe you!"

I hadn't meant to shout it, but the words ripped from my lungs as I stumbled backward.

The trance I'd been in snapped.

Revulsion surged where that pang of lonely fear had been. I could finally see him for what he was.

A predator.

A monster.

"Believe it," Garrat said softly.

I didn't want to. My mind rebelled, grasping for anything solid—but memories rose unbidden.

Alice's house filled with photos of me.

Alice in the front row of every recital.

Alice encouraging me to leave, to grow, to live.

Alice leaving me everything.

Alice saying I would come back someday.

Because Alice knew I had to.

Voss stepped fully in front of me now. "What do you want with her?"

He pointed the gun at Garrat and inched forward. I was too stunned to move. To think.

"What I want," Garrat said lightly, "is exactly what you'd expect. And now that I know who she is, delivering her becomes much easier."

"She's the Guardian," Voss said flatly. "She'll close it."

"Will she?" Garrat's gaze slid back to me. "Or will she be too distracted trying to figure out who her father is? Who Alice was hiding from? Why she gave away her own child?"

"Stop," Owen said. Another crack of thunder.

"The truth hurts, doesn't it?" Garrat stepped backward, into shadow, into bubbling dark. "Until next time, my dear. We have so much more to discuss."

Then he vanished.

The woods seemed to inhale.

The sludge at the base of the tree surged again, angry and alive, as if whatever doorway Garrat used had made it worse.

My knees gave out. I hit the ground hard, breath shuddering out of me as the world narrowed to sound and heat and disbelief.

"Piper?" Owen dropped beside me.

"Leave me alone." My voice shook. "I want to be alone."

"No," Voss said sharply. "It's too dangerous here in the woods. The crossing is still open."

"Then I'll seal it." The words came out raw. Furious.

Tani clapped her hands. "We'll make another potion—"

"I will make another potion." I didn't hide the razor's edge to my voice as I looked at the fairy. "Go back to your realm, fairy queen. I don't need your help."

Tani's face fell.

"Piper—"

"Don't, Owen," I said when he opened his mouth. "Are we going to pretend that didn't happen? That he didn't tell me my whole life has been a lie?"

No one argued. The only sound in the woods was cicadas, birds chirping overhead, and the wet, sick bubbling at the tree behind us.

"That's what I thought."

I got to my feet and ran.

I was going to confront my parents for the truth.

If it were true, it would explain so much. It would explain why my mother seemed to hate me and treated me differently and why I never felt part of the family even after all this time.

If Alice was my mother, then who was my father?

"Piper, wait." Owen panted as he caught up to me, shoving past tree limbs as he went. He caught my arm, pulled me to a halt. "Let me drive you."

"No." I shoved him away. "I don't want you to drive me anywhere."

"Then how are you going to get back?"

"I'll walk!"

"Piper—"

I put my hands on either side of my head and squeezed my temples. "Owen, please. I don't want to be with you or anyone right now." I needed to be alone long enough to turn grief into anger and anger into questions.

"I'm trying to help you."

"I don't want it! Not right now. Take Voss to the bed and breakfast."

His face fell, creasing with pain I had intended to give him. "What about Tani?"

"She has wings. She can fly. Or use fairy dust. Or whatever it is she does."

Before Owen could reply, I broke into a run. I reached the road and started down the blacktop—heading straight for my parents' house.

The walk burned.

Heat and sweat and fury tangled together until my skin felt too tight, my lungs too full. Every step closer to the house made the truth press harder against my ribs, demanding space it didn't have.

When I reached the porch, I didn't hesitate.

The door flew open under my kick, slamming into the wall with a crack that echoed through the house.

"Piper! Dear Lord, you scared me half to death." My mother quickly recovered from her fear and then it turned to outrage. "What is the matter with you? Coming in here like that. You ought to be ashamed."

"Ought I, Mother?" I sneered. "Maybe you're the one who should be ashamed."

"I don't know what you're talking about." She resumed her position on the sofa and picked up her knitting. Ignoring me. As if I didn't even exist.

"Alice was my birth mother, wasn't she?" I blurted.

Her needles halted their clickety-click, and she looked up at me, meeting my gaze. My mother's face was stricken with shock. "Who told you that?"

"So it's true?"

"I don't know who's been filling your head with these notions," Gladys said stiffly, reaching for denial like a lifeline.

"Answer the question!"

The words hit the room like a slap. For a long moment, no one spoke. Then Gladys stood, abandoned her knitting where it lay.

"I will not have you talking to me like that in my house."

"Your house. Right. Because you're the only person who matters."

"You are out of line, young lady."

"Am I? Why don't you tell me the truth, Mother. I'm not yours. I never was. The only thing I can't make sense of is why. Why would Alice give me to you to raise?"

She stared at me. Her face devoid of all emotion. Even hate. She said nothing when she stalked out of the room and up the stairs.

"You coward," I shouted.

But I would find out the truth.

"I can tell you why." My father's quiet voice made me spin around to face him. He stood outside the kitchen, a cup of coffee in his hand and his pipe stuck between his teeth. "Sit down, Piper."

I moved into the living room and perched on the edge of the same chair I sat in when I learned Alice had willed me everything. My father took his place on the sofa, setting his cup on the nearby table.

"You shouldn't have talked to her that way," he said in his quiet scolding way.

Perhaps not. But I had been through a lifetime of disappointment with that woman. Even so, I felt the need to apologize.

"I'm sorry, Dad."

He leaned back and puffed on his pipe. "I understand why you think she hates you, though. She's not the most affectionate woman. She never has been."

Cold was the word that came to my mind. I leaned forward. "Tell me the truth, Dad. Was Alice my mother?"

"Yes." He said it without hesitation and I knew it to be true.

I leaned back in the cushion of the chair, exhaling a breath I hadn't realized I had even sucked in.

"I don't understand. Why did she never tell me?"

"We were sworn to secrecy," he said. "She made us promise that we would never tell you."

"But why?"

He puffed out a cloud of white smoke. "When Alice learned she was pregnant, she knew she could never keep you. She begged your mother to take you and raise you as her own. She was afraid."

"Of what?"

"Losing you."

I considered this. If Alice was a witch, then what did that make me? "Dad, is Mom a..." I paused, unwilling to squeeze out the word.

"A witch? No. Gladys is not a witch. But Alice was. She feared you would be one, too."

I glanced at my father, wondering. Had he and Alice had an affair? Was I half his? I had to ask.

"Are you... my father?"

"No." He cut a glance to me. "I mean, yes. But not your biological father. I've always thought of you as my own, though. Since the day Alice handed you to us."

"Why did she? Why did she do that and then stay in Hickory Hollow?"

"She thought she'd be safe here. It was so isolated from the real world back then. She was sure she could watch you grow up."

"That's why I spent so much time with her," I mused. "But then why did Mom make me stop seeing her? I was in high school then."

"Your powers were starting to manifest. Gladys felt that if you were with Alice, then you would start to suspect and you'd want her to teach you."

"So why didn't she?"

"Because she didn't want you to know what you were. She wanted you far from that life. As far as possible."

He was quiet then, his mouth tightening around his pipe. "She didn't hide you because she was ashamed. She hid you because she was afraid your father would find you."

That got my attention. I stared at him. "My father?"

"That's all I know about that."

But something told me he knew more and wasn't saying. Maybe because it was an old wound he didn't want to reopen. There was no knowing.

It was another secret I would have to crack open.

Things must have started to go wrong for Alice after I left for college. Or maybe things were going wrong for her all along and I didn't know it.

She'd changed her will to leave me the estate. She'd written me the letter telling me I was the only one she trusted. She must have known that something was going to happen to her and she had to find a way out. Someone to avenge her death or at least discover who the true killer was.

"How did Alice die?" I asked.

"Heart attack," my father said. "You know that."

So he must not know the truth. Only I, Owen, and Mr. McAllister did. And how much did my father know about the town anyway?

"Alice was always secretive about some things, Piper. I've been worried about you ever since you inherited her estate."

"There's nothing to worry about, Dad," I said.

"Are you sure?"

"Yes."

I couldn't bring myself to tell him there were shadow-things out to kill me. Or an open crossing in the woods. Or that I was the new Guardian of this magical place. He may not believe me. And if he did, he'd try to talk me out of it.

"Be careful, okay?"

"I promise."

But the promise rang hollow even as I said it.

Garrat hadn't come looking for me by accident. He'd appeared at the antique shop to test if the grimoire answered me. He'd appeared here to weaponize the truth about Alice.

Someone had known who I was long before I did. Long before Alice died.

And now that I knew the truth, I had the sickening certainty that whatever was hunting me had only just begun.

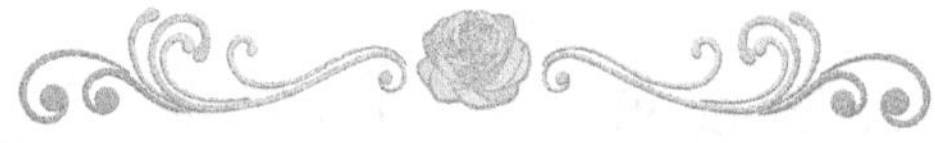

Chapter Eighteen

"I'll drive you home, kiddo." He snuffed his pipe in the nearby ashtray and then rose.

I got to my feet, trying not to acknowledge the pounding exhaustion through me. "You don't have to do that."

But what was my alternative? Walking home in the late afternoon heat? The thought made me wince.

"Piper, it's much too hot for a walk." He was already reaching into his pocket for his keys.

I didn't argue.

"How did you know I walked?"

"I didn't hear a car drive up." He gave me a knowing grin.

Together, we walked out of the house and climbed into his truck. I said nothing as I buckled my seatbelt and we were away, leaving the house I grew up in behind. I wasn't sure if I'd ever go back. Why would I? There was truly nothing there for me.

As we drove to the other side of town, I saw Hickory Hollow with new eyes. Though the town hadn't changed, I had.

Alice was my mother. Alice was a witch.

It was a hard thing to accept. The gaping hole of loss I felt when I learned of her death was bigger now. More substantial. More meaningful. I hadn't lost the aunt who loved me best. I lost the mother I'd never known and always wanted.

Ahead, the pavement shimmered with the heat of the day and something else. I squinted, wishing I had my sunglasses to block out the glare.

But it wasn't burning afternoon Texas glare.

It was something more.

A faint golden shimmer traced the length of the blacktop road—not sunlight. Not mirage. It moved wrong, like a seam catching the light when you turn fabric.

A feeling coiled tight and bright in my chest. It buzzed beneath my skin, humming there like it always belonged there. And suddenly I understood.

Magic.

Not around me.

In me.

Like it was claiming me. Like the truth had unlocked something in me that had been dormant for years. Telling me this was the way of things now. Like it had... awakened.

I inhaled a soft breath.

"You all right?" my father asked.

"Yes, I'm..." I faltered, clutching my hands in my lap. "Yes."

I thought of my life in Hickory Hollow before leaving for college, before leaving for Manhattan. Aside from Alice, the one steady constant—the one person who loved me unconditionally—was my father, George Wakefield. He was steady. Calm. A giant among men who soothed me when Gladys made me feel small and inconsequential.

He was the one person who taught me how to be a decent human.

"Dad?" My voice was quiet in the confines of the cab.

He gave me a sideways questioning glance. "Yes?"

"Thanks."

He blinked, his gaze firmly planted on the road ahead. "For what?"

"For raising me."

"You're welcome." His voice cracked only a little as he said it. But I saw his reaction. I saw how he gripped the steering wheel tighter as though it was a defense against the emotion.

He pulled into my driveway and came to a halt.

There, parked in my driveway, was Owen's blue pickup.

The second George stopped and put the truck in park, Owen was already climbing out, rounding the hood with long, purposeful strides. Worry etched his face until his gaze locked on me. Then his shoulders loosened. Relief softened something tight in his eyes.

George didn't cut the engine. He sat there, hands on the wheel, studying Owen through the windshield.

"I'd ask what his intentions are with you," George said mildly, "but I think I already know."

Despite everything weighing on my chest, a laugh slipped free. "I think I do, too."

George nodded once, as if confirming something to himself.

"He waited," he said. "Didn't barge in. Just stayed close."

I swallowed.

"He's a good man," my father went on quietly. "The kind who shows up when things get hard. Your mother would've liked him."

That did it. My throat tightened. Such a simple thing for him to say, but it cracked me wide open.

Your mother. Not Gladys. Alice.

And Alice did like him. She'd written it in her letter. *Be nice to Owen. I think he's always liked you.*

I cleared my throat, forcing away the sudden prick of tears. "Thanks for the ride."

I unlatched my seatbelt, opened the truck door and started to slide out.

"And Piper?"

I paused, looking back at him.

"Come see me, huh?" he said, eyes fixed on the windshield. "Don't make me wonder how you're doing."

My chest tightened. "I won't," I promised.

Then I was out of the truck, closing the door and stepping aside. He put it in reverse and backed out of the driveway with a slow, familiar ease. Then he was disappearing down the dusty country road.

I stood there for a moment, my heart a riot in my chest.

He might not be my biological father, but he would always be my dad.

Slowly, I turned to face Owen.

He leaned against the cab of his pickup, thumbs hooked in the front pockets of his jeans, waiting.

Maybe it was the shock of the day, but for the first time, I saw him clearly.

Someone who had never left this town when I ran. I remembered his face from our high school days, remembered the boy—but this wasn't him anymore. This was the man who stayed.

The sleeves of his white shirt were rolled to his elbows, revealing a golden expanse of sun-warmed skin. His jeans were faded. His boots scuffed and well-loved.

We stared at each other across the stretch of dirt driveway between us, the moment stretching thin and taut—

—and then my feet moved before my brain realized I'd given them permission.

Before I even reached him, he opened his arms.

I went into them without hesitation. Because going to him didn't feel like falling apart. It felt like relief.

He wrapped me in his strength, tucking me close, my forehead fitting easily beneath his chin.

He held me there, saying nothing for a long, quiet moment.

And that was all right by me.

It was like he understood I needed a bit of space to get the truth from my parents. He didn't question me. Didn't need to.

"I'm sorry I yelled at you," I murmured against his chest.

"It's all right."

"Did you know?" Because if he did, I wasn't sure I could handle that bit of truth right now.

His arms tightened around me. "No."

There was weight in that one word—and with it, relief flooding me. I closed my eyes for a moment, listening to the faint beat of his heart and the cicadas humming overhead.

Then they stopped.

Not slowly. Not naturally.

Like someone had reached down and pinched the sound out of the air.

The breeze shifted around us—humid Gulf air to something thinner, sharper. Wrong.

Owen stiffened, still holding me tight, as his body went rigid. I tried to remain perfectly still as a shudder skipped down my spine.

"You feel that?" he asked, his voice a rumble beneath my ear.

"What... is it?" My voice was a whisper against him.

I shifted in his arms to turn and look back toward the road. He never let me go, keeping me close, as we both peered toward the street.

The shimmer was back.

A faint, gold-threaded distortion crawled along the blacktop like a seam being pulled open—quiet, deliberate—sliding toward the driveway.

My skin prickled. The magic in my chest answered it, humming in recognition, like it had been waiting for this exact frequency.

And then I knew—knew with the same sick certainty I'd felt in the woods.

The crossing was calling.

Not the tree itself.

The thing behind it.

Listening.

Reaching.

"Piper," Owen said, sharper now, and I felt the shift in him—the druid in his blood waking to the threat. "We need to go. Now."

My pulse hammered. "The tree," I whispered. "It's getting worse."

He nodded once. "Yeah."

I pulled back enough to look up at him, panic rising fast. "Voss said it's loud. If it's loud enough to follow me home—"

"Then we don't give it time to get comfortable," Owen cut in. Determination hardened his mouth. "We go shut it down."

"How?" I asked.

"I have an idea. Something we can use."

He didn't wait for me to ask more questions.

"I'll drive. Get in the truck."

His keys were already in his hand as he rounded the front while I slid into the passenger seat, my body a bundle of nerves.

I didn't know what waited for me in the woods.

But I knew one thing with terrifying clarity.

Whatever was in those woods, it had my town in its sights. I wasn't running anymore. Not from Hickory Hollow. Not from what I was.

Chapter Nineteen

The shimmer followed us from the driveway onto the country road. A thin, gold-threaded distortion that clung to the blacktop like a seam coming undone.

As if it was tracking us.

I peered in the sideview mirror, my stomach in knots as I watched it stretch longer behind the truck, brightening whenever my pulse jumped.

"Owen... it's following us." My voice shook as I said it.

"I see it." He mashed the gas and pushed the truck faster.

I gripped the door handle so hard my hand cramped, holding my breath in the short drive from the house toward town. When he parked the truck, we both jumped out at the same time.

Movement across the street caught my attention.

There was Rylyn closing up the flower shop for the night.

I froze, staring across the way as guilt slammed into me hard.

I hadn't even thought about the flower shop since all chaos broke loose. I'd been too preoccupied with the crossing, the sludge in the woods, the thing that stepped out of shadow like it owned my name—and learning Alice was my mother.

Rylyn—still in goth attire—locked the door and then turned to head to her car parked on the side of the building. Our eyes met from across the street. The girl stared at me, but I wasn't sure what her expression was under all the eyeliner and black lipstick.

"Piper, come on," Owen urged.

I forced my feet to move and jogged around the front of the truck.

"I see how it is, Piper!" Rylyn shouted from across the pavement.

Remorse pounded through me. I'd have to explain later to Rylyn—maybe she'd understand. It was clear she was actively caring for the shop while I was trying to save my own skin.

I hurried after Owen who held the door to the antique store open waiting for me. Once I was inside, he threaded his way through the rows and rows of antiques toward the back.

"Owen? That you?" Dougal called. He popped out from the private office at the back. "What are you doing here? I was about to close the shop."

"Dad, I need the Sun Disk," Owen said, voice urgent.

Dougal's brows drew together. "The what?"

"No time to explain." Owen stepped around him and continued on his path toward the back of the shop.

Dougal looked at me, question in his eyes. I gave him a shrug and a sheepish grin as I hurried after Owen.

"What's this about, son?" Dougal fell in step behind me.

But Owen was already at the back of the store, popping open a ladder and pushing it under a round, gold-inlaid talisman mounted high on the wall.

In the late afternoon light, it looked decorative—beautiful, old, and harmless.

Except it wasn't.

The moment my gaze landed on it, something hummed deep and low under my skin. Recognition. Magic.

Owen climbed up the rungs of the ladder to the top and leaned over, but he still couldn't reach it.

"Owen, stop," Dougal said, voice firm and unrelenting. "This isn't a good idea."

Owen moved up one more rung, standing precariously at the top of the ladder and leaned over as far as he dared. I held my breath. The last thing I wanted to see was Owen toppling off.

"Got it!" His hand wrapped around the disk as he pulled it from the wall with a swift jerk.

But that nearly cost him. He almost lost his balance and fell backward. He grabbed the top of the ladder with his free hand and waited until he got his bearings before he moved again. Then he climbed down with the talisman in one hand. At the bottom rung, he leapt off and turned to me.

"Let's go."

He tried to breeze by his father, but Dougal caught his arm and pulled him to a stop.

"I can't let you take it." His face was hard, his voice stern. He meant it.

Owen's jaw tightened. "Dad, we need it."

"Why?" Dougal's gaze shifted between us, hard and searching.

"Because something is using the crossing," Owen said. "And it followed her home."

Dougal's eyes snapped to me. "What followed you?"

I swallowed, my voice quieter than I meant it to be. "A pressure. A shimmer on the road. It tracked us from my house."

"Whatever's on the other side that's been listening," Owen added, voice grim.

Dougal's grip tightened on Owen's arm. "That thing is dangerous, son. Whoever wants it—whatever wants it—knows it."

"I know," Owen said. "But if we don't use it, the crossing won't hold."

I looked between them, heart hammering. I didn't know what the Sun Disk did. Didn't understand how a talisman mounted on a wall could help seal a portal that was bleeding darkness into the woods.

But Owen did. And I trusted him.

Dougal studied his son for a long moment, jaw working. Then his gaze shifted to me—assessing, measuring.

"You understand what this means?" he asked me quietly. "Once it's drawn to you, there's no going back."

I didn't understand. Not fully. But I nodded anyway.

"I understand."

That seemed to stop Owen in his tracks. He angled his body so he could see his father and me. He glanced between the two of us and I sensed it then.

His hesitation.

He wanted to do what his father wanted.

But he wanted to help me, too.

"There isn't another choice," Owen said finally, voice quiet but firm. "I'm sorry, Dad."

Owen handed off the disk to me.

The moment my fingers closed around the gold, the feeling shot through my arm to my shoulder. I sucked in a sharp breath and staggered back a step.

Like something inside me clicked into place.

A dizziness swept through me so quick and so fast my vision dotted with black.

"Piper?" Owen was there in a second, his hand on my back as he reached for the talisman.

I snatched it back, clutched it to my chest. "I'm fine. It was weird for a moment."

Dougal stepped closer, his gaze fixed on me now. His voice dropped low, urgent. "Don't hesitate when the time comes," he said, as though he sensed something horrible was about to go down. "Once it's drawn to you, there's no going back."

I met his eyes, still clutching the Disk that hummed against my ribs. "I won't."

Owen's hand stayed on my back, steadying me. "Dad... the grimoire already recognized her. Will the Disk—"

"It's keyed to the same bloodline," Dougal said, cutting him off. His gaze stayed on me. "Guardian relics answer to Alice's line. The grimoire woke when you touched it. The Disk will bind to you the same way."

"Bind?" My voice came out smaller than I meant it.

"Acknowledge you," Dougal corrected gently. "The grimoire called across the veil. The Disk will anchor you to the Crossroads itself—make you visible to the land, not to what's trying to break through."

Owen's grip tightened. "So when she uses it—"

"It'll recognize her as Guardian," Dougal said. "Properly this time. Not inheritance—choice."

"We need to go," Owen said.

Dougal held my gaze a moment longer, then nodded once. "Go."

Owen ushered me toward the door.

We were out of the shop and back in his truck in minutes. I scanned the parking lot across the street looking for Rylyn. She'd disappeared into the night, leaving me with nothing but my raw regret.

I needed to do better.

I would.

Right after I stopped whatever was turning my life into a hunting ground.

I gripped the disk between both hands as Owen drove like a race car driver from town toward the woods. I didn't have time to worry about his driving—I was too busy trying to understand the feeling coursing through me while I held it.

It was ancient. As though it knew me, which was insane. Whatever was humming through the talisman and into me was tuning itself to me. Sensing me. Merging with me.

That wasn't possible.

Was it?

It was as if it knew I was Alice's blood.

Owen pulled the truck to a halt and cut the engine. Seconds later we were out, moving fast through the woods as the sun dipped dangerously close to the horizon.

I noticed it then—the shimmer on the leaves and the trees and the ground. Not frost.

A gold-threaded distortion that led us deeper, tugging like a thread in my ribs.

The woods were unnaturally quiet, too. No birdsong. No cicadas. No rustling of underbrush.

As we approached the clearing, the shimmer thickened, gathering at the base of the old hickory tree where the crossing still stood open—black sludge bubbling like a wound that refused to close.

And someone stood near it.

Garrat. Tall, dark, too still and half a step away from the bubbling edge, as if the crossing itself had spit him out and he hadn't bothered to hide the fact.

Garrat.

He turned his head slowly, like he'd been waiting for us.

His smile was precise. Calculated.

"Oh," he said softly. "You came back. Good. We finish together."

Owen's body went rigid beside me. "Back off."

Garrat's gaze slid to the Disk clutched in my hands, and something hungry sharpened in his expression. "Clever." He tilted his head. "Your mother did love her safeguards."

My stomach lurched.

I tightened my grip.

The talisman flared.

Not light like a flashlight. Light like a boundary.

A pulse rolled out from my hands into the ground—down, down, down—into the roots of the hickory tree. The earth answered, a low vibration I felt in my teeth.

Garrat took a step forward—

—and stopped short.

His smile faltered.

He pressed his hand forward as if testing invisible glass. The air in front of him rippled. He hissed under his breath, jaw tightening like he'd hit resistance he hadn't expected.

"What is this?" he snarled.

I didn't know. Not fully.

But the words bubbled up anyway, older than my fear, steadier than my shaking hands.

"The land answers to only one," I heard myself say. "The Guardian. Not you."

Owen's head snapped toward me, shock rolling off him.

Garrat's eyes widened a fraction—then narrowed, furious. "So it's true," he murmured. "The Crossroads chose."

The Disk flared brighter in my grip, the hum beneath my skin tightening, pulling downward—into the earth.

Garrat tried again to step forward.

The boundary held.

He recoiled as if burned.

His gaze lifted to mine—still hungry, but now edged with something colder.

Calculation.

"Very well," he said softly. "Keep your pretty little key."

The sludge behind him bubbled harder, throwing off a stink of rot and sulfur.

He smiled again, slow and obscene. "This isn't the end, Piper. It's only the beginning."

Then he stepped backward—into shadow, into the wrongness at the edge of the crossing—and vanished.

Silence rushed in to fill the clearing.

The sun had slipped fully below the horizon, leaving only indigo shadows and the soft, steady glow of the Disk in my hands. The shimmer on the ground lingered, reluctant—like the world itself was still listening.

Owen exhaled beside me.

I stared down at the gold in my palms, watching the light pulse in time with my heartbeat. The boundary—whatever it was—had come from this. From me holding it. From the way it answered when I touched it.

"It stopped him," I whispered.

Owen moved closer. "Yeah."

"I don't..." I looked up at him, searching his face in the dying light. "I don't understand what this is. What it did."

"A ward," he said quietly. "One of the old protections. Guardian relics are keyed to bloodlines—passed down through families who guard the Crossroads. When you touched the Disk, it recognized Alice's blood in you."

"Like the grimoire did," I said.

He nodded. "The grimoire broadcast that you existed. The Disk claimed you as the Crossroads' keeper. That's why Garrat can't cross the boundary now—the land knows you, and it won't let anything through that you don't permit."

The words should have felt too big. Too impossible.

But the Disk hummed warm against my skin, and somewhere deep in my chest, something hummed back.

I let out a shaky breath.

"Well," I said, my voice thin but steady. "That's not weird or terrifying at all."

Owen's mouth curved faintly. "Yeah."

I tightened my grip, feeling the weight of it settle into something that felt less like a weapon and more like a key I didn't know I'd been missing.

And for the first time, I understood—

weird wasn't the problem.

Understanding what I was supposed to do with it… that was the problem.

Chapter Twenty

"Piper?"

I dragged my eyes up from the Sun Disk and met his. He had a look of wonder on his face. Wonder and... admiration?

"That happened," I said. Not a question. A statement trying to become real.

"Yeah." His voice was soft. "It did."

I held the Disk so tight in my hands they cramped. It continued to glow, the only light between us as darkness shrouded the forest.

"A ward," I repeated, testing the word. "So this thing... it can keep them out?"

"For now." Owen's expression shifted, something cautious entering his eyes. "But wards aren't meant to hold forever. They're meant to buy time."

Time.

The word settled heavy in my chest.

"How much time?" I asked.

He shook his head. "I don't know. My father would know better than me. We should go," he said then. "I'll take you home."

He started to turn away and head back to the truck.

"Owen?" My voice warbled.

He paused, looked at me over his shoulder. But it was dark and his eyes were nothing more than black orbs. Not the dove gray.

"I don't know how to do this."

He smiled—a soft smile—and offered his hand. "You don't have to know yet."

I hesitated, then shook my head. "I do," I said quietly. "Or at least... I need to start acting like it."

He studied me a long moment, then nodded. "You are."

But his agreement wasn't condescension. It was respect. Like he understood what I had to do and he didn't—wouldn't—argue the point. Maybe he didn't know what I was up against. Maybe I didn't either. But he acknowledged it for what it was.

My job.

I took a deep breath and nodded. "Okay."

Only then did I take his hand and let him walk with me from the clearing, through the woods, back to the truck. When we arrived, he opened the door for me and I climbed in, still clutching the warded relic like it might keep my ribs from cracking open.

He got in, started the truck, put it in drive.

As he rolled away, I said, "What do I do with this thing?"

"Keep it tonight," he said. "We can return it to the shop tomorrow."

I nodded. "Yes, that's a good idea." Then fought off a yawn.

The word tomorrow landed heavy. Tomorrow meant the flower shop. Rylyn. Lights on. Doors open. Responsibility I'd been dodging since Alice died—since Alice handed it to me.

Magic or not, that didn't go away.

"Tomorrow," I echoed. "I—" I paused, pressing my lips together as the weight settled in. "I need to open the shop. I own it. I need to act like it."

His hands tightened on the steering wheel as if he'd forgotten about the shop, too. "Yes," he said quietly. "Of course."

When he pulled into my driveway, he cut the engine. I was out before him.

"Night."

"Wait—" he said as I closed the door.

He was out, rounding the hood of the truck. "I can stay."

"You don't have to. I'll be fine." I half decided I'd sleep with the Disk under my pillow like a deranged, newly-minted magical homeowner.

I had to stop leaning on him so much. Not because he pushed. But because it was time I stood on my own.

Plus, I owed it to Rylyn and the shop to show up like the owner I was. I had a lot of responsibility now with Alice gone.

"At least let me walk you to the door."

He was Southern gentleman to the core. I nodded.

At the door, I turned to him, decision steady now.

"About tomorrow," I said. "I'll get this back to your father. After work."

He nodded again. Said nothing.

Because something had shifted—the Crossroads had chosen me and I knew it. I felt it. And it was time to stop pretending otherwise.

I leaned in and kissed his cheek, gentle and deliberate. "Good night."

Then I went inside, closing the door behind me. I stood in the dark, listening to his footsteps fade. The truck door. The engine. And then he was gone.

With deliberate steps, I moved through the house, flicking on a lamp as I passed by. I set the Sun Disk on the kitchen table as I made my way out the back door. Then to the greenhouse.

My heart fluttered with nerves as I opened the door and stepped inside. There was a soft glow from the string of lights overhead. Inside, it was warm and damp, rich with the loamy scent of dirt and plant life. Flowers in pots stood along the workbench like sentries.

I paused inside the door looking for the telltale sign of pink fairy dust.

There. Pink fairy dust hovered at the end of the table, tucked inside a tiny garden house built her size.

"I owe you an apology." My voice was loud in the quiet, small space.

Pink dust flickered. Then, Tani's voice, sharp as glass. "You owe me more than that."

"I do. I was—it was a shock, that's all." How could I make the Queen of the Fae understand learning Alice was my mother from a monster was the worst. "I didn't know."

Tani flittered out from her fairy home trailing glittering light. Then she poofed and made herself life size. Her hands were on her hips, her gaze razor sharp. She wasn't ready to forgive me yet.

"Anyone with two eyes can see you're her daughter." Then she dropped her hands to her sides and puffed out a breath. "But... I suppose I can see why that'd knock you sideways."

"I'm sorry, Tani. Can you forgive me?"

She crossed her arms over her chest and looked out through the panes of glass into the night. "I suppose I'll have to if I want your help to get Oberon back."

Which made me grin. "And you have my word. I'll do what I can to help you."

Her gaze shifted back to me, narrowed. "Good. You're in it for good now, girlie." Then she dropped her arms and scanned the area behind me. "So... where's Mr. Hottie?"

I laughed. "I sent him home."

"Spoil sport." She pouted.

"It's time I start figuring this out on my own," I added.

"Sure," she said, "but you could let him help." She put air quotes around help and waggled her eyebrows.

I huffed. "Good night, Tani!"

"I'm just saying!" she called as I walked away.

As I turned to leave, laughter bubbled up despite myself. But it didn't loosen the knot of resolve in my chest.

Tomorrow was coming.
And this time, I would be ready.

Chapter Twenty-One

I arrived at Enchanted Blossoms as the sun crested the rooftops. The only way I could face the early hour was armed with a latte, a bag of scones, and determination.

The scones were a peace offering to Rylyn.

Morning light spilled across the black and white tile floor, creating slashes of light and catching on colorful vases in the nearby case. Inside, the shop smelled like earth and greenery and possibility.

And it was mine.

For the first time since Alice died, I didn't hesitate on the threshold.

I flipped the sign to OPEN and claimed the day.

At the counter, I set down the coffee and scones and peered at the mess of handwritten invoices. Rylyn had been busy the last few days while I was trying to save the town from impending doom. Guilt slashed through me at leaving her alone when she made her promise to stay through the summer.

Then I wandered to the back to check inventory. The coolers were filled with the usual. Roses, lilies, carnations in various colors. The work table in the back was littered with greenery, baby's breath, floral tape, and flower petals. As if Rylyn didn't have the wherewithal to clean up after a long day.

More guilt.

The bell signaled an arrival. I turned toward the door and saw Rylyn standing there staring at me with an unreadable expression. She was still dressed in the goth attire. Black clothes from head to toe, black choker. Heavy eyeliner and black lipstick and her hair cascading over her shoulders.

"You decided to show up, huh?"

The girl wasn't going to make this easy on me.

I walked from the coolers to the front of the store, the click-click of my kitten heels the only sound on the tile. I regretted the shoes immediately.

I'd been thinking about what to say to her since last night. I could make excuses and tell the girl I'd been busy, but excuses were no longer going to cut it.

"Rylyn, I'm sorry," I said and meant it. "I should have been here. It won't happen again."

"You should have." The girl gave a jerky nod.

I reached for the bag of scones and held it out toward her. Her gaze flicked to the bag then back to my face.

"A peace offering," I said. "Blueberry scones from Honey & Crumb."

Her gaze went back to the bag as she considered the idea of what might be inside. Honey & Crumb had been in business since before I was born. It was absolutely legendary for its baked goods and run by Adelaide Collins for as long as I could remember.

"Honey & Crumb?" She stepped closer and took the bag from me. She opened the top, peered inside and then inhaled the buttery, sweet scent of blueberry. Then her gaze flicked back up to me. "My favorite. How did you know?"

The truth was, I didn't. But I smiled anyway.

"Lucky guess. I promise to do better," I said.

Rylyn reached into the bag and pulled out a scone. She broke off a corner and popped it into her mouth, closing her eyes and savoring the flavor. She chewed, swallowed, then gave me a nod.

"Good. Let's get to work."

While she went to work checking phone orders and printing delivery tickets, I moved to the back to check the coolers.

The stems stood in deep plastic buckets, each one labeled in a precise hand with the delivery date. Roses in tight spirals. Lilies still closed and green. Carnations fluffed and cheerful despite their reputation.

I tugged open the cooler door and cold air rushed out, carrying the sharp, green scent of fresh-cut stems. Condensation slicked the metal shelves as I checked water levels out of habit, topping off a bucket here, stripping a yellowing leaf there.

The cooler hummed steadily—a sound I'd grown up with, familiar as breathing.

Everything looked right.

Almost.

A flower at the back of the cooler caught my eye. With the door open, I stared at it for a long moment, trying to make sense of what I was seeing.

It wasn't anything I recognized. Not a rose, or a lily, or a carnation—or anything else I'd ever arranged. The neatly stacked stems sat in an unlabeled bucket. Several of the buds were still tightly closed, their petals sealed as if waiting.

But one or two were open.

Thriving.

As if the cold was giving them life.

I reached for one in full bloom. The instant my fingers closed around the stem, a sensation shot up my arm—familiar enough to make my breath catch. Not unlike what I'd felt at the Crossroads the night before.

Similar.

But different.

Purer. Cleaner.

I glanced toward the front of the shop. Rylyn was busy rotating the window display, oblivious.

I closed the cooler door and studied the flower in my hand.

The petals were delicate—pale pink brushed with the faintest hint of blue, their edges translucent, curling upward instead of outward. They smelled faintly of rain and stone rather than pollen or sweetness.

And even as I watched, the bloom began to sag.

I opened the cooler and returned it to the bucket.

The petals lifted.

Color deepened.

Alive again.

I frowned.

As if being out of the cooler wasn't what it wanted at all.

The door chime sounded and then the sound of a familiar voice drifted through the shop. My head snapped up.

There he was. Standing at the front of the counter, hands in jeans pockets, chatting easily with Rylyn. And Rylyn, leaning toward him... flirting? Twirling a lock of hair around her forefinger. Laughing at something he said while he smiled that smile he gave everyone.

And then he saw me.

His expression shifted. Recognition lit his eyes. The smile he gave me was different. As if he'd been waiting to see me, and now that he had everything else faded.

Rylyn straightened, cut a glance back over her shoulder and then drifted away from the counter. She busied herself at one of the displays keeping her head tipped enough to eavesdrop.

I made my way to the front, my heart doing a ridiculous dance in my chest.

"Hi," I said. "What brings you here?"

"Thought I'd come by and pick up that thing," he said. "Save you a trip after working all day."

That thing. The Sun Disk. My gaze flicked to the antique store across the street. "It's not like it's out of the way."

Owen shrugged like it was a great excuse to come by and see me.

"It's in my trunk." I was already reaching for my keys before my decision was made. "I'll get it."

"I'll come with you."

Like he sensed goth girl listening in and didn't like it.

"I'll be right back, Rylyn."

"Sure." Her tone was bored and annoyed.

Owen followed me out of the shop into the mid-morning heat to my car parked on the side of the building.

"You two make up?" he asked.

"Sort of. I bribed her with scones."

"A good bribe if they came from Honey & Crumb."

"Of course." I flashed a smile as I popped the trunk.

The Sun Disk lay wrapped in a dish towel between a tire iron and a jack—ridiculous and sacred at the same time. I lifted it out carefully. Even in daylight it seemed to hold a faint warmth, like it remembered the earth answering my hands.

"Here you go."

When he grasped it, his hand lingered a second longer than necessary. He didn't tug it away, just held it while he held my eyes.

"Dad wants it back in the shop," he said quietly. "And... I wanted to see you."

My heart did a ridiculous dance in my chest.

Then he added, like it was no big thing, "Come to dinner."

"Dinner?" My heart kicked into overdrive. "Tonight?"

"Sunday," he corrected. Like he'd changed his mind last minute. "After church. At my parents'."

Oh.

That wasn't dinner. That was intention. That was intimate.

"At your parents?" I repeated as if I couldn't grasp the concept.

Sunday after church dinner was the kind of invitation that screamed *I more than like you and I want them to know it.* And maybe even *I want them to approve.*

Of course, I knew Dougal McAllister, but I hadn't seen Madeline McAllister since high school graduation. Last I heard Owen's mother was fighting a battle with cancer.

A hot flash seared through me.

Oh, I was so not ready for that.

"Don't answer now," he said, perhaps sensing my commitment phobia. "Think about it."

I swallowed hard. "Okay."

He slid the Sun Disk fully into his grip. "Oh—and tomorrow, Mrs. Rollins can see us at one."

The grimoire. I'd forgotten about it until that moment. "Tomorrow?"

"I'll pick you up."

He flashed a grin as he started back across the street to the antique store.

I stood unmoving, my breath stilled and my heart racing. He'd hit me with all he had, smiled, and walked away.

If his plan was to throw me off kilter, it worked.

Finally, I closed the trunk and headed back inside. A numb feeling took up residence in my chest. Rylyn finished up her phone order and hung up.

"What's wrong with you? Mr. Perfect asked you out or something?"

Rylyn said it like she could sense the unease rolling off me. Did I look that out of sorts? I certainly felt out of sorts.

Though I didn't know why. It was Owen, for Pete's sake.

"Yes," I said absently.

Rylyn blinked, surprised that her sarcasm-laced barb was true. "You said yes, right? You'd be crazy not to say yes."

There was a bit of longing in the girl's voice.

"I didn't say yes. Or no."

She sucked in a breath. "Wow. You said nothing? Ouch. Poor guy." She started toward the back of the shop. "Delivery is here. I'll get it. Your turn to man the front."

And then she was gone leaving me to contemplate the consequences of my non-answer—and why something as simple as dinner felt so complicated.

I shoved away the thoughts. I had work to do and that didn't include pining away for my high school crush.

Which I seriously thought I was over.

Thank goodness a customer came in to distract me. Mr. Evans was a haggard old man with a squint and frizzy gray hair about his head. And though he looked like Scrooge's brother on his best day, he was a kind soul.

"Well, I'll be. Look who it is!"

"Hi, Mr. Evans." I couldn't stop the eruption of a smile. "How are you?"

"Come here and let me hug your neck, girl." He waved me around the counter.

Laughing, I walked around the counter to hug him. He smelled like old wood. Then he held me at arm's length to get a good look at me. Mr. Evans taught World History at the high school but had long since retired. Owen and I were both in his class when we were juniors.

"Heard you were back," he said with a nod. "Thought it was a story."

"Not a story, Mr. Evans. I'm back."

He leaned in close. "Say, sorry to hear about Alice, God rest her. She was a real gem."

"She was." I swallowed hard, then steered the conversation back to business. If not, he'd stand there all day and chat. "What can I do for you?"

"It's my anniversary. Fifty years! Can you believe it?" He laughed and scratched at the stubble on his chin. "Hard to believe the old girl put up with me for so long."

"Well, then. Let's make Mrs. Evans something special," I said, reaching for the order book.

"Nah, don't go to any trouble. I know what she likes." He shuffled to the display case and picked up a white vase full of vibrant stargazer lilies.

He prattled on about nonsense as I rang him up and he paid in cash—a hundred-dollar bill, of all things. I opened the cash drawer to give him change. But I had to lift the tray to get to the extra twenties. When I did, I froze.

A scrap of paper was nestled under the bills, the edge peeking out. The familiar handwriting hit me cold in the chest.

Mr. Evans didn't notice as he continued to talk about the latest shenanigans with his chickens.

I quickly counted out the change and handed him the bills, the coins, and the receipt. I wanted to shoo him out of the shop so I could investigate that paper closer.

"Have a great day, Mr. Evans, and congrats again," I said warmly, but my heart was racing like it was about to beat out of my chest.

He started to leave but then paused at the door and turned back. "Whatever happened with you and that Owen McAllister? Nice, good-looking kid."

I flushed. "Happened?"

"You two always in competition." He chuckled then. "Thought you'd end up together somehow."

Oh, for the love of—

"Hoped you would anyway," he added as an afterthought.

My mouth turned dry. "You did?"

"You two seemed to fit. Welp, I better run. I'm having my annual summer barbecue next weekend. Y'all should come."

Y'all—me and Owen.

"Oh, I—"

And then he was out the door before I could decline.

As soon as he was gone, I opened the cash drawer and picked up the tray. The scrap was still there. I hadn't imagined it. I slid it out with shaking fingers and stared down at the familiar handwriting.

It was Alice's.

Chapter Twenty-Two

I stared at the scrap of paper, my heart in my throat, my hand shaking.

The page had been ripped in half—and ripped from something. The left edge was jagged, like it had been torn straight out of a book.

The words were faint pencil. Scrawled like an afterthought.

Or intention.

My first impulse was to run across the street to Owen. I didn't—because Rylyn's footsteps were already behind me. I shoved the paper into my pocket to examine later.

Then I did what I always did when my world tilted.

I worked.

Filling orders. Answering phones. Creating arrangements.

By late afternoon, Halle arrived on a breeze of vanilla and afternoon sunshine.

I stiffened. We were supposed to grab lunch, and between portals, grief, and the minor detail of my life exploding, it had slipped right past me.

Halle didn't miss a beat. "I was hoping you'd be here."

"You were?"

"I realized when I saw you the other day I didn't give you my number." She pushed her business card into my hand.

One glance down and I saw she was a real estate agent—specializing in historic homes in the area. Quite a niche.

"You can text me or call me anytime," she said.

I reached for a pen and a scrap of paper and scribbled down my number. "Here's mine."

She smiled down at it, then asked, "What are you doing tonight?"

The unexpected question made my head pop up. "Why do you ask?"

Because my initial thought was, I'd be alone with Willow, a chatty Tani, the Red Queen, and too many worries to put away on a Friday night.

"Thought we could go out and have some fun. You look like you need it."

"I do?" I ran my hand over my short hair, wondering if something was out of place.

Rylyn busied herself at a display case as Halle stepped closer to the counter and lowered her voice.

"And I know you want to talk about..." She nodded to the shop across the street.

Owen. Why was everyone so interested in my love life?

"I don't."

She grinned. "Sure. Come out with me. I'm heading to Neon Cowboy after my last showing. First round on me."

Hesitation crawled through me. I glanced down at my chic capris, strappy sandals and gauzy peasant top. So not Neon Cowboy attire.

"I don't know. I don't have anything to wear."

Halle snorted. "Wear your big city clothes. Those guys won't know what hit them when you walk in."

"If I walk in like this, I'm going to look like a Vogue intern who got lost on the way to Coachella."

"I know but it'll be fun to watch." She grinned again. "What do you say? We have some catching up to do."

I cut a glance to Rylyn still fussing with a vase and clearly listening. I thought of the scrap of paper in my pocket. My grimoire outing with Owen tomorrow. The possibility of Sunday dinner with his parents.

And it was all so overwhelming.

Halle was right. I needed a distraction. I needed some fun. I needed to blow off steam.

"All right. We close up in an hour. I'll meet you there."

"That's perfect! See you there."

And then Halle was heading out of the shop before I had a chance to change my mind.

I quickly busied myself with the last receipts of the day, but Rylyn was watching me intently. Finally, I looked up.

"What?"

The girl smirked. "Neon Cowboy?"

"What about it?"

She shrugged, giving me a once-over. "Nothing. I wouldn't have figured you for a honky-tonk."

I laughed. Perhaps not since I'd returned home with a Manhattan wardrobe. But maybe, since I was here to stay, it was time to embrace that small town girl again.

After closing the flower shop, I returned home to change.

I couldn't wear my big city clothes—as Halle put it—to Neon Cowboy. I'd stick out like a Vegas showgirl at a church potluck. I opted for a faded pair of jeans, a loose-fitting top with flowing sleeves, and my worn sneakers.

Before I left town, I'd donated all my boots because I swore I was never coming back and wouldn't need them.

The universe, clearly, decided to play trickster.

I tucked the scrap of paper I found in my wallet for safekeeping. Seemed like the best place for it and not lying around at the house.

I drove my aunt's oversized Cadillac to the outskirts of town where the weathered sign for Neon Cowboy flickered in red and blue—what else?—neon. The parking lot was already full of muddy pickup trucks and dusty SUVs. The music thumped through the walls and for a moment, I sat staring at the aging exterior that hadn't changed a bit since the last time I saw it.

Inside, I knew the floor was littered with peanut shells. The bar would be crowded with the locals and regulars laughing and drinking cheap beer on a Friday night. In the back, the rattle of balls as someone racked them and then the crack as they broke. The dancefloor was nothing but a small square hardwood floor covered in sawdust for the best boot scootin'. And the old jukebox in the corner hummed between songs—country, rock, or whatever someone felt like paying for—the glow casting lazy shadows along the walls and floor.

It was old. Not fancy.

But familiar.

The kind of place where everyone knew your name, your face, your business. And nobody cared as long as you bought the next round.

I smiled, pushed open the car door and stepped out into the balmy summer night.

When I heard my name and looked up. There, walking across the gravel parking lot, was Halle. Waving like she was ten miles away instead of ten feet.

"You showed up!"

Golden hair hung in lazy waves over her shoulders. Green eyes sparkled with life and mirth underneath her straw cowboy hat.

Her off-the-shoulder boho sundress was paired with a pair of worn cowboy boots and accessorized with a wide belt, a fringe bag, and silver jewelry.

For a moment, I stopped cold as I gaped at my friend. This was a look featured in fashion magazines. A look that women tried to recreate in the city. A look that cost thousands in SoHo. While here was Halle doing it in her effortless way and it probably cost less than a hundred bucks.

If I still worked at the magazine, I would absolutely insist on a spread of boho cowgirl chic.

"I made it," I said.

"Good! Tonight is about nothing but fun." She hooked her arm in mine and together we entered.

The music was loud. The air was stale. The beer was flowing. The laughter was boisterous. And for a moment, I soaked it all in and let it thrum through me. This was home. This was right.

Halle led me through the bar to the back with the pool tables. I hadn't played in so long, I was sure I was rusty. But my heart was thumping with George Strait and for the first time since I arrived in Hickory Hollow, I felt something akin to joy.

The second we made it to the back with the pool tables, I stopped short.

There, with a sweating bottle of beer in one hand and a pool cue in the other... was Owen.

My pulse did something stupid. Of course he'd be here. Of course my hometown would pick tonight to mess with me.

Halle stopped next to me following my line of vision.

"Well, look at that. Don't tell me this town doesn't love a set up. Let's go over!" She started to drag me toward them.

But my feet refused to move. "No, Halle. We should go."

"What? And miss out on all the fun? We can all shoot pool together. Have a few laughs. Come on. It'll be fun."

Halle gave me another tug and practically dragged me into the back with the pool tables, right toward Owen and his mysterious friend.

As we approached, he caught sight of me. His eyes widened in surprise and then he smiled which made my insides turn to jelly.

Halle came to a halt next to the pool table. “Well, look who it is. Owen McAllister and Luke Bennett.”

Luke Bennett. Of course. Quarterback star who was destined for a Heisman. Yet here he was still in Hickory Hollow.

“Ladies,” Luke said with a tip of his hat.

But I couldn’t take my eyes off Owen. The sleeves of his white shirt were rolled to his elbows, the top buttons undone. Like he’d just got off work and was trying to reset after a long week.

“You remember Piper, don’t you, Luke?”

“Yes, ma’am.” He grinned at me, showing off deep dimples that were still killer even all these years later. “Welcome back, Piper.”

“Ma’am?” I said with a laugh. “That makes me feel old.”

Halle, being the sociable one, said, “How about I buy us a round? Luke, come with me.”

She grabbed him by the arm, not giving him a chance to say no, and dragged him toward the bar, leaving me alone with Owen.

“I didn’t expect to see you here,” he said.

“I didn’t expect to be here,” I said with a grin. “But Halle... well...”

He chuckled. “She talked you into it.”

I glanced over at the bar to see Halle leaning back on her elbows talking to Luke and laughing at something he said. He was leaned in close. Intimate. Friendly.

“She did.”

He handed me the pool cue. “How about a game of 8-Ball?”

“Sure.” I couldn’t refuse.

Because the last time I played a game of pool with Owen was when we were still in high school and I was still competing.

I intended to compete again. Old habits and all.

He took a swig of his beer and then set it aside to re-rack the table. I watched him. The way he methodically slipped the balls within the rack, ordering them precisely like it was something he'd done all his life.

"We used to play pool," I said before I could stop the words.

Still bent over the table, he looked up at me, light glinting in his soft gray eyes. "We did."

But what I didn't say was we used to get Owen's older brother, Colt, to buy us beers while we played. Back then, I thought we were being nothing but rebellious teenagers. Colt kept an eye on us and let us drink while we shot pool and tried to outdo each other.

After he graduated high school, Colt disappeared out of Hickory Hollow.

"Do you ever hear from Colt?" I asked.

His expression changed. Like it was a sore subject he didn't want to talk about.

He shrugged. "Not as much as Dad would like."

I took that to mean he didn't visit on holidays.

Interesting.

But I couldn't stop thinking about me and Owen back then. I competed against him then because I wanted his attention. I wanted him to think I was one of the cool kids who could drink and play pool.

And back then, he never ever acted like he had an interest in me.

Back then, all the girls chased him and Gretchen, AP Chem genius, managed to catch him.

"You always beat me," I added, thinking about our previous games.

"You always wanted to beat me." He finished racking and reached for another cue. "Do you want to break?"

"I'd love to." Even as I said it, my heart fluttered.

My palms broke into a sweat as I lined up the cue ball and took my stance. Before I could shoot, though, he leaned down close enough to brush against me.

"Let's see what you got, Wakefield," he murmured, his breath sliding warm over my ear.

My brain promptly forgot how to operate my limbs. He was trying to distract me, and it worked.

I glanced up. He grinned as he stood straight, clearly proud of himself.

"You'll pay for that," I said.

I regained my focus and smacked the cue ball with all I had, then watched the balls scatter across the table. I sank two solids right off the bat. I cut him a smug glance.

"I still got it," I said.

"We'll see about that," he said on a laugh.

By then, Halle and Luke were back, each carrying two beers. She handed one to me.

"I propose a toast!" Halle announced, holding her bottle over the pool table. "To old friends and good times." She looked right at me as she said it.

"Hear, hear!" Luke added.

But Owen never took his gaze off me as we clinked bottle necks. I took a swig of the cheap, cold beer. Nothing ever tasted so good.

Then I took my next shot and missed.

"Are we playing pairs?" Halle asked.

"Yes, and we're solids," I said to her.

Halle took up a pool cue, handed it to Luke. Then grabbed one for herself. Owen leaned down to the table, his focus intense as he lined up. He sank two more balls with one shot. Then stood straight, grinning at me as though he won the lottery.

"How's that?"

"Lucky shot, that's all," I said with a laugh. "Bet you can't get another one."

"I'll take that bet."

He leaned down, lined up with the cue ball… and CRACK. He sank his third.

"You lose, Wakefield," he said with a laugh.

"You sink another, McAllister, and I'll buy you another beer," I said.

He laughed. "You're on."

"But—" I added. "You gotta call this one."

He lifted a brow, trying desperately to hide his smile. "All right then. Twelve ball in the left corner pocket."

"Tough shot. You'll never make it," Luke said, heckling him.

And as I looked up at him, I saw he had his arm slung over Halle's shoulders. Casual. Comfortable. Like he'd been doing it all his life.

I blinked. Halle grinned.

Halle—head cheerleader and Luke—star quarterback.

Just like old times.

And it felt good to be home.

"We'll see about that," Owen said as he leaned down to the table.

His gaze was intense as he lined up with the cue ball. Then took his shot. The twelve ball smacked against the eight and missed the pocket by a long shot.

"Oh, too bad, McAllister. You owe me a beer," I said with a grin.

He moved to stand next to me. "You're up, Halle."

She untangled herself from Luke's arm and handed him her beer. "Get ready to weep, boys. I'm going to sink the rest."

Halle lined up but all I was focused on was how close Owen was standing to me. How I felt his body heat. Smelled that faint twinge of cologne I scented in his truck. And how I wanted him to sling his arm over my shoulders.

Tonight, I wasn't a Guardian. I wasn't an heiress. I wasn't a walking target.

I was a girl in her hometown, shooting pool and drinking cheap beer with people who still knew her name.

And for the first time since I'd come back, that felt like enough.

Chapter Twenty-Three

After Halle and I obliterated Owen and Luke two out of three, I slid the cue back into the rack, fighting off a yawn and the warm buzz of cheap beer.

Owen was at my side like he'd been there the whole time.

"Want to dance?" he asked. His voice slid over me smooth as silk.

And immediately my cheeks flushed. "Oh—"

"One dance," he said, already taking my hand. "Then I'll walk you to your car."

Such a gentleman. It was hard for me to resist. I conceded.

"One dance, McAllister. Then I'm done for the night."

As we stepped onto the dance floor, George Strait crooned about crossing his heart and promising to give it his all. Which felt far too fitting for the man who was putting his hand on my waist and holding the other against his chest. I was acutely aware of the slow, steady beat of his heart. And something else... something that seemed to recognize me.

Magic. His. Humming under the surface curling toward me.

It was such a heady feeling that dizziness swept through me.

But I filed it away with everything else I wasn't ready to unpack. Because I wasn't sure if he was doing it on purpose or if it was a thing that happened.

His head bent low next to mine, his breath warm at my temple. And for that one suspended moment, there was no one else in Neon Cowboy except him and me and George Strait.

He said nothing. I said nothing. We held onto each other as the words hit me like he was saying them to me himself. Which did something to me. Made my throat tighten and my eyes burn.

I didn't want to wait anymore. My high school crush was a man, and he was holding me in his arms making me feel safe and warm and cherished. Even Mr. Evans thought we'd end up together.

And now that I was home, now that he was still here, maybe it was time to stop fighting those feelings and lean into them.

"Owen?"

"Yes?" His voice was soft in my ear.

The song was ending and I knew it was now or never.

"Will you drive me home?" And before I lost my nerve, I added, "And stay?"

He pulled back, those gray eyes landing on me with question and a hint of uncertainty. "Are you sure?"

I nodded. "Yes, Owen. I've never been more sure of anything in my life."

And as I said that, AC/DC's *Thunderstruck* detonated from the jukebox.

Like it was planned.

Owen's mouth curved like the universe had decided to heckle us. I laughed—half-mortified, half-exhilarated—and he leaned in close, one hand still on my waist.

"Sure you don't want another dance?" His breath was warm on my cheek.

Another laugh bubbled out of me. "With AC/DC? I don't think so."

His other hand was still clutching mine. "Then let's go."

He led me off the dance floor. At the bar, Halle and Luke were sitting side by side, their heads together like they were sharing a secret. For half a second, I thought I should tell her I was leaving—then Luke kissed her, and Halle slid an arm around him like she'd been waiting all night.

Well. That solved that.

Owen sensed my hesitation and glanced at the bar. "That's new," he said.

My head snapped to him. "I thought—"

"No." He shook his head. "He's been chasing her for years. At least he waited until the divorce was final."

"Divorce?" I blinked. "His or hers?"

"His," he said.

There was still so much I didn't know about this town.

Outside in the balmy night, he led me to the oversized Cadillac.

"Want me to drive?" he asked.

I was already handing him the keys.

He took them without a word, opened the passenger side for me, then slid behind the wheel. The radio was on low, playing some old classic rock tune from my youth I'd forgotten I liked. He left it on—didn't even adjust the seat or mirrors—just settled into the driver's seat like he was born to it.

Then we were off, heading down the dark two-lane highway back to my house.

My heart pounded hard, my pulse erratic, and I wasn't sure I remembered how to breathe.

When we were sixteen, I'd dreamed about kissing him. He never gave me a sideways glance. I guess that's why I was determined to beat him at everything—grade point average, pool, and whatever else I could do to get his attention.

Now that I'd kissed him as a full-grown adult, that fantasy turned into something less sweet.

I glanced his way. His focus was on the road ahead, one hand on the wheel like this was a casual date. While I was coming apart at the seams, he seemed perfectly calm.

Which was annoying.

He caught me staring.

"What?" A smile pulled at the corner of his mouth.

"In high school..." I started, then stopped. Pressed my lip together and shook my head. "Never mind."

"What about it?" He sounded half amused.

"I thought you didn't like me."

He cut me a glance. "I told you. I've always liked you, Piper."

Since kindergarten. Yes, I remembered.

"But you never—"

"Things were different then," he said. His hands tightened on the steering wheel. "You made it clear you were leaving town."

Oh.

I chewed on my lower lip. But what he didn't say—because maybe he didn't want to remember—was that he was dating Gretchen. The brainiac with the perfect GPA like him.

"And you had a girlfriend."

"Not exactly. She liked me more than I did her. And I didn't know how to say no."

"You went to senior prom together." Why did I sound bitter?

He cut me a glance. "I didn't think you'd go."

His voice softened, like it mattered. Like he'd wanted to ask me... and didn't.

That caught me off guard.

And I didn't go. I stayed home because no one asked and I played it off like it was my choice.

I said nothing else as I stared through the windshield like I could will myself into composure.

But something settled deep inside me—quiet and certain. This wasn't casual. It was going to mean something. Maybe not to him. But definitely to me, because suddenly I couldn't imagine my life without him in it.

And that was a staggering—no, sobering—thought.

"Are you changing your mind about tonight?" he asked, voice quiet in the car.

"No, I'm..." My words trailed off. I wasn't ready to share those intimate thoughts with him yet.

"What?"

I swallowed hard. "I like you, Owen."

Four simple words that held more meaning than he could ever know.

He reached for my hand across the console and laced our fingers. "That's good to know."

Then he lifted my knuckles to his mouth and kissed them. A little sizzle went straight through me, right into my heart.

He kept my hand in his for the rest of the way.

When we pulled into the drive, Owen cut the engine.

For a long moment, neither of us moved. We sat there staring at the house—the porch light glowing yellow, washing the steps in soft, familiar gold. June bugs and moths dive-bombing the light like the deranged insects they were. It looked so normal. So quiet. Like nothing strange or magical or downright unhinged could possibly be waiting inside.

Then I pushed open the door and stepped out into the night.

Owen followed, keys in hand, and together we climbed the steps. A minute later we were inside, the front door clicking shut behind him.

And there, sprawled on my sofa like she paid taxes here, was the Red Queen eating Cheez-Its out of the box while watching QVC.

Willow was perched on the arm of the nearest chair, her golden eyes peering at us with boredom.

We both halted and stared, then exchanged a stunned look. It had completely ruined the moment.

I didn't even know what to say.

"What are you doing?" Finally, I found my voice. And was deeply relieved she hadn't found my hidden credit cards.

The queen glanced up, one hand still buried in the box. "I was hungry. And this woman is selling an emerald bracelet the size of a pigeon egg. I need it."

"You don't," I snapped, clutching the strap of my handbag tighter.

Owen made a strangled sound that was a laugh. I shot him a look. He straightened his face, but was still actively trying to keep it together.

I pressed a hand against my head. "It's late," I said. "Do not summon anyone from Wonderland to redecorate or help you buy anything off television."

She shrugged. "I make no promises." Then she shooed us away. "Be gone. The host is about to demonstrate the versatility of this handbag. I must watch."

"Fine," I said. "Stay here. Watch your show but do not touch anything that sparkles or hums."

"Do not command me, or off with your head."

I sighed. "That doesn't work in this realm, Red."

She gave a dismissive wave and reached for a another handful of crackers. Clearly we'd been dismissed.

Owen's hand landed on the small of my back, warm and steady, and guided me toward the stairs. I let him. Away from cheddar dust, QVC, and the absurdity that the Red Queen was making herself at home in my living room.

He took my hand and lead me up the stairs. My legs felt like rubber and for one strange moment I felt like this was a dream—that any second, I'd wake up alone in my bed.

But his hand stayed tight on mine as we went up, then to my bedroom, still in darkness.

He pushed the door closed with a soft click and pulled me against him again—hands on my waist, mouth on mine.

When we broke, his hands came up, cupping my face, his thumb sweeping across my cheek. The intensity in his gaze was too much. A breath shuddered out of me.

"I told you before," he said softly, "I wanted you. And I meant that. But I want you to be sure it's what you want, too."

I pressed a hand against his chest and felt the wild thumping of his heart.

He was... nervous.

Like me.

"I want you," I whispered.

Then he kissed me.

He'd kissed me before, but this was different. Calmer. Surer. Sweeter—until the underlying need turned the edges of it dangerous. I leaned into him, my mouth yielding to his. He tasted faintly of cheap beer and peanuts and yearning.

Heat swept through me, threads of desire pulling taut.

My fingers fumbled with the buttons of his shirt. One. Then two. Enough to graze the warm skin beneath. The tips of my fingers found the hollow of his throat. A soft touch. A reverent touch.

He made a low, appreciative sound as his hands slid into my hair. His mouth left mine for my cheek, then my neck—right over my hammering pulse. This time, there was no careful distance. Only choice. Only this. Only us.

He deepened the kiss. Slow. Methodical. No hurry at all.

It unraveled me.

And for the first time, I opened myself to this, to him. Let myself feel everything. Let myself hold on. Let myself have this one perfect moment where there were no monsters or flower shops or Crossroads demanding my attention.

Him and me and the dark.

I awoke cocooned in warmth—the steady hum of the air conditioning through the vent, and the soft snore of the man holding me like he'd never let go. My head was still on his chest, right where I'd fallen asleep. He hadn't moved. I hadn't moved. Still tangled together without so much as a breath between us.

I didn't want to move, and for the longest moment, I didn't. I lay there and listened to his rhythmic breathing, the steady beat of his heart beneath my ear, and the certainty settling deep in my bones—

this wasn't casual.

This wasn't some temporary comfort or a no-strings distraction.

This was something more. Something real. More real than anything I'd had with that guy in Manhattan—who would henceforth be known as *that guy* because he had nothing on Owen McAllister.

That guy had been handsome. Sure.

But he wasn't steady. He wasn't kind. He wasn't here, wrapped around me like I mattered.

And the worst part was… it was deep. Deeper than I wanted to acknowledge at this early stage of whatever it was we were doing.

Which, frankly, was terrifying.

I shifted. Enough that he noticed and moved, his arms tightening a fraction around me.

"Not yet." His voice was thick with sleep.

"Owen—"

"Let me have this." One hand slipped through the short locks of my hair. "Five more minutes."

I stopped breathing. Then whispered, "Okay."

All the tension bled out of me.

"That's better," he said, sounding smug.

Like he was waiting for me to relax.

"You fit here," he said. "I knew you would."

Everything inside me stilled. Every nerve ending sizzled. He said it—me, fitting against the hard planes of his body—like he'd been thinking about it a long time.

Why did he have to say something so wrecking when I was already in a weakened state? I didn't know what to say. I kept telling myself not to break the moment.

So, of course, I broke the moment.

"We meet Mrs. Rollins today," I said.

"I know."

"Shouldn't we get going?"

"I have three more minutes, missy."

I couldn't help it. I laughed.

"Three minutes and then what?" I asked, pushing.

"Then I make you breakfast."

"You want to cook for me?"

"Yes."

"In my house?"

"Yes."

"No," I said. "I don't even know if I have pots and pans."

"You have a coffeemaker."

"I do."

"And you do have pots and pans," he said.

"How do you know?" I lifted my head to look at him. And his dove-gray eyes were lit with amusement. "Have you been snooping in my kitchen, McAllister?"

He hauled me closer, his mouth a breath away from mine. "I love it when you call me that."

"You're incorrigible."

"I am."

He kissed me before I could retort. A kiss that made me melt against him and forget we were supposed to be doing things outside of the bedroom. I pulled away, tried to disentangle myself from him. But he held on tight.

"Time's up," I said and my voice came out breathy. Then, because I wanted to tempt fate, "McAllister."

"You're bad," he growled.

He tried to hold onto me, but I squirmed free and slid out of the bed with less dignity than I envisioned. My feet hit the floor, my gaze landing where there was a trail of clothes. I found his shirt first, snatched it up and tugged it on. Then bounced out of the bed and headed for the bathroom.

"You're trying to emotionally destroy me, woman," he called.

My response was to flash him a grin over my shoulder before I closed the door.

And now that I was sealed behind the door, I leaned against the bathroom counter trying to catch my breath.

I looked at the woman in the mirror—the girl with the short-cropped hair who thought her life would be New York City glam—and I realized something. I wasn't that girl anymore.

I was just a small town girl falling for her high school crush.

Chapter Twenty-Four

I pulled on my favorite pair of faded jeans, an old, worn t-shirt that had *Fashionably Late and Questioning Everything* scrawled across the front in faded script. As I headed for the bedroom door, my phone buzzed on the nightstand.

A text from Halle.

You left without telling me bye

I typed back. *You were in a lip lock with Luke*

Her reply: *And you were on the dance floor with a certain charming someone. His truck is still in the bar parking lot. Care to share details?*

I stared at the text for the longest time. Then, *Absolutely not*

I closed the messenger, but she was still typing back a reply, so I pocketed the phone to deal with her later. I started to leave the room when I halted, thinking about the scrap of paper I'd found in the cash register drawer. I retrieved it from where I'd tucked it into my wallet. Maybe Owen could help me figure out where it came from.

Downstairs, the smell of bacon, eggs, and coffee permeated the air. In the kitchen, fun-size Tani lounged against the kitchen counter on her stomach, her chin in her hands, giving Owen moon eyes as he cooked.

He was at the stove in his rumpled clothes from yesterday—I'd given him back his shirt before my shower—a dish towel slung over one shoulder looking like a Food Network chef. Barefoot. Far sexier than he had any right to be. In my kitchen.

I paused there, watching this quiet domesticity with my heart in my throat.

"I like your rumpled appearance," Tani was saying. "Very morning after chic."

Owen smirked, amused. But I was scandalized.

"Tani!" I admonished.

He chuckled as he scooped eggs onto a plate.

"Morning, sunshine," she said, never taking her eyes off Owen. "Your boyfriend is sexy when he's cooking."

Heat flooded my cheeks. Owen froze long enough to give me a sideways look of mild curiosity. Like he was waiting to see what I'd do with that word—but he didn't rescue me.

"He's not my boyfriend," I said, too quickly.

And I wasn't even sure what we were other than in serious like with each other.

Owen's smirk deepened. Still not helping.

"Sure," Tani said brightly. "Whatever you say, chica."

"Don't you have some place to be?" I snapped.

She huffed. "Fine."

And then she was gone in a puff of pink fairy dust.

"Sorry about my fairy," I muttered.

He handed me a cup of coffee. "She doesn't mean any harm."

And we both avoided the word *boyfriend* like it was a loaded gun.

Willow sat at the kitchen door, her tail curled around her, like she was waiting for her next meal. Owen grabbed a box of cat treats and shook several into his hand. The cat was on her feet, tail flipping in the air. He put them in front of her.

I dropped into a chair at the table.

"What do you have there?" He eyed the paper in my hand as he placed two plates. One in front of me. One next to me.

I slid it across to him. "I found this in the cash register. It's Alice's handwriting."

He sat, leaned back in the chair with the paper in his hand as he studied it.

"Alice wrote this?"

I nodded. "I don't know where it came from."

I watched him with an ache in my chest I hadn't expected. Like this could be any normal morning between the two of us. If there was an us.

"But this isn't English," he said.

"You noticed that, too, huh?" I scooped up eggs with my fork.

"Bring it to Mrs. Rollins. Maybe she can read it." He slid it back toward me with his calm efficiency.

I nodded. I broke a piece of bacon in half for something to do with my hands. But that word kept turning over in my head—boyfriend. I didn't know why. I wasn't ready for that. But I wasn't ready to let him go, either.

When I moved to New York, I was prepared to leave behind everything. The town, my parents, Alice. Him. I'd had a long stretch of homesickness as I poured my heart and soul into the magazine job. I had friends, yes. I had a live-in boyfriend, too. But it all felt... empty. And now, here, back in town sitting with Owen at my breakfast table it felt... different. Warm. Happy.

I wasn't sure what to do with that.

"What is it?" he asked, as though he sensed my internal spiral.

I stabbed eggs with my fork, gave him a weak smile. "Nothing."

He reached for me, placing his hand on my wrist. I met his gaze and my heart turned over.

"Do you regret last night?" he asked, low, serious.

"God, no," I said on a breath. Then, "Do you?"

A corner of his mouth lifted. "No. Never."

We stared at each other in silence.

"Is it what Tani said?" he asked.

Everything inside me froze.

"Because we don't have to name anything, Piper," he said, steady and clear. His fingers tightened a little on my wrist. "I want to be with you."

Oh.

Well, that did terrible things to my insides.

"And," he added as an afterthought, "I want you to come to dinner tomorrow. Mom wants to see you."

Rylyn's voice boomed in my head. *Mr. Perfect ask you out?* Because he was. Perfect. In every way. With a charming smile.

"Okay," I said finally.

His response was to kiss my fingers.

And then I knew—something was happening between us.

And I was going to let it.

***

After breakfast, I grabbed the grimoire and we left. Owen wanted his truck, so I drove us back to Neon Cowboy.

In the car, he said, "I need a shower and a change of clothes."

"At your parents'?" I asked.

He grinned. "No. I have a place. A cottage."

I gripped the steering wheel. "A cottage?" Like the words were foreign.

"The old caretaker place. It's been in the family a few generations," he said. "Near the woods."

"I didn't know you had a place."

"It didn't seem relevant until now."

I glanced at him as he reached for my hand, his fingers wrapping around mine.

"Follow me there? We can drive together to see Mrs. Rollins."

He had a place. A cottage near the woods. I don't know why but it settled somewhere deep and quiet inside me.

"Okay."

In the empty parking lot, I watched him climb into his truck and then he was off back down the highway. I followed close because I hadn't a clue where we were going. He turned down a one-lane tree-lined road and then slowed as he came to a driveway that was practically hidden between the trees.

I turned, following him up the dirt road. In the distance, trees from the distant woods rose up behind the white-walled cottage with the wraparound porch. It was simple and well-cared for. Like someone spent a lot of time and effort on upkeep. It was smaller than the monstrous house I'd inherited.

And it was delightful.

I loved it on sight.

I parked and got out and paused there beside the old Caddy. The air here was clean, fresh. Full of pine and earth and something that seemed wholly his. Like he'd conjured this perfect little place from his own breath and magic.

"You live here?" I asked.

He nodded.

It was well off the beaten path. Far from town. On the edge of the woods where the old hickory tree was gasping for life. Where the Crossroads came to an intersection.

"You didn't tell me you were so close to the Crossroads," I said.

"It never came up in conversation." He gave me one his winning grins as he headed to the steps of the wood porch.

I followed, clutching the grimoire against my chest. He opened the door and stood aside for me to enter.

Inside, it was no bachelor pad.

It was decorated with the same care as the outside upkeep. Quiet. Beautiful. Bamboo floors covered in a plush jewel-toned rug. Comfortable furniture that looked almost new. It smelled like cedar with traces of coffee and some citrus cleaner lingering in the air.

A small kitchen with a dining table and chairs. One hallway that led to the bedroom and bathroom.

He was tidy.

Not a speck of dust. Not a pile of clutter anywhere. Only a stack of books on the coffee table. One with a bookmark sticking out of the top. Boots lined up at the door. The mantel hosted family photographs. His mother, father, brother.

It felt like stepping into someone's private, personal space and I wasn't sure I was worthy.

He dropped keys in a bowl on the table by the door, then caught me staring.

"It's not as big as yours—"

"It's perfect," I said.

He kissed my cheek. "Make yourself at home. I'll be ten minutes."

And then he disappeared down the hallway. A few minutes later, water came on.

I was in his cottage. Tucked neatly into the side of the woods. And it was charming, like him.

I wandered the living room looking at family photos. One of young Owen when he was twelve, maybe thirteen, and his older brother, Colt, when they were on a fishing trip with their dad. Owen proudly holding a string of perch like he'd caught a great white shark. A family photo with Colt in his high school cap and gown. Owen's graduation photo with his parents, but without his brother.

Everything about those photos said family, warmth, love. Everything about the photos on the mantel at my house said I was the center of Alice's universe.

She had me and no one else. And something my dad said came back to me. *She hid you because she was afraid your father would find you.*

She hid me. Kept me close. Loved me from a distance.

Who was he? Where was he? And why did she hide me from him?

For half a second, I wondered what it would be like to be part of a family—a real one.

"Hey." Owen's soft voice pulled me back to the present.

I turned to see him standing in the middle of the living room with damp hair smelling clean and looking rakishly handsome in faded jeans, a navy t-shirt and boots. Like he'd stepped off the cover of Casual Cowboy.

"Ready to go?" he asked.

"Yes."

But I was still distracted as I followed him back out the door. He locked up and then we were in his truck.

"You okay?" he asked.

He sensed my distraction.

"I keep thinking about something my dad said when I talked to him," I told him. "He said Alice hid me because she was afraid my father would find me."

I paused, glanced his way. His hands were tight on the steering wheel.

"My biological father," I said. "What does that mean, Owen?"

"I think it means she was afraid of him for some reason," he said.

"Do you think..." I paused, chewed on my lower lip. "What if everything happening at the Crossroads has something to do with him?"

He shook his head. "I don't know."

I leaned back against the seat as he drove. "I need to find out."

"How?"

I huffed out a breath. "No idea."

"We can figure it out together," he said.

He sounded so sure, so confident that it made my heart squeeze. And yet that old armor snapped back into place. The one that was headstrong and determined to do things on my own without asking for help from anyone.

"You don't have to do that."

"I want to." Absolute determination edged his tone.

I glanced his way. He was still gripping the steering wheel, focused on the road ahead. I couldn't stop myself. I reached for him, placed my hand on his thigh. His head snapped toward me, surprise then delight in his eyes.

"Then I want you to."

He gave me that smile that always made me melt.

We arrived at Mrs. Rollins house. I got out, clutching the grimoire to my chest feeling a little nervous. It warmed against me. I didn't know why. Owen looked calm and controlled. Like he was visiting an old friend to catch up, not asking our former English teacher to translate a magical book.

We climbed the steps together of the old red-brick house. He rang the bell. A few minutes later, the door opened and there was Mrs. Rollins on the other side of the door.

She looked exactly the same—well, maybe with a few more wrinkles—as she did our senior year. Tall with a wild mess of black curls around her oval face, big brown eyes behind thick glasses, straight pert nose, and thin lips. Her face broke into a brilliant megawatt smile the second she saw us.

"Well, bless my soul," she said with a wide smile. "Get in here, you two."

She waved us inside the small living room that smelled like antiques, old people, and lemon oil. The hardwood floors creaked as walked inside and she waved us to the worn sofa along the wall. We sat together. Owen's leg brushed against mine.

It was hard not to notice and it felt deliberate.

"Thanks for seeing us, Mrs. Rollins," Owen said.

"Of course." Then her gaze swung to me. "Piper, I heard you were back in town. It's good to see you."

"Thanks. I'm glad to be back," I said and meant it.

"And I was sure sorry to hear about Alice. What a dear of a lady."

I nodded agreement and clamped down on words that wanted to burst forth. Like she was my mother and I never knew it. "She was."

She looked at Owen then. "You said you had a book you wanted me to look at?"

"Yes and thanks for seeing us on a Saturday afternoon," he said.

I handed the book over as he spoke. She took it, held it in her hands for a long minute as she looked down at the cover. She ran her hand over it with a swish.

"Where did you find this?"

I glanced at Owen. We hadn't talked about that beforehand and I didn't know what our story was. But he was unflappable.

"In the town archives," he said simply. "It's on loan."

Slowly, she opened the cover. It cracked with its age. "It's old."

We both nodded. And my heart climbed to my throat in the hopes that I was going to finally—*finally*—get some real answers.

Her black-rimmed glasses perched on the end of her nose as she turned the pages with gentle care. Her gaze went over the strange words on the pages. The weird drawings. I watched intently as she turned the pages.

Owen sat stiff next to me.

Finally, Mrs. Rollins shook her head. "I'm sorry, dear," she said. "This isn't any language I recognize."

"It's not?" My voice was weak.

"No. Not Old English. Not Latin. Not even Gaelic," she said. "I can read a fair amount of Old English and Latin and I know Gaelic when I see it, but this..." She shook her head again. "This I don't know. It's something older. Something... specific. Whoever wrote it used an archaic language I've never seen. It reminds me of a mixture of cuneiform and ogham."

"Ogham?"

"You know. What the old Celts used. The Druids."

We both stared at her in silence. My heart climbed it's way back to my throat. Owen's whole body went still beside me—like she'd called him out. He coughed into his hand like he had a sudden allergy attack.

I finally got my brain back on track and asked, "So, you can't read it?"

"No, I'm afraid not."

All the air went out of my lungs along with the hope I'd been hanging onto like a lifeline. Next to me, Owen's hand brushed the back of mine. Like he was silently telling me everything was going to be okay.

She handed the book back to me. I laid it in my lap and glared down at it like it was nothing but a foreign object I'd never seen.

"Well, thanks for giving it a try," Owen said. "We appreciate it."

"I wish I could help," she said, then tilted her head with a soft smile. "You know, I used to watch you two compete in my class. All that energy between you—I knew it would turn into something eventually."

It seemed everyone in town had decided Owen and I should be a couple.

Heat crawled up my throat and settled in my cheeks.

But Owen took it all in stride as he got to his feet. "We appreciate the vote of confidence, Mrs. Rollins," he said with his easy charm and a flirty smile.

God, why was he so charming?

She walked us to the door. "If you do find someone who can read it, let me know. Scholarly curiosity, you know."

"We will," he said. "Thanks again."

And then we were back out in the afternoon heat walking to his truck. But I couldn't help but feel defeated.

"Don't give up yet," he said as he opened the car door for me.

"Who says I'm giving up?"

"I do because I can read the look on your face."

I frowned as I climbed into the truck. "You can?"

"Yes, and it's adorable." He closed the door and then rounded the back. A second later, he was getting in behind the wheel. "How about dinner?"

"Dinner?" I asked.

"Yes, Piper. You know. Food?"

"Oh." A breath escaped me. Like my body didn't know which feeling to feel first. The exhilaration of him asking me to dinner or the disappointment of not knowing what the book said.

"I'll cook for you," he said. "At my house."

That seemed awfully forward. Then he reached for my hand and pressed his lips against my fingers. "Bring your toothbrush."

Warmth spread through me the second he said the words. My throat went dry.

"I... I'm not sure I should leave the Red Queen and Tani alone together. Might be disastrous. And then there's the tree thing."

"You're making excuses," he said good-naturedly. "Then come for dinner. Or I'll cook at your place."

"Owen—"

"I'm moving too fast for you, aren't I?"

"No." I stared down at the grimoire like it might have the answer. Then, quietly, "Maybe a little."

The truth was, he *was* moving too fast and I wasn't ready for all that... togetherness. I'd already agreed to dinner at his parents tomorrow.

His hand never released mine. "I'm sorry. I'll slow down." He kissed my fingertips again, his mouth soft and warm against my skin. "I guess I'm making up for lost time."

Oh, he was killing me.

"Maybe I am making excuses," I said quickly, "but that doesn't mean I don't want to be with you."

His expression softened as he continued to hold my hand.

"I think you should know I had a someone in New York and... well, it didn't end well."

And that was all I wanted to say about that. There was no need to rehash that past or that he was a lying, cheating wretch.

"Oh," he said quietly. "You don't want to get hurt again."

I wanted to look away from him, but I didn't. I watched his profile as he kept his gaze on the road ahead. His expression was careful, thoughtful.

"Piper." He said my name so many different ways, but this one sounded reverent. "I will never hurt you."

Something deep in my chest twisted. I squeezed his hand.

"And," he added. "I don't want to rush you, either." His gaze flicked to mine for one second, then back to the road. "Because I respect you and I—"

He cut himself off, pressing his lips together. Like he was about to say something he was afraid to admit out loud.

"You...?"

"I'm glad you're back," he said. "That's all."

But I had the sneaking suspicion he wasn't telling me everything. So, I changed the subject in a hurry.

"I'm not saying no," I said. "Just... not tonight. If I leave Red and Tani alone together too long, I'm afraid I'll come home to the house covered in pink fairy dust and the possibility that Red has learned how to shop on the Internet."

He laughed at that. "That is a real possibility."

He pulled into his driveway and put the truck in park, still holding my hand. Quiet. Patient. The epitome of the perfect man sitting beside me and I had commitment issues.

But he was still looking at me like I was the best thing that ever happened to him and that did something funny to my insides.

"We'll try again tomorrow," he said. "After you come to dinner at my parents."

"Oh," I said on a breath. "Yes. Tomorrow."

"You're still coming, right?" He sounded worried.

I met his gaze. "Of course."

Relief creased his features. "Good. I'll pick you up at noon."

I reached for the door and exited the truck. He was out, too, rounding the hood and stopped in front of me. He reached for my hand.

"Sure you won't change your mind about dinner?"

I grinned. "You'll see me tomorrow, McAllister."

He made a low, appreciative sound in his throat, then pulled me closer. "You keep calling me that and you won't be able to leave."

Before I could reply, he kissed me. Long, slow, thoughtful. Deep. Determined to keep me in his orbit for as long as possible.

"I'll see you tomorrow," I said.

He released me.

And as I got into the car to drive away, back to the house on Snapdragon, my heart ached with regret.

It was late afternoon by the time I returned home.

A strange car was in my driveway and Agent Voss was standing on my front porch looking furious with his hands on his hips. Like he was angry I wasn't home. I frowned. He was not a welcome visitor. And I didn't have the energy to deal with him.

I steeled my nerves as I got out the car holding the grimoire cradled in one arm.

"Where's your guard dog?" he asked.

Not the best way to start a conversation with me. "If you mean Owen," I snapped, "he's home."

His gaze flicked over me, pausing on the book.

"What do you want, Voss?" I climbed the porch steps, my steps weary, clutching my keys in my fist. I didn't want to open the door and invite him in. He wasn't welcome.

"The Crossroads is still open."

"It's currently contained and will be closed soon enough," I said, thinking of the Sun Disk.

His gaze flatlined as he stared at me. "It doesn't appear you're taking this job as Guardian seriously, Miss Wakefield."

"I am."

"You're too busy trying to get a date rather than do your job. The flower shop was closed today."

I glared at him. "I know," I snapped. "I had to. I was trying to get—"

I bit off my retort because he didn't know about the grimoire and I didn't want him to.

He didn't even notice.

"That's unacceptable. The Council—"

"You and the Council can mind your own business. I have everything under control."

I was tired of this pushy guy.

"The Council," he continued as if I hadn't spoken, "has made a motion to remove you as Guardian and replace you with someone who can handle the Crossroads."

I stiffened, staring at him. "That is unacceptable. Alice—"

"I explained to them Alice was dead and you've failed."

"How dare you—"

"However," he continued, talking over me. "I told them you were trying your best given that you had no knowledge of the Crossroads prior to Alice's death."

"Gee, thanks." I wasn't sure that was a win.

"And," he said, "they've agreed to give you seventy-two hours to return the Red Queen and the fairy queen back to their rightful realms as well as close the Crossroads."

"Seventy-two hours," I said, my voice flat. "You think I can do all that in three days?"

"You have no choice," he said. "I told them I'd monitor the situation and will report back. If you fail again, Miss Wakefield, you will be removed."

And he sounded delighted by that fact. Like he was expecting failure.

I lifted my chin. "Do what you must, but I'll see that the Crossroads are closed for good before your deadline."

He gave me one curt nod. "See that you do."

And then he was stepping down off the porch and heading to his car. I stood there in the late afternoon heat, sweat rolling down my back, watching him pull away and disappear down the country road.

"Jerk face," I muttered.

Seventy-two hours. I had seventy-two hours to close the Crossroads and push two queens back to their respective realms. One I wasn't so sure would go.

I stood there for the longest time with the grimoire clutched in my arm breathing through the urge to panic. I could do this. I *had* to do this because now I had no choice.

The problem was, I had no idea where to start—and the clock didn't care.

Chapter Twenty-Five

I entered the house to late afternoon sunlight slashing across the worn living room. I expected to find one of the queens lounging there, but neither were present.

No broken lamps.

No fairy dust littering the floor.

Just an empty box of Cheez-Its on the coffee table.

I closed and locked the front door, then headed to the basement still clutching my handbag and the grimoire.

The place was still a disaster zone from my previous potion-making—I hadn't had time to clean it up. I made space for the book and placed it on the counter, then opened the drawer and started going through papers.

"There you are!"

Tani exploded in front of me in a shower of pink fairy dust scaring me half to death. I sucked in a breath and pressed my hand to my chest.

"Tani! We talked about this."

"Sorry. Was excited to see you." She landed on the counter next to the book and lounged against it. "So, you and Mr. Hottie...?"

"Owen," I corrected. "And?"

"He cooked you breakfast," she said. "Does that mean he spent the night?" She waggled her eyebrows.

"That's none of your business." I flipped a page in one of the folders, scanning it. Nothing.

"Sure it is. I live here, too."

"You live in the greenhouse," I reminded her. "And if Voss has his way, not for much longer."

That got her attention. She straightened. "What does that mean?"

"It means," I said, turning another page. "He was on the porch when I got home with an ultimatum. He expects me to send you and Red back to your own realms."

"I have to find Oberon first," she said. "That was the deal."

I ignored her grousing. "Also, the Council has given me seventy-two hours to figure this out or I'm gone as Guardian."

Silence. She didn't move. Her wings didn't even flutter. Then she poofed full-size in a burst of glittery fury.

"Then we better figure this out, chica. What are you looking for?"

That gave me an idea. I stopped my frantic search and pointed to the book. "Know what that is?"

"A book."

"Very funny." I flipped open the cover. "Can you read it?"

She squinted down at it, flipped a page. Then shook her head. "No. Where did you get it? I've never seen it before."

"Doesn't matter," I said quickly. It mattered, but I didn't want to explain it. "If you can't read it, I have to find someone who can. Or something in these files that will help translate it."

Tani reached into the drawer, pulled out a file, and slapped it on the counter like she meant business. "I can help."

I hesitated, staring at her.

Trust was a luxury. But so was doing this alone.

"Fine," I said, shoving another stack of folders toward her. "Then start reading."

Tani slapped open the file and started humming as she flipped pages like she was looking for her favorite dinner recipe instead of a decoder to a magical book.

At least, I assumed it was a magical book.

The grimoire sat on the counter beside her—innocent-looking, if you ignored the fact that it felt like a live wire every time I got too close.

"Receipts. Lists. Nothing important," Tani announced. "Human realm is obsessed with paper trails." She paused and heaved a dramatic sigh, as if she was offended by accounting.

Then she eyed the book. "What do you suppose it says?"

"I have no idea," I said. "That's why I need to figure out how to read it."

"And you think this book has something to do with closing the Crossroads?"

That was a good question.

I reached for the grimoire without thinking to steady myself, to have something solid.

The leather warmed under my palm.

Not heat from the room. Not friction.

Warmth like recognition.

My breath caught. I snatched my hand back like it had burned me.

Tani's eyes narrowed. "It likes you."

"I think," I said slowly, forcing my voice to stay normal, "I'm running out of options."

Tani closed the folder and shoved it aside. "Fine. Next victim." She reached for another file.

"MM," she read aloud. "Who's MM?"

I looked over at the folder she held. The label was in Alice's handwriting—the two letters, neat and deliberate.

"I don't know," I said.

Tani opened it.

Inside were notes written in Alice's hand—but not in English. The same strange language that filled the grimoire.

"Oh," I breathed.

"Like the book." Excitement danced in Tani's eyes, like she'd found the secret menu.

"But this does us no good," I said. "I still can't read it."

"What do you suppose MM means?" she asked. "Initials?"

Initials. Maybe. I nodded. "Someone Alice knew. Someone helping her."

Tani pointed to a place further down the page. "This handwriting is different. More loopy."

She was right. Not Alice's sharp precision. Someone else's.

"Maybe MM's," I said.

Tani nodded, pleased with herself. "So your dead witch-mom had a pen pal."

"She had an ally," I corrected.

"Same thing," Tani said, and flipped to the next page.

"Let's keep looking," I said.

We kept searching. Papers scattered everywhere. File folders stacked two and three deep. Every drawer emptied. Every page shuffled.

Delivery receipts that were at least a decade old. Phone orders from people in town that she'd kept for years. A sketch of the greenhouse out back—like she was trying to envision it before it was built.

"Hoarder," Tani muttered as she shuffled more papers.

"Thorough," I corrected, though by the piles of papers everywhere I was starting to agree.

I peered down in the drawer I'd emptied to make sure I got everything out when I noticed a seed catalog at the bottom. Like it had fallen out of the folder and Alice never noticed. The cover was bent at odd angles. I rescued it and placed it on the counter in front of me. I don't know why but I started flipping through it.

There, stuck against the crease in the middle of the book, was a scrap of paper folded in half. Like it had been stuck there absently.

I unfolded and read it.

MM. Old ways. Crossroads. Stellar convergence.

What did that mean?

Tani peered over my shoulder.

"Stellar convergence?" Tani asked.

"Something about the Crossroads and a stellar convergence—but what? Planetary alignment?" This was, of course, rhetorical. Tani wouldn't know.

To prove me right, she shrugged.

Someone knew the old ways. Someone was helping her. Someone with the initials MM.

"Maybe it's like astrology," she said.

My brows drew together. "What do you know about astrology?"

"You know. Like Mercury retrograde. Don't sign contracts. That sort of thing."

I stared at her. How did she know about that?

"Maybe." And then I forced away a yawn.

I glanced down at the book again and froze. All my thoughts fled as I stared down at the open page.

Staring back at me was a picture of the mystery flower in the cooler. The one that preferred to be in the cold with pale pink petals brushed with blue translucent edges. The name of the flower was Moonpetal.

I had a name for the mystery blooms in the flower shop. And now I had a place to buy the seeds.

"Oh." It came out on a breath.

"What is it?" Tani peered over my shoulder at the open page.

"Moonpetal," I said.

Maybe the note was related.

"Alice grew those in the greenhouse."

My head snapped up. "She did?"

"Got them started," she said around a yawn. "Then moved them to the flower shop cooler. The blooms are winter flowers."

This felt significant. I closed the seed catalog. Then picked it up with the scrap of note and the grimoire.

"Let's call it a night," I said.

"Good idea."

She poofed into fun-size Tani and vanished in a flash—leaving me alone in the basement with a stack of questions and one bright, clear thread.

Moonpetal.

Alice had been planting them long before I came home. And now I needed to find out why.

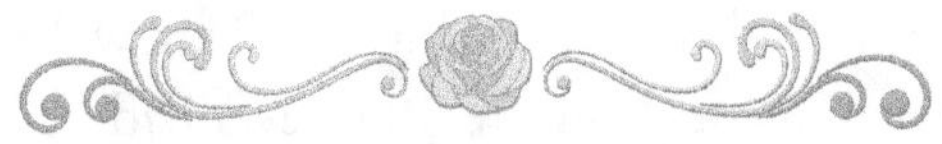

Chapter Twenty-Six

Sunday arrived, and my stomach twisted in knots.

Owen said he'd pick me up at noon, which gave me ample time to go to the flower shop and make an arrangement for his mother. I'd closed the shop for the weekend—a much needed break for me and Rylyn. While there, I paused outside the cooler and peered at the Moonpetal flower in the unmarked bucket. The open flower was exactly like the one in the seed catalogue.

"What was the plan for that, Alice?" I asked.

Silence answered me back.

Busying myself with making the arrangement helped keep my mind off everything I'd found in the basement. I'd chosen a tall, clear vase for a vibrant arrangement with orange roses, hot pink carnations, yellow snapdragons, Asiatic lilies and filled it in with assorted greenery and purple statice. It looked happy and cheerful and I was rather proud of it.

I gave one last glance at the Moonpetal—stopping to snap a picture with my phone—before I closed the shop.

Back at the house, I stared at the clock that said 11:53 like it was a dare. Sunday dinner—which is what good Southern folk called the midday meal—at his parents' house was a big deal. I chose an airy sundress in pale blue, sleeveless, with a sweetheart neckline and my favorite strappy sandals with a kitten heel. I'd even shaved my legs which meant I was taking this more seriously than I should.

I reminded myself this was not a big deal. I knew the McAllisters. Had known them most of my life. But never had I been invited to Sunday dinner after church.

I was also bursting at the seams to tell Owen what Tani and I discovered last night in the basement. I was still wired about that because, despite my fatigue, I didn't get much sleep.

I used my best concealer to fake rested human, swiped on my favorite pale pink lip gloss and hoped that was enough to keep me from looking like I'd been up all night.

The crunch of tires on the driveway caught my attention. Somehow, I managed to keep my composure calm as he rang the doorbell. The perfect gentleman. Impulse wanted me to bolt for the door, but I forced my feet to take normal steps.

He stood on the other side of the door looking far too handsome and far too cool for a hot summer afternoon—clean dark jeans, a blue button-down (funny how we seemed to match without trying), sleeves rolled halfway up his forearms, and his favorite scuffed, well-loved boots. The collar was open at his throat, giving me a hint of what I knew was underneath.

He'd even shaved.

Which was frankly unfair to my raging hormones.

"Hi," I said, which was a ridiculous opening line.

"Hi, yourself." His appreciative gaze swept over me, one corner of his mouth lifting. "Maybe you should come to Sunday dinner more often. It'll make the dinner table a whole lot prettier."

I flushed at that.

"Ready to go?" he asked.

I waved him inside. "Yes. I need to grab my purse."

I closed the door after him. He waited with his hands in his pockets as I slung the crossbody bag over my shoulder that contained everything I'd found last night plus the grimoire and the scrap of paper in Alice's handwriting. I intended to talk to him about that on the way.

Then I picked up the vase of flowers.

"Flowers?" His brows lifted.

"Yes. I do own a flower shop, you know." As he eyed them, I thought maybe they weren't a good idea or it was too forward or too... something. "They're for your mother. Is that okay?"

He stared at them for the longest time, then his gaze traveled back to mine. His throat worked once. "She'll love them. Did Rylyn do the arrangement?"

"No, I did."

He stilled as he looked at me. "Beautiful and talented."

Such a simple compliment but it made me blush.

Then he was turning toward the door and opened it for me. But I was fumbling with my keys trying to lock the door.

"Let me."

He took the keys from me, locked the door, then put his hand on my elbow and guided me down the steps.

And for some reason that gesture made my heart skip. Ridiculous.

He opened the truck door for me but it was going to be awkward to climb inside in a dress holding a vase of flowers. Without asking, he took the vase from me. We stood there in the open truck door for a long minute, the midday breeze ruffling his hair and something inside me nearly cracked.

For the briefest of seconds the thought that Owen McAllister was too good for me pounded through my head.

He held out his other hand to help me climb inside and I did all sorts of ridiculous adjustments to my skirt, fluffing it over my knees. He watched with an intense amusement that made me regret my choice of outfit.

Once I was settled, I held out my hands for the vase. He handed it over, our hands brushing and my heart flipped. Then he leaned in and kissed me.

"Oh," I breathed. "What was that for?"

"For being you."

Then he closed the door, rounded the hood, and climbed in the driver's side. My heart was pounding hard now, my nerves on edge.

He started the truck and pulled out of the driveway and then we were off down the road. The truck smelled like him—faint traces of his cologne and country road dust and something that reminded me of being tangled up with him in his arms. That didn't help my nerves. The radio played low—a country song I half-recognized.

"Voss paid me a visit yesterday afternoon," I blurted.

His gaze cut toward me. He didn't look happy. "What did he want? Why didn't you call me?"

I ignored his last question and forged onward. "He told me if I didn't get the Crossroads closed in seventy-two hours, the Council was replacing me as Guardian."

His hands tightened on the steering wheel. A muscle ticked in his jaw.

"Also," I added before he could say anything, "I have to return Tani and Red to their realms."

"You should have called me," he said.

"So you could do what? Glare at him appropriately?"

"Piper—"

"You couldn't have done anything," I said. "He was there with a ticking clock and an ultimatum. I have to find a way."

"Piper," he said again, more slowly. "I thought we were a team."

He never looked away from the road as he said it and something in his voice told me his pride was wounded.

I didn't know what to say to that, so I said nothing as trees flashed by.

We were a team? All this time I'd been operating from the fact that I was figuring this all out on my own. Even though I knew he was there to help me, I didn't want to depend on him like a safety net.

"I did want to call you," I admitted. "But I... I don't know. I thought I could find something in Alice's files. And I did. Tani helped."

This time he did glance my way. "What did you find?"

"Someone with the initials MM was helping Alice," I said. "I found a note. Something about the old ways and stellar convergence. It was tucked into a seed catalogue on a page with a particular flower. One that's in an unlabeled bucket in the flower shop cooler. I think they're all connected, Owen."

He was silent as he stared straight ahead, his hands gripping the steering wheel. He turned down a tree-lined road that gave way to houses dotting the rolling grasses.

"MM," he finally said, calm and careful.

There was something about the way he said it that gave me pause. Something that suggested he might know something.

"Do you know who that is?"

"Maybe." He still wouldn't look at me. "I don't want to get your hopes up if I'm wrong."

"Oh," I said. And then pressed my lips together.

I peered out the windshield as he turned into a drive and went through an iron gate that was already open with a big initial M in the center of it.

The sprawling single-story ranch house fit against the landscape like it had always belonged there. The gabled roof stretched wide and low and the deep front porch ran nearly the entire length of the front of the house. A swing was on one end, drifting lazily in the faint breeze. Large windows on the front invited natural light into the home. Flower beds lined the front of the house with a riot of antique rosebushes—Mrs. McAllister's pride and joy.

Mr. McAllister's old pickup coated in red dirt was parked out front in the gravel drive. A four-door sedan next to it.

I knew where his parents lived, of course. But I had never been to the house. Most of my interaction with his parents had been at school functions like open house and PTA meetings.

But now that I was seeing it and he was parking, my mouth turned dry.

He put it in park and cut the engine and we sat there, neither of us moving.

"Piper, about my mother..." he started, turning to face me. His voice had that grave edge that made my stomach tighten. "She's still fighting the cancer."

My chest went tight. "Owen..."

"She's in chemo," he said. "So—she's tired a lot. Some days are better than others." His jaw flexed once. "And she lost her hair."

"Oh." I swallowed hard. "I didn't know."

"We haven't exactly been... doing normal updates," he said quietly. Then he looked at me, eyes steady. "Here's what you need to know."

I nodded, heart thudding.

"She hates pity," he said. "If you ask how she's doing, she'll tell you. If she doesn't bring it up, don't make her talk about it." A faint, humorless smile tugged at his mouth. "And don't say 'you look great' like it's a consolation prize. She'll eat you alive."

Despite myself, a tiny breath of laughter escaped.

"Follow her lead. Let her set the tone."

I nodded again. "Okay."

"And one more thing," he said, softer. "If she offers you a hug, take it. If she doesn't—don't force one. She's careful right now."

"Got it," I said. "I can do that."

His shoulders loosened a fraction, like he'd been holding his breath.

"She's going to love you," he added. Then he glanced away, back toward the house. "She already does. She's been asking about you."

"She has?" That surprised me. I could count the times I'd met her in person on one hand.

He nodded. "Since you came back to town."

Well, that wasn't disconcerting at all.

"Ready?" he asked.

I nodded.

We climbed out, and Owen took the vase from my hands so I could manage my dress and dignity.

At the porch steps, he handed the flowers back with a grin. "I don't want her to think those are from me."

Together, we walked toward the house.

Before we even reached the porch, the door opened. A tall, slender woman stood framed in the doorway. She had the same gray eyes as Owen, the same smile, and my chest tightened.

Her head was wrapped in a colorful scarf, and a simple cotton dress hung too loosely on her frame.

But her eyes were bright. Her smile was warm. She looked genuinely happy to see us.

"Owen, it's about time you brought her here," she said, voice strong. She waited while we climbed the steps. "Look at you, Piper. All grown up."

"Hi, Mrs. McAllister."

"Oh, call me Madeline, please. Mrs. McAllister is my mother-in-law."

My hands tightened on the vase. Everything inside me froze.

Madeline McAllister.

MM.

I looked at Owen, but his face was impassive.

Owen's mother had to be the one helping Alice. The one who knew the old ways.

"Are you two going to stand there all day in the heat or come inside?" Madeline asked.

"These are for you," I managed, handing her the vase.

She took it, eyes lighting with delight. "Oh, Piper. They're lovely. From your shop?"

I nodded.

Owen said, "She did the arrangement."

"Of course she did." Madeline grinned. "You have a talent for it, like Alice. Now come inside. It's hot enough to scald a lizard out here."

Inside, the house was cool and smelled like Sunday dinner—pot roast, fresh bread, and something sweet baking in the oven. The living room had a lived-in, comfortable home look with furniture that had been well-worn and well-loved. Family photos were everywhere, which was such a contrast to the house I grew up in.

The living room had built-in bookshelves on one end that were filled top to bottom with books. Old ones. And as we entered, Madeline put the vase of flowers on the coffee table and motioned for us to sit.

But my eyes were still on the bookshelves because I thought I saw something familiar. Something with the same lettering as the grimoire stamped on the spine, the gold glittering in the lamplight. I couldn't stop staring at it.

Madeline followed my gaze, then she looked back to me.

"Owen," she said, "why don't you help your father in the kitchen. I want to get to know this young lady."

He hesitated, glancing between the two of us but I was frozen in place. The last thing I wanted was to be left alone with his mother.

Finally, he nodded, pressed a kiss to my temple, and then was gone.

When he was out of the room, she looked me over with a critical eye.

"He likes you," she said.

I nodded. "Yes, I think so."

"Good. That will make things easier." She held a hand out to me. "Come sit with me."

I wasn't sure what that meant, but I took her hand, anyway—it felt frail in mine—and we crossed the room to the sofa and sat together.

"What do you know?" she asked, point blank.

I blinked. "I'm sorry?"

"About the Crossroads," she said, as if that cleared everything up.

I stared at her, my mind blank.

"What did Alice tell you?"

"Very little," I said.

She was silent, her mind working, then she nodded once. "Then we have a lot to discuss."

Chapter Twenty-Seven

Madeline's gaze swept over me once as she leaned back into the cushions of the sofa. Her expression was unreadable but if I had to guess I'd say she looked like she was trying to decide what to tell me and where to start.

Owen had disappeared into the kitchen with no hope of rescue. I wasn't sure what to do with my hands so I sat there, ramrod straight and waited for her to say something—anything.

"I was helping Alice," she said finally.

That spurred me into action. I reached into my oversized handbag and brought out the grimoire, the seed catalog and the scraps of paper I'd found. The first one—the one with her initials—I unfolded and handed to her.

"I found this."

She took it, stared down at Alice's handwriting, her gaze sweeping across the scrawled line. Then she looked at me.

"Does Owen know?" I asked before she said anything.

"No," she said. "And neither does my husband."

I blinked. She'd been helping Alice and never breathed a word to either Dougal or Owen.

"Why?"

"I didn't tell them because Alice didn't want anyone else to know about her struggle," she said.

"Dougal was helping her, too," I pointed out.

She nodded. "I know about the treasures she hid in the shop."

"Why was she hiding them there?" I asked, my heart clanging in my chest hoping for answers.

She shook her head. "I only know she was hiding them to keep them out of someone else's hands."

That didn't help at all. I sank back into the cushion.

"Alice knew the Crossroads was failing. That's why I was helping her. We patched it up," she said. "More like covering it with a bandage than fixing it permanently. The fix only lasted one moon cycle."

I stared at her. "You know what I need to do, don't you?"

"I know what you can do to hold it back." She nodded. "Stellar convergence. There's a celestial event when the planets align—a planet parade, if you will. Mercury, Venus, Saturn, Jupiter, Uranus, and Neptune will appear to line up. That's when you need to act."

"When does that happen?"

Her eyes didn't flinch. "Tonight."

Of course.

But something else clicked in my head. If the planet parade was happening tonight, and Voss gave me the ticking clock—then did he know it was happening? Did he know my window of opportunity was shrinking? Did he intend to remove me as Guardian no matter what?

I flipped open the seed catalog to the page I found with the note and turned it to show her. "That note was stuck between these pages."

Madeline peered down at it for the longest time. "Moonpetal." Then her gaze flicked up to mine. "Do you have some?"

"Yes, in the cooler in the shop."

"Good."

She rose and crossed the room to the bookshelf. She pulled down a weathered book with a cracked leather spine, then returned to me, flipping it open. The language was exactly the same as in the grimoire. My heart pounded so hard I thought it would beat out of my chest.

Madeline paused at one of the pages, then placed it open with care on the coffee table next to the vase of flowers.

"You need this." She tapped the page with her fingernail.

"What is it?"

"An enchantment. And you'll need the Moonpetal flower but I'm afraid I can't help with the potion. Only Alice knew that."

So there was an enchantment and a potion. But I was still lost.

Madeline looked at me, then reached for me. She placed her cold hand on mine and gave it a little squeeze.

"You don't know what to do."

I shook my head.

That got me thinking about the other scrap of paper I found and the grimoire. I pulled the book from my bag.

"Owen and I found this in the town archives." I showed her the book.

Recognition flickered through her gray eyes. "The town archives?"

I nodded. She took the book from me and started flipping pages. "This belonged to Alice, though I don't know why it ended up there."

"Maybe for safekeeping?" I suggested.

As she flipped pages, I saw it. The torn page.

"Wait," I breathed. "Go back."

She flipped back and there it was, sticking out of the binding of the book like a puzzle piece waiting for its mate.

"The page is missing," she said.

My hands were shaking when I reached into my bag once more. I opened the folded page that I'd found in the cash register and held it up. The jagged edge looked like a perfect fit to the book.

Oh.

With a shaking hand, I placed the page against the torn one.

It fit.

A perfect fit.

My pulse kicked into high gear. Madeline breathed in quick through her nose.

And then we both watched as the torn page fused with the one in the book. Gold light danced along the jagged edge leaving nothing but a faint line. The pencil marks came together, as though forming one complete sentence. One complete thought.

Relief hit first. Then annoyance because the letters might as well have been star charts.

This didn't help me at all. But at least I knew where the page belonged now.

Beneath my hand, the grimoire warmed. As though it recognized me and the page.

"Piper," she said slowly. "That's the instructions for the potion."

My head snapped up. "The potion?"

"For the Crossroads. The one you'll use with the enchantment."

"You can read it," I said, still stunned.

Of course she could read it. She could read the book she showed me.

"Yes."

"I can't read it."

"Then I'll translate it for you." She smiled then. "I'm glad Owen brought you."

"So, am I."

Madeline ran her finger down the page as she read it, her gaze intent as it focused on every word. I waited, holding my breath.

"The potion requires essence of Moonpetal," she said. "Mixed with a teaspoon of vervain, a tablespoon of hickory sap, and a single drop of Guardian blood."

"Blood?" I swallowed hard. "Mine?"

She nodded, "Yes, Piper. Yours. To bind it to you and the land."

The realization hit me hard. Hickory Hollow wasn't just a place I lived—it was tied to me bone-deep.

I pulled out my phone and opened the notes app, typing quickly with the tip of my finger to get down the ingredient measurements before I forgot. "What else?"

"The Sun Disk," she continued. "You'll need it to place at the crossing while you recite the enchantment during the planetary alignment." She was still looking at the page as she spoke. "Then pour the potion over the roots of the tree."

I abandoned trying to use the tip of my finger and went for both thumbs to type faster. I got it all down.

"And this will seal the Crossroads?" I asked.

"Only for one lunar cycle." She looked up at me then, her dove gray eyes meeting mine. "Thirty days. Less if the contamination is worse than Alice realized."

I dropped the phone into my lap. "Only thirty?"

Thirty days wasn't enough time to mend the Crossroads, deal with the chaos living under my roof, or even find Alice's murderer… but it might be enough time to keep the town from being obliterated.

"It's only a temporary binding but that should buy you some time to figure out how to close it permanently. Time to discover who's poisoning the tree. And," she paused, took a deep breath, "who killed Alice."

The words hung between us and her tone of voice was soft, reverent, emotional.

"You were close?" I asked.

Her eyes were watery and it was clear she was trying to hold back the tears. "There at the last we were. She was… worried. I think she knew something was going to happen to her."

I eased back into the cushion of the sofa, my hand gripping the phone so tight it ached. "Did she… talk about me?"

That seemed to brighten her. "All the time. She loved you, Piper."

Then she reached for me, her cool hand on my cheek. "I see her in you."

And that nearly did me in. My throat closed. I swallowed hard. "She was my mother."

I don't know why I told her that. I hardly believed it myself. Her hand never moved from my cheek as she looked at me, her eyes going soft and her mouth curling at the ends.

"I know," she whispered.

That caught me off guard. It was deeply unfair that the entire town—even Tani—could see I belonged to Alice before I did.

"You did?"

"She never told me. But I knew. The way she talked about you. Worried about you." She dropped her hand back to her lap then.

"I wish she'd told me." It was too much to bear.

"She was protecting you from whatever was happening," she said. "And that's why you have to be the one to finish it." Then she turned all business. "Now, here's what you need to do. The planetary alignment will be visible in the western sky at 10:47 pm tonight. You'll need to be ready and at the Crossroads before then."

I picked up my phone and started tapping again making notes.

She walked me through it, step by step. The enchantment words—which she made me practice until I could say them without stumbling.

"You'll need to memorize them," she said.

I nodded. She kept going, giving me the order of the ritual, where to place the Sun Disk, how to pour the potion, what to expect once it was all done.

"The boundary will feel different than before," she warned. "Stronger. But also... hungry. It will want to pull magic from you to sustain itself. Don't let it take too much."

"How do I stop it?"

"The Sun Disk," she said. "It anchors you. As long as you're touching it, the seal can't drain you dry."

I wrote it all down. Every word.

When she finished, I looked up. "What if it doesn't work?"

Madeline's expression softened. "Then you call me. And we try again."

"You'll help me?"

"Honey," she said, "I'm not letting Alice's daughter face this alone."

Footsteps sounded in the hallway. Owen appeared in the doorway, two glasses of sweet tea in his hands.

"Dinner's ready," he said, looking between us. His gaze lingered on my face. "Everything okay?"

"Everything's fine," Madeline said smoothly. "We were getting to know each other."

She patted my leg like we were old friends. Owen didn't look convinced, but he handed me a glass anyway.

I took a sip, grateful for something to do with my hands.

Tonight. I had to seal the Crossroads tonight.

And I had less than nine hours to figure out how to make a potion I'd never made before, using a flower I barely understood, with magic I was still learning to control.

And Owen didn't know yet what tonight was about to ask of me.

What it might ask of us.

Chapter Twenty-Eight

Dinner was slow-cooked pot roast—fall-apart tender—served with buttery mashed potatoes and a rich gravy made from the cooking juices. There were green beans with bacon that tasted like the best thing that ever happened to me, and of course, Madeline's homemade biscuits—hot, soft, and unfairly perfect, especially considering she'd "somehow whipped them up" while I was having an existential crisis in her living room.

And then, as if she wasn't already showing off, dessert.

Homemade peach cobbler with Blue Bell vanilla ice cream.

I was pretty sure I'd died and gone to heaven. If heaven came with homemade cobbler, I'd like to file a formal complaint for being kept from it this long.

I was also so stuffed I didn't know how I was going to get up from the table again without assistance and a forklift.

Between bites, I was regaled with tales of Owen and his older brother, Colt, growing up and getting into all sorts of trouble. Owen, however, looked less than amused—chin tipped down, that familiar warning in his eyes.

"... the time Owen decided he could jump the creek on Colt's ten-speed," Dougal was saying.

"Dad," Owen groaned. "Please, stop."

"What happened?" I asked, smiling.

Dougal ignored him with the confidence of a man who knew how to embarrass his children. "Didn't make it. Fell right in. Came home dripping wet and covered in mud."

I giggled.

"Maddy made me hose him off before she'd allow him to step foot in the house," Dougal added.

He reached for Madeline's hand and gripped it. She was grinning at him—soft and bright, like the story lived somewhere warm inside her.

"I'd just mopped," she said. Then her gaze met mine. "And there was no way I was allowing muddy footprints on my clean floors." She sounded indignant even now.

I laughed.

"Colt was mad for weeks," Dougal said.

"Why?" I asked.

"Because I ruined his precious bike," Owen said, a grin breaking through despite himself.

"He'd saved all summer for that bike," Madeline said.

"How old were you?" I asked.

"Eight. Colt was fourteen," Owen said. "I thought he was going to murder me. He didn't talk to me for days."

As I sat there listening, I realized something that made my throat tighten.

This was what had been missing from my childhood. Family that felt warm instead of... managed.

Iris wasn't exactly fun to grow up with, and Clay only cared about rodeos and when he could start riding bulls. And my parents?

They were never like this—casual, playful, trading stories like they liked each other.

The longing hit me harder than I expected.

Because I'd built an entire life pretending I didn't need this.

And sitting at the McAllister table, it was obvious I was lying to myself.

I blinked hard and lifted my tea glass to my mouth like I could drink my emotions back down.

Owen noticed, because he noticed everything.

"We should probably go," he said then.

"Let me send you home with some leftovers," his mother said.

Madeline pushed up from the table and grabbed her empty dessert plate. Then reached for mine. But Owen snatched it up before she could along with his and his father's. He gave her warning look, one that said he'd done this before and she better not argue.

"That's not necessary," I said.

"Nonsense," she said as she started for the kitchen. "I cooked enough food for a small army."

I glanced up at Owen who gave me a nod. "She did."

Then he headed off to the kitchen with the dirty plates. I sat there with his father listening to the clink of dishes and their low murmuring voices.

"Today was a good day," Dougal said, almost to himself. Then he added, "The visit and the flowers made her day."

And something about that one sentence warmed everything inside me.

"I'm glad," I said.

Minutes later, Owen returned with his mother. She carried several clear containers with lids. Inside, pot roast, gravy, potatoes. In another container, green beans. Biscuits. Cobbler.

"Mrs. McAllister, you're going to make me fat," I said with a laugh as she handed it over.

"Nonsense. And I told you to call me Madeline."

Then she stunned me by kissing my cheek and hugging me. I glanced at Owen over her shoulder. Surprise then delight crossed his face.

Like he'd won a prize.

"Owen, you bring her back here to see me, you hear?" she said.

"Yes, ma'am." He grinned, then kissed her cheek and hugged her.

"You two best get going. The Crossroads are waiting," she said.

Owen's smile faded at the word Crossroads. His gaze sharpened as if flipping a switch.

"I'll tell you on the way," I said.

I gathered my things and then we were out the door. It was already early evening as we walked to the truck in silence. He opened the truck door for me. Before I climbed in, his hand wrapped around my arm and stopped me. I turned to him. His hand rested on my waist, his gaze fixed on mine.

"She loves you," he said softly.

"Oh," I breathed. "Well... that's good, isn't it?"

He leaned in, kissed me, and said against my mouth, "Yes. I knew she would."

"I love her, too."

It was an admission I hadn't intended to make, but now that the words were out, I didn't want to take them back. His hand tightened on my waist. The way he was looking at me made my heart jolt and for a second, I stopped breathing. Like he wanted to say something but somehow kept it back.

"I'm glad."

Then he took the containers from my hand so I could climb into his truck. When I was settled and my seatbelt on, he handed them back, shut the door and rounded the hood of the truck.

I watched him. The easy way he walked. The way his held himself with confidence—the same way he'd always held himself even in high school. That hadn't changed. What had changed was he was older and even more attractive than I remembered from those days.

It was a good and bad thing. Good because, well, he was attractive. Bad because I didn't want to think of him with anyone else.

Once he was in the truck, he started it and put it in reverse.

"Your mother told me how to temporarily seal the Crossroads."

He hit the brakes hard enough to jar me and then turned to face me. "That's what you were talking about before dinner."

"Yes," I said with a nod. "She's MM but you knew that, didn't you?"

His hands tightened on the wheel. He regarded me then finally nodded.

"I suspected, but I wasn't sure."

"She was helping Alice. She didn't tell anyone. Not even your dad."

He swallowed hard and looked away, back through the windshield at the house. Like his mind was trying to understand that his mother was helping Alice like his father. They were both entwined with Alice in different ways. He said nothing.

"We have to go to the Crossroads tonight," I continued. "I need the Sun Disk and a flower from the shop."

His gaze traveled back to mine. "She told you this?"

I nodded. "The torn page I found was part of the grimoire."

He stared at me, then blew one breath out through his nose. "What else?"

"It's a lot." Honestly, I didn't know where to start.

"Then you better tell me everything."

He backed the truck, then turned and headed down the driveway toward the road.

"I will. And Owen?"

"Yeah?"

I studied his profile. "You're right. We *are* a team."

"Good," he said. "I wouldn't want it any other way."

As we drove, I told him everything his mother and I talked about—the grimoire, the potion, the planetary alignment, the fact that we had to be there to say the enchantment at exactly 10:47 pm. The sun was already burning toward the horizon and soon it would turn the sky into that pinkish-indigo of dusk.

We stopped at the antique store and picked up the Sun Disk. Watching Owen climb the ladder again and reach was not my favorite thing. Then we went to the flower shop and I picked two Moonpetal flowers. One that wasn't open yet and another that was. In case I screwed up the potion and needed a do-over.

The second I removed them from the cooler, they started to wilt.

"Are they supposed to do that?" he asked.

I shrugged. "I think so?"

"Then we better hurry and get back to your house so you can make that potion."

I couldn't agree more.

Back at my house, the Red Queen was lounging on the sofa. She'd traded her enormous red gown for sweatpants and one of my navy t-shirts. She had the remote in one hand—QVC again—and a package of cookies—my Chewy Chips-Ahoy—in the other.

"Red, where did you get those clothes?" I demanded.

"Tani helped," she said, her tone accusatory.

"I raided your dresser," Tani called from the kitchen.

"Oh, God," I groaned.

These two were getting far too comfortable here.

Next to me, Owen chuckled, but I was already on my way to the kitchen. He was right behind me.

"You didn't ask permission to do that," I said.

Full-size Tani lounged against the counter, her chin in her hand, flipping through one of my fashion magazines while waiting for the kettle to boil. The second she saw Owen, she straightened.

"Oh, you brought Mr. Hottie." She beamed.

He snickered.

"Please stop calling him that," I said as I pulled open the fridge and placed the leftovers inside. "And stay out of those containers."

She eyed the fridge with a curious glint in her eyes. "Why?"

"It's my food."

Then I took Owen's hand and led him out of the kitchen to the basement.

"Those two are going to be the death of me," I muttered.

He laughed.

The basement was still a terrible disaster—papers and file folders everywhere. I hadn't bothered to clean it up after last night, and I wasn't going to start now. I shoved stacks to one end of the worktable, then cleared off a space I could use.

Owen stopped at the edge of it. "What do you need?"

I pulled out the grimoire and placed it on the table, then flipped to the torn page—now fused back together like it had never been ripped.

He leaned over to look at it and went still. Then he reached out, his fingertip tracing the healed seam.

"This book was Alice's," he said.

I winced. I'd forgotten to tell him that part. "Yes. And your mother thinks she hid it in the town archives."

"Hoping you'd find it?" he asked.

"Or it would find me," I said with a shrug. "Either way, I have it. And now I know how to make the potion to temporarily close the Crossroads." I tapped the page. "But we have to move fast. We need to be there before the planetary alignment."

Owen pushed his sleeves up higher to his elbows. "Put me to work, boss."

Together, we made the potion—adding one drop of my Guardian blood like Madeline said.

And shockingly—I didn't mess it up.

I measured, poured, stirred, and followed Madeline's translated instructions like my life depended on it. Because it did. When the last ingredient hit the vial, the liquid shimmered a pinkish-blue, almost luminous.

We both stared at it.

"I sure hope this works," I whispered.

"Me too." Owen checked his watch. His expression tightened. "We should go."

"Right. Give me a minute to change." I pressed the vial into his hand. "Guard that with your life. And do not let Tani anywhere near it."

He nodded once, serious as a vow—and followed me anyway, up the stairs.

As we passed through the living room, Tani and Red were sitting side by side on the sofa watching *How the Universe Works*.

Willow was on the back of the sofa, her long orange body stretched out. Neither queen seemed to care she was there.

I halted. Stared.

Then blinked.

"At least they're not throwing things at each other," Owen murmured near my ear.

"Valid," I said faintly.

They didn't even look up. Or if they did, they refused to acknowledge us like two teenagers sneaking out past curfew.

Owen loitered in the hall while I changed out of my cute sundress into something more Crossroads/might-die-in-the-woods appropriate: faded jeans, my favorite *I'm Optimizing Joy* T-shirt, and comfortable shoes.

I ran a brush through my hair, checked my pockets—phone, keys—and decided that was as ready as I was going to get.

Ready to face whatever waited at the Crossroads.

I opened the bedroom door and met Owen's eyes.

"Here goes nothing," I said. "I hope this works."

"It will." He sounded confident.
Together we headed for the stairs.
Ready or not, the Crossroads was waiting.

Chapter Twenty-Nine

We made a quick stop at Owen's cottage so he could change out of his Sunday shirt into something else—a collarless three-button henley.

No matter what he wore, he looked good. And I was noticing it far too much.

Back in the truck, he drove us toward the Crossroads. I gripped the potion vial in one hand. The Sun Disk sat heavy in my lap. It was fully dark now and my stomach was in knots.

When he parked, he reached into the glove box and pulled out a flashlight.

"You're prepared," I said.

"Always," he replied, a brief smile cutting through the tension.

I started to reach for the door handle, but he stopped me with a hand on my arm.

"Piper—if anything goes wrong—"

"Nothing will," I said, too quickly. It couldn't. I wouldn't allow it. I needed this to work.

He stared at me in the dim cab, his dove-gray eyes nothing but dark orbs in the shadows. His hand stayed on my arm like he didn't trust the world not to steal me.

"I don't want anything to happen to you," he said.

The words tugged at me. I reached up and cupped his smooth cheek. "Don't worry. I've got this."

I sounded far more confident than I felt.

He caught my fingers in his hand and kissed my fingertips.

"We do this together," he said.

"Together," I agreed.

"And if anything happens," he murmured, low, "I'll be there."

I nodded.

Then he released me, and we climbed out into the night.

I clutched the Sun Disk and the potion and kept running the enchantment words through my head like a prayer I couldn't afford to forget.

Owen clicked on his flashlight and led us through the trees.

The clearing opened ahead—and the sick hickory tree waited like a wounded giant.

The smell hit first.

Rot and sulfur and something worse—something wet and wrong.

"Oh," I rasped, immediately regretting breathing. "That's awful."

"The tree is worse than we thought," Owen said.

He swept the beam down to the base of the trunk.

Black gunk oozed from the roots, bubbling and gurgling like a wound that refused to scab over. A foul-smelling miasma lifted from it and drifted into the still, humid air. More bark had been carved away from the trunk, leaving pale wood exposed.

I checked my watch. Just before ten.

Then I looked up at the sky. Without city lights, the stars were sharp and bright. Madeline said the planetary alignment would be visible in the western sky at 10:47.

I could already see the brighter points gathering—planets beginning to stack themselves into a line like the universe was holding its breath.

"All right," Owen said quietly. "You've got forty-seven minutes. Then it's go time."

I took a deep breath—which was a mistake because of the stench—and forced it out through my mouth.

"Should I place the Sun Disk now?" I asked.

"Yes," he said. "Get it ready."

I approached the bubbling ground, careful not to step in it, and certainly not to kneel in it. Owen's beam slashed across the mess, searching.

"There," he said, angling the light.

A narrow sliver of green clung near the base of the tree, like the earth was refusing to surrender completely.

I picked my way toward it. Owen stayed at my shoulder, close enough that I could feel him without looking.

"Place the Disk as close to the roots as you can," he said.

"I'm not sure I can with all this muck," I muttered.

I crouched, trying to find a stable spot. Owen lowered himself beside me, the white beam holding steady on the place he wanted.

I stretched my arm out, but it was out of reach.

"I can't reach it."

"Here—hold this."

I traded him the Sun Disk for the flashlight and aimed the beam where he'd had it. Owen leaned forward to place the Disk—

—and the light flickered.

My gut clenched.

"Hold it steady," he said.

"That wasn't me," I said, voice turning cold. "We're not alone."

A twig snapped.

Owen's head came up at the same time the darkness shifted at the edge of the clearing—taller, denser—like a shadow deciding to become a body.

Garrat stepped into the beam. This guy was wearing out his welcome in my town.

His smile was slow and knowing.

"I've been waiting for you, pretty," he said.

I shot to my feet. So did Owen, the Sun Disk still in his hand. He moved between me and Garrat without thinking.

I tightened my fist around the potion vial until my fingers cramped.

"Your ward wasn't going to keep me bound forever, druid," he purred.

"I'm here to send you back to wherever you came from, Garrat," I said.

I was proud of how steady my voice sounded. It didn't waver.

He tilted his head, amused. "You think so?"

"I know so."

The flashlight carved harsh angles across his face, turning beauty into something terrifying. He frowned—lines etching into shadow like a warning.

And the ooze at the base of the tree bubbled faster.

Garrat was using his magic on it—I felt it deep inside me. Not just on the ooze. On me.

A pull tightened behind my ribs and dragged forward.

Compelling.

My body started to obey before my mind caught up. I took a step, and Owen's arm snapped out, blocking me.

"Piper." My name—sharp as a warning.

I blinked hard, trying to clear my head.

"She's coming with me," Garrat said. His voice was rough now. Harsh. Like nails on a chalkboard.

"No," Owen said.

But I stepped forward anyway.

My foot landed at the edge of the bubbling goo, my shoe sinking into it with a wet, sickening sound.

"Piper," Owen said again—tighter, more urgent.

"That's right," Garrat murmured. "You want to come with me."

The pull was too strong. My throat tightened. My skin prickled. I couldn't resist.

He held out his hand. I reached for it.

Owen slapped my hand down—hard enough to sting—then shoved me backward behind him.

I came back to my senses, realizing what I'd almost done.

"You'll have to go through me," Owen said.

His voice had changed—darker, dangerous, like something old had stepped forward.

I blinked, still gripping the flashlight in one hand and the potion vial in the other. "Owen?"

"Then I'll go through you," Garrat said.

He lifted one hand. Not a grand gesture. Barely an effort.

A force slammed into Owen.

He flew backward like he'd been yanked by an invisible rope. The Sun Disk spun from his hand, skittering across the ground.

Owen hit with a terrible thud—and for a heartbeat, he didn't move.

"Owen!" I lurched toward him, panic punching through the compulsion.

"He can't help you, pretty," Garrat said, stepping closer. "Only I can."

My feet locked.

My thoughts went fuzzy at the edges, like cotton stuffed into my skull.

"If you come with me," he said, voice low and poisonous, "I can take you places you've only dreamed of. I can show you wonders. I can teach you magic."

Warm fog spread through me—sweet and false.

I turned toward him, swaying like a flower toward the sun. Garrat stood in the middle of the bubbling ooze as if it couldn't touch him, hands loose at his sides, patient.

Then he extended his hand again.

"Come, Piper. There's someone you need to meet."

Thunder cracked.

So loud the ground vibrated.

The sound punched straight through the fog. I jerked my head, startled back into my own body.

Owen was on one knee, one hand braced on the ground, the other flat to the earth like he was holding it down by sheer will. His face was thunder itself.

"She's not going with you."

I'd never heard him sound that ferocious.

Lightning streaked overhead, a jagged white scar across the sky.

"Get the Sun Disk, Piper!" Owen barked.

The ground vibrated again—and Garrat froze mid-step, teeth bared. Like Owen had pinned him to the earth.

I didn't think. I moved.

I scurried to where the Sun Disk had fallen. I dropped the flashlight—I couldn't afford to drop the vial—and snatched the Disk up with my free hand.

"Place it at the tree!" Owen said, voice still dark and dangerous.

Garrat strained, snarling, but he couldn't move. Owen's druid magic held him like a fist around his throat.

I clutched the Sun Disk in one hand and ran back to the sliver of green by the roots.

My shoes were already ruined, so I stepped into the oozing blackness and tried not to gag—or think about the smell—then dropped to my knees.

I stretched the Disk out and pressed it against the roots.

Instantly, it lit—gold blooming in a perfect circle, bright enough to paint the underside of the leaves.

I checked my watch.

Ten minutes to go.

Too much time between now and the planetary alignment. Too much time for Garrat to find a way out. Too much time for anything to go wrong.

I wasn't sure what to do next.

In my hand, the vial warmed. I glanced down at it. The potion had started to... glow. I sucked in a breath.

"Uh..."

"Piper." Garrat's voice. I lifted my gaze to him. "Don't you want to know what happened to your mother? Who killed her and why?"

I stared at him, my heart clawing its way to my throat.

"Y-yes."

"Don't listen to him, Piper!" Owen said. "He's trying to trick you."

"I have all the answers," Garrat continued as if he hadn't spoken. He lifted his hand toward me once again. "Come. And I will give them all to you."

The compulsion was so strong, I almost reached for him.

"She *will not.*"

Owen. His voice was feral. His face still a mask of thunder.

I glanced his way. Saw the blood dripping from his nose. Whatever he was doing to keep Garrat away from me, it was hurting him. A pang of terror went through me.

I had to do something. To act. Instead of standing here frozen like a weak lamb.

In my hand, the potion continued go glow brighter.

What did that mean? Did the ritual want to begin early?

On impulse, I reached for the Sun Disk, my free hand landing on it. The second my fingers touched it, it pulsed bright gold. So bright, in fact, that Garrat flinched and shielded his eyes.

And when that pulse subsided, the black ooze started to abate. As if the Sun Disk had something to do with its retreat.

That gave me hope.

"You fool," Garrat sneered. "You think you can defeat me?"

"Yes." I lifted my head and met his terrifying gaze. "I can and I will."

As I said the words, my chest burned bright and hot. The Sun Disk flared. The potion in my hand flared brighter—pink-blue light trapped in glass—until the vial was too hot to hold.

Overhead, the planets were beginning to align—though I couldn't spare a glance.

I didn't want to lift my hand from the Sun Disk, so I hooked the cork with my teeth, yanked it free, and spat it into the dirt.

"*Crossroads, hear me—hold and heed,*" I began. "*Take my blood, but not my need.*"

"NO!" Garrat shouted—and for the first time, real panic cracked through his voice.

The black ooze fizzed, like it recognized the words.

"*Hickory root and Moonpetal flame, I bind this gate in Guardian's name,*" I continued.

"Stop, Piper!"

"Keep going," Owen growled, his voice tight with strain. "Don't you stop."

"*Shut the seam and still the roar—*" My breath hitched as I tipped the vial. "*One moon's turn, and nothing more.*"

The last drop splashed against the roots.

The Sun Disk pulsed—gold so bright it turned the clearing white.

A hiss split the air.

Garrat screamed as the ground beneath him fractured open, a blinding fissure yawning like a mouth. Shadow and ooze and magic dragged downward at once—hungry in reverse.

Garrat clawed for purchase, but the earth took him anyway.

The bubbling blackness slurped into the crack as if the wound itself was drinking it.

Then the fissure snapped shut. The light vanished.

And the clearing went still. The Sun Disk stopped glowing.

I knelt there with my hand on it and the empty vial clenched in the other, afraid to move—as if the spell might snap the moment I breathed wrong.

The air smelled... cleaner. Not good. But less dead.

Somewhere in the trees, a single cricket chirped—hesitant, like it was checking whether it was safe to exist again.

My mind tried to make sense of what happened and came up with one ridiculous thought.

Huh. That worked.

Then reality followed, as it always did. I still had two queens living in my house.

A groan—and I sucked in a sharp breath.

Owen.

He'd collapsed on the ground. I dropped the empty vial and rushed to him. He was on his side, blood dripping from his nose.

"Piper?"

"Oh, God, Owen. Are you all right?" I reached for his hand, held it in mine. "You're bleeding."

"I'm all right." His voice was hoarse as he gripped my hand. "You did it."

I glanced up at the place where Garrat stood, where he threatened me, where he tried to take me. Where he promised me answers to questions I had about Alice.

"For now."

I helped him to a sitting position—though truthfully he didn't need my help. He swiped the back of his hand across his nose. It came away smeared with blood.

"It's still not over," I said.

"No, but now we have time to figure it out."

We. I loved that he said we.

The Crossroads still wasn't healed. Alice was still dead. The danger hadn't vanished.

But Hickory Hollow was still standing.

And for the first time since I came back, staying didn't feel like a sentence. It felt like a choice.

He reached for me, cupping my cheek. "The potion worked."

"Thanks to your mother's translations."

He pulled me close, his mouth a breath from mine. "See? Team effort."

Then his lips brushed mine.

We held onto each other as we both got to our feet. His arm went around my waist. My shoes were ruined. My knees were caked in that disgusting black ooze. And I smelled.

But Owen. He looked tired. Drained.

"That took a lot out of you," I said.

"Yes." He puffed out a breath as though he didn't want to admit it. "But I couldn't let him get his hands on you."

My heart swelled. He'd protected me so I could complete the enchantment.

"Maybe I should drive you back to your place," I said.

His arm tightened around me. "Maybe you should. And stay the night."

Oh.

Hot pinpricks exploded all over my skin. "I didn't pack an overnight bag."

A feeble excuse. He knew it.

He grinned. "That's ok. You won't need clothes."

Heat crawled up my neck and settled into my cheeks and I was profoundly grateful it was dark so he couldn't see.

"Owen..."

"Stay with me tonight." He pressed his forehead against mine. "The queens will be all right. They're watching the Science Channel."

And the thought of that made me snicker. Still, I had objections.

"But I... have the shop."

"Take the day off."

He was persistent. I swallowed hard.

How could I resist him?

"Okay but you take me home first thing in the morning."

"Mm. You drive a hard bargain, lady."

I smiled. "And you're persistent."

"It's one of my better qualities," he said.

He released me to retrieve the Sun Disk. I watched with relief flooding me. I may not have permanently closed the Crossroads—but I'd bought us time.

One thought kept circling back, quiet and persistent under all the relief.

There's someone you need to meet.

Who? The question burrowed in despite everything else. Garrat had dangled it like bait, which meant I probably shouldn't want the answer. But Alice had hidden me my whole life. From what, from whom—I still didn't fully know. My father was out there somewhere. And Garrat, apparently, knew exactly where.

That was either very useful or very dangerous.

Probably both.

As he took my hand and I followed him in the dark, I had only one thought. If I could survive the Crossroads, I could survive whatever came next.

Hickory Hollow. The magic. The fight still ahead of me.

And Owen McAllister.

Chapter Thirty

Morning pressed against the bedroom windows, washing the room in soft gray light with the promise of day.

I didn't sleep much. How could I when I was tucked into bed with the one person who seemed determined to keep me for himself? Owen hardly let me go all night.

And lying there beneath his ceiling, his arm heavy across me, it was impossible not to acknowledge what had taken root between us—the safety, the steadiness, the way he'd stood beside me at the Crossroads and shielded me when he didn't have to.

In high school, I'd wanted Owen to notice me. I think he did, in his own shy way. I think he held himself back because I'd been so vocal about leaving Hickory Hollow for my big-city-glam life.

But I was back now.

I wasn't leaving.

I had a mystery to solve, my aunt—no, my mother—to avenge, a flower shop to run.

And I had Owen.

I closed my eyes and let that sink in. My life had changed so drastically in the last few weeks it was hard to fathom—but I realized, with a strange calm, that I could accept it. Even the parts that had made me want to run.

The Crossroads had chosen me. The grimoire had chosen me.

And, it seemed, Owen had chosen me too.

Deep in my chest, something stirred. Emotion—yes. But something else. Something sharper, brighter.

My eyes flew open.

Magic.

It was magic inside me.

And it wasn't alone.

Next to me, it sensed Owen's druid magic—recognizing it the way the Sun Disk had recognized my touch. The way the grimoire warmed like it knew my name.

I turned my head to look at him.

His eyes were open. He was awake, watching me.

"You feel it," he said, voice rough with sleep.

"Yes," I whispered.

The magic in me reached toward him like it had at Neon Cowboy when we danced—like it couldn't help itself.

"Why does it... do that?" I asked.

"Magic calls to magic." He nuzzled my neck. "It means you fit me."

He planted one featherlight kiss against my skin.

"It means you're mine."

Oh.

Oh.

"It's too early for you to be this romantic, McAllister."

He chuckled against my throat. "It's never too early for that, missy."

And then he wrapped me closer like he had no intention of letting go.

Maybe it was the magic humming between us making me dizzy. Or the fact that he'd brought me to his cottage, handed me clean clothes—his—and let me shower off the stench of the Crossroads. Or the way his leg slid over mine and we were still tangled together like we belonged that way.

Whatever the reason, the feeling rose in me—hot and unsteady—threatening to spill over.

"Owen?" I asked quietly.

"Mmm?"

"I..." The words died.

Fear flared. Because if I said the thing I wanted to say, it would make everything real in a way I wasn't sure I was ready for.

So instead, I offered the safest truth I could manage.

"I like you more than I thought."

It was the closest I could get to the other words. Maybe it was close enough for now.

He went still against me, his face pressed to my neck. His arms tightened a fraction.

"I like you a lot, Piper," he said softly. "And I'm glad you're here. With me."

It should not have unraveled me as much as it did.

My eyes drifted closed.

And then, without thinking too hard about it, I whispered, "Me, too."

Eventually we had to get up. He loaned me a pair of sweatpants that were a bit too big and a shirt that was too baggy. But at least I didn't have to wear my ruined jeans that smelled like something had died on them.

When I dressed and headed into his kitchen—small, warm, comfortable—he was pouring a mug. Then handed it to me, the corner of his mouth lifted.

"I like you in my clothes," he said.

"Ha. Don't get used to it."

"I think it's too late for that." He smirked. "You also look good in my kitchen."

My cheeks heated. "Owen..."

"What? You do." He feigned innocence.

Which was adorable.

He was dressed, too. Wearing faded jeans, his boots, and an old faded t-shirt that was as soft as it looked. I sipped my coffee. He sipped his. And something about standing there in the early morning with the smell of freshly brewed beans did something to me. It was... domestic. And for a flash of a second, I could see us doing this every morning.

And that was terrifying and exhilarating at once.

"I should get home," I said. "Check on the queens."

He nodded. "I know." He reached a hand toward me. I took it. "But we can finish our coffee first."

My heart swelled. "Yes," I agreed. "We can."

Owen pulled into my driveway, put it in park, and then cut the engine. I gave him a curious look.

"I thought you were dropping me off?" I said.

"I thought I was coming inside with you to make sure the queens haven't destroyed anything."

I wanted to laugh but the way he looked at me made my heart melt. "All right then."

We exited the truck and he followed me up the porch steps. I clutched my still smelling clothes under my arm as I opened the door and pushed it open.

Red was still sitting on the sofa, her legs folded underneath her watching a cooking show on Food Network. Willow sat on the cushion next to her, paws tucked under her round body. Eyes closed. Purring. Tani was in the kitchen making tea.

My house was weird.

"Well, well, well!" Tani called from the kitchen. "Look what the cat dragged in."

Willow meowed a protest.

"No offense, Willow. I didn't mean you, specifically."

She replied with another meow-yawn.

Red looked at us both, blinked, and went back to watching her celebrity chef.

Tani, in full-size, leaned against the kitchen doorway, arms crossed. She eyed me in Owen's clothes with a smirk on her face.

"Don't start," I said.

"Start what? Looks like you two had a busy night." She waggled her eyebrows.

"The evidence does support that," Red said.

I rolled my eyes.

Next to me, Owen snickered. I turned to him. "You're not helping."

He shrugged. "We did have a busy night at the Crossroads."

"Crossroads?" That perked up Tani. She dropped her arms and stood straight.

Before I could answer, the doorbell rang.

"Early morning visitors are never a good thing," Tani said.

She wasn't wrong. I dropped my clothes in the nearest chair and went back to the door to open it.

Agent Voss stood on the other side.

"Miss Wakefield," he greeted with a nod of his head.

Owen was instantly at my side. Next to me, his magic flared like a bright hot flame that made mine react to him.

That was... new.

"What are you doing here?"

He practically snarled the words. I reached for his hand, wrapped my fingers around his.

Voss's gaze flicked from me to him and back again. "The Crossroads is different this morning."

"Oh, so you've already been there? How fun," I said.

His mouth flatlined.

"Would you like to invite me in so we can discuss the Crossroads like civilized people?"

Owen stiffened. I squeezed his hand.

"Not really," I said, "but since you're standing on my porch being a giant pain, I suppose I will."

Behind me, Tani laughed.

He stepped inside, his gaze instantly landing on the Red Queen, Tani, and Willow still perched on the sofa.

I closed the door. Owen and I remained there as he turned to face us.

"Part of the agreement," he began, "was to return the queens to their rightful realms."

"Yes, I know that," I said, my tone as haughty as I intended. "However, the most important thing was to get the Crossroads closed. And I did."

"You closed the Crossroads?" Tani moved into the living room now taking up a spot close to me. She gave Voss a proper glare.

"It's temporary," Voss said, folding his arms across his chest.

"One crisis at a time, eh?" Owen snapped. "She, at least, got it closed for now."

"Did she now?" Tani's gaze never left Voss. "For a rookie, I'd say that's pretty good."

"I'd agree." Red stood up and moved to stand next to Tani.

Solidarity. I loved it.

Even Willow yawned, stretched, and hopped down off the couch. She parked her furry body between us and Voss, blinking up at him with her golden eyes.

It seemed he wasn't exactly popular.

Voss eyed the Red Queen who still wore my borrowed clothes and her ruby and diamond crown perched on top of her head. Then his gaze drifted to Tani and her rumpled ren-faire clothing.

"They belong in their own realm," he said.

"I met your ridiculous deadline," I said slowly, "and I'll get them back when I have time. Right now, I have to get ready to open the flower shop and you have a date with never coming back here."

Voss's jaw clenched.

"In the meantime," I said slowly, "they're perfectly fine here and not hurting anyone."

Owen squeezed my hand as if to say he was in full agreement.

"And I'm not leaving until I can rescue Oberon," Tani announced, her arms folded across her chest. "Alice promised."

"Which is now my promise," I added. "The Fae treasures are safe in Dougal's storeroom. When we're ready, they'll be there."

Tani went still. Her eyes softened as she looked at me, relief creasing her features.

"And," Owen added, "she has me to help her, too."

Voss's expression tightened as he stared at me. I wasn't certain he was happy with the turn of events—and the fact that this motley crew that included two queens, a charmed cat, and a druid were against him.

But I didn't care what he thought as long as he was out of my house and leaving me alone.

Finally, he said, "I will report to the Council that the seal is adequate. On my authority, they'll accept it as temporary compliance."

"How generous of you," I said, deadpan.

"And," he continued as if I hadn't spoken, "you still have thirty days to complete the closing of the Crossroads, return the queens, and find out who murdered Alice."

"I'm aware."

"We want answers, Miss Wakefield," he said.

"So do I," I snapped.

She was my mother and I never even knew it. She was the one person who could have told me everything about the Crossroads, who my father was, and my life in general. But she was gone and that was something I was going to have to come to terms with.

"And one more thing," he said, his voice tight.

I stiffened.

"We need to find out who's poisoning the tree."

I nodded, growing weary of his list of demands. "I'm working on it."

"Work faster."

At this point, Owen released my hand and took one threatening step toward the agent. "She *said* she's working on it."

I was silent as I watched the two of them standoff. Like two roosters sizing each other up. Owen looked far more menacing that Voss. Especially when his druid powers were activated.

"For what it's worth," Voss said, low and quiet. His gaze flicked to me. "You did well. I am... impressed."

"Gee," I said, "Thanks for the vote of confidence."

I stepped toward the door, opened it. "Maybe you'll relay that to the Council, too."

He stepped to the door. "Maybe I will."

And then he was gone. I shut the door and blew out a breath.

"He's an absolutely charmer," Tani said. Then her gaze slid to mine. "You'll help me with Oberon?"

"I will," I said.

"We both will," Owen corrected.

Tani's grin went from ear to ear. "Well, if that's not the cutest thing I've ever seen, I don't know what is."

I flushed.

Willow wound around my legs in a figure eight and meowed.

"Willow agrees," Tani said. "Also, she wants her breakfast."

"Oh, right."

Red stood and stretched. "And I need my morning nap."

Then she headed upstairs to the spare bedroom.

"And I have a date with a greenhouse."

Tani poofed away in a cloud of pink fairy dust.

That left me and Owen and Willow, who was trying her hardest to get my attention.

"Come on," I said to the cat.

She galloped ahead of me into the kitchen.

Owen followed. He paused at the counter, leaning against it as I placed kibble in Willow's bowl and refreshed her water. Willow glanced at the kibble, then up at me like I had personally offended her.

"You can have tuna later," I said.

Willow paused and looked back at me over one elegant shoulder. Those gold eyes held mine for a beat too long to be ordinary cat.

"I haven't forgotten," I said quietly. "About the hex. I just—I need a little more time to figure out how."

She blinked once, slow and regal. Then she turned and walked away.

Which, from Willow, I was choosing to interpret as gracious patience rather than judgment.

She sauntered off to find a patch of morning sun with a mournful meow. I'd never seen a cat turn its nose up at a bowl of food. But Willow wasn't any cat.

When she was gone, I looked at Owen standing in my kitchen.

"Willow is hexed?" he asked.

"Yes," I said. "And, apparently, the witch from the fairy tale, *Hansel & Gretel*."

His gaze drifted from mine to Willow lounging in the sun. He was quiet for a moment, watching her the way you watch something when you're rearranging what you thought you knew.

"Thirty days," I said. "That seems like a long time, but I know it isn't."

"You can do it." He pushed off the counter and stepped toward me, placing his hands on my waist. "I know you can."

"I'm glad *someone* thinks I can."

He kissed the tip of my nose. "You can do anything, Piper."

I couldn't stop myself from sliding my arms around his waist and resting my head on his shoulder.

"And my father," I said. "I need to find out who he was. Or is—if he's still alive."

"You will."

He held me there in the peace of the morning, and I didn't want him to let go. I didn't want to get ready to open the flower shop. I wanted to stand right there for the rest of the day.

But then I thought of my customers. Of Mr. Evans. Of normal life insisting on showing up.

"Mr. Evans was in the shop this week," I said, "and he said we should come to his annual summer barbecue next weekend. Halle will probably be there, too. She keeps texting me about that lunch we keep not managing to have."

I don't know why I said we should go to the barbecue, but there it was. And I wasn't taking it back.

Owen pulled back, holding my hands in his.

"Are you asking me on a date, Wakefield?"

I started to deny it. Then I decided to throw out all caution and take the plunge.

"Yes, McAllister," I said. "I am. An informal summer barbecue where half the town will see us together." I paused, took a deep breath. "If that's okay with you."

He smiled, his eyes glinting with something I didn't want to name. "Yes, ma'am. It's definitely okay with me."

I looked around my inherited house—the worn furniture, the photos of Alice on the mantel, the queens making themselves at home, the cat purring in a patch of sun.

This was my life now.

Guardian of the Crossroads. Owner of a flower shop. Keeper of secrets. Daughter of Alice.

And maybe—probably—dangerously—in love with Owen McAllister.

Also by Michelle Miles

Age of Wizards (Epic Fantasy)
In the Tower of the Wizard King
On the Hunt for the Wizard King

Dragon Protectors (Paranormal Shifter Romance)
Desiring the Dragon Lord
Seducing the Dragon Knight
Tempting Her Dragon Bodyguard

Dream Walker (Paranormal Romance)
Call of the Dark
Blood and Bone
Flame and Fury
Smoke and Ashes
Light of the World

Dream Walker Related Novels
Guardian of the Soul (Coming Soon)

War of the Brotherhood (Dark Paranormal Romance)
Set in the Dream Walker Universe
Dark Night of the Soul
Fall of the Forsaken
Immortal Everlasting (Coming 2026)

Enchanted Realms (YA Fantasy Romance)
Once Upon a Midnight Clear (Cinderella)
Once Upon True Love's Kiss (Snow White)
Once Upon an Enchanted Kiss (Sleeping Beauty)
Once Upon an Enchanted Castle (Beauty and the Beast)
Once Upon a Midnight Dreary (Poe's The Raven)

Enchanted Realms Related Novellas
Once Upon an Ancient Curse (Red Riding Hood)
Once Upon a Silver Strand (Rapunzel)
Once Upon a Woven Wish (Rumpelstiltskin)

Enchanted Realms: Crossroads (Cozy Fantasy)
A Spin-off Series of the Enchanted Realms
Petals and Portals (Coming 2026)

Five Towers (YA Fantasy Romance)
The Sorcerer's Daughter

Highland Destiny (Paranormal Romance)
Desiring the Highland Laird
Loving the Highland Warrior
Captivating the Highland Rogue

Legends of the Five Crowns (Romantasy)
with Misty Evans
The Lost Kingdom
The Flame and the Dragon
Tide of Stolen Thrones

Realm of Honor (Fantasy Romance)

One Knight Only

Only for a Knight

A Knight to Remember

A Knight Like No Other

Shadows of the Knight

Watch for more at MichelleMiles.net

About the Author

Michelle Miles is an empress with a war map in one hand and a romance vow in the other—writing fantasy, paranormal, and young adult adventures where magic crackles, danger prowls, and love refuses to back down. From fairy-tale retellings to angels and demons to Fae, elves, and time travelers, she builds big-hearted worlds full of quests, curses, kisses, and chaos—often in that order. When she's not plotting her next emotional ambush, Michelle narrates audiobooks and hosts Miles Beyond the Page, a podcast spotlighting writers' real journeys. A proud Texan, she's usually reading, hiking, rewatching favorite movies, or savoring a glass of wine while sharpening the blade for the next adventure.

Magical Worlds, Daring Adventures, Unforgettable Romance

Read more at MichelleMiles.net

www.ingramcontent.com/pod-product-compliance
Lightning Source LLC
Chambersburg PA
CBHW051549030726
47592CB00001B/208

* 9 7 8 1 9 6 9 1 6 4 1 2 5 *